Israel Zangwill

The Old Maids´ Club

Outlook

Israel Zangwill

The Old Maids´ Club

1. Auflage | ISBN: 978-3-73261-730-2

Erscheinungsort: Paderborn, Deutschland

Erscheinungsjahr: 2018

Outlook Verlag GmbH, Paderborn.

Reproduction of the original.

Israel Zangwill

The Old Maids´ Club

Outlook

THE
OLD MAIDS' CLUB

THE

OLD MAIDS' CLUB

BY

I. ZANGWILL

AUTHOR OF

"THE BACHELOR'S CLUB," "THE BIG BOW MYSTERY," ETC.

WITH NUMEROUS ILLUSTRATIONS

BY

F. H. TOWNSEND

NEW YORK

TAIT, SONS & COMPANY

UNION SQUARE

1

INTRODUCTION.

THE READER MY BOOK.

MY BOOK THE READER.

THE OLD MAIDS' CLUB.

CHAPTER I.

THE ALGEBRA OF LOVE, PLUS OTHER THINGS.

The Old Maids' Club was founded by Lillie Dulcimer in her sweet seventeenth year. She had always been precocious and could analyze her own sensations before she could spell. In fact she divided her time between making sensations and analyzing them. She never spoke Early English—the dialect which so enraged Dr. Johnson—but, like John Stuart Mill, she wrote a classical style from childhood. She kept a diary, not necessarily as a guarantee of good faith, but for publication only. It was labelled "Lillie Day by Day," and was posted up from her fifth year. Judging by the analogy of the rest, one might construct the entry for the first day of her life. If she had been able to record her thoughts, her diary would probably have begun thus:—

"*Sunday, September 3rd:* My birthday. Wept at the sight of the world in which I was to be so miserable. The atmosphere was so stuffy—not at all pleasing to the æsthetic faculties. Expected a more refined reception. A lady, to whom I had never been introduced, fondled me and addressed me as 'Petsie-tootsie-wootsie.' It appears that she is my mother, but this hardly justifies her in degrading the language of Milton and Shakespeare. Later on a man came in and kissed her. I could not help thinking that they might respect my presence; and, if they must carry on, continue to do so out of my sight as before. I understood later that I must call the stranger 'Poppy,' and that I was not to resent his familiarities, as he was very much attached to my mother by Act of Parliament. Both the man and the woman seem to arrogate to themselves a certain authority over me. How strange that two persons you have never seen before in your life should claim such rights of interference!

There must be something rotten in the constitution of Society. It shall be one of my life-tasks to discover what it is. I made a light lunch off milk, but do not care for the beverage. The day passed slowly. I was dreadfully bored by the conversation in the bedroom—it was so petty. I was glad when night came. O, the intolerable *ennui* of an English Sunday! I divine already that I am destined to go through life perpetually craving for I know not what, and that I shan't be happy till I get it."

Lillie was a born heroine, being young and beautiful from her birth. In her fourth year she conceived a Platonic affection for the boy who brought the telegrams. His manners had such repose. This was followed by a hopeless passion for a French cavalry officer with spurs. Every one feared she would grow up to be a suicide or a poetess; for her earliest nursery rhyme was an impromptu distich discovered by the nursery-maid, running:

Woonded i crawl out from the battel,
Life is as hollo as my rattel.

And her twelfth year was almost entirely devoted to literary composition of a hopeless character, so far as publishers were concerned. It was only the success of "Woman as a Waste Force," in her fourteenth year, that induced them to compete for her early manuscripts and to give the world the celebrated compilations, "Ibsen for Infants," "Browning for Babies," "Carlyle for the Cradle," "Newman for the Nursery," "Leopardi for the Little Ones," and "The Schoolgirl's Schopenhauer," which, together with "Tracts for the Tots," make up the main productions of her First Period. After the loss of the French cavalry officer she remained *blasée* till she was more than seven, when her second grand passion took her. It was a very grand passion indeed this time—and it lasted a full week. These things did not matter while Lillie had not yet arrived at years of indiscretion; but when she got into her teens, her father began to look about for a husband for her. He was a millionaire and had always kept her supplied with every luxury. But Lillie did not care for her father's selections, and sent them all away with fleas in their ears instead of kind words. And her father was as unhappy as his selections. In her sixteenth year her mother, who had been ailing for sixteen years, breathed her last, and Lillie more freely. She had grown quite to like Mrs. Dulcimer, and it prevented her having her own way. The situation was now very simple. Mr. Dulcimer managed his immense affairs and Lillie managed Mr. Dulcimer.

He made one last effort to get her to manage another man. He discovered a young nobleman who seemed fond of her society and who was in the habit of meeting her accidentally at the Academy. The gunpowder being thus presumably laid, he set to work to strike the match. But the explosion was not such as he expected. Lillie told him that no man was further from her thoughts as a possible husband.

"But, Lillie," pleaded the millionaire, "not one of the objections you have impressed upon me applies to Lord Silverdale. He is young, rich, handsome ——."

"Yes, yes, yes," answered Lillie, "I know."

"He is rich and cannot be after yourmoney."

"True."

"He has a title, which you consider an advantage."

"I do."

"He is a man of taste and culture."

"He is."

"Well, what is it you don't like? Doesn't he ride or dance well?"

"He dances like an angel and rides like the devil."

"Well, what in the name of angels or devils is your objection then?"

"Father," said Lillie very solemnly, "he is all you claim, but——." The little delicate cheek flushed modestly. She could not say it.

"But——" said the millionaire impatiently.

Lillie hid her face in her hands.

"But——" said the millionaire brutally.

"But I love him!"

"You what?" roared the millionaire.

"Yes, father, do not be angry with me. I love him dearly. Oh, do not spurn me from you, but I love him with my whole heart and soul, and I shall never marry any other man but him." The poor little girl burst into a paroxysm of weeping.

"Then you *will* marry him?" gasped the millionaire.

"No, father," she sobbed solemnly, "that is an illegitimate deduction from my proposition. He is the one man on this earth I could never bring myself to marry."

"You are mad!"

"No, father. I am only mathematical. I will never marry a man who does not love me. And don't you see that, as I love him, the odds are that he

7

doesn't love me?"

"But he tells me he does!"

"What is his bare assertion—weighed against the doctrine of probability! How many girls do you suppose Silverdale has met in his varied career?"

"A thousand, I dare say."

"Ah, that's only reckoning English Society (and theatres). And then he has seen Society (and theatres) in Paris, Berlin, Rome, Boston, a hundred places! If we put the figure at three thousand it will be moderate. Here am I, a single girl——"

"Who oughtn't to remain so," growled the millionaire.

"One single girl. How wildly improbable that out of three thousand girls, Silverdale should just fall in love with me. It is 2999 to 1 against. Then there is the probability that he is not in love at all—which makes the odds 5999 to 1. The problem is exactly analogous to one which you will find in any Algebra. Out of a sack containing three thousand coins, what are the odds that a man will draw the one marked coin?"

"The comparison of yourself to a marked coin is correct enough," said the millionaire, thinking of the files of fortune-hunters to whom he had given the sack. "Otherwise you are talking nonsense."

"Then Pascal, Laplace, Lagrange, De Moivre talked nonsense," said Lillie hotly; "but I have not finished. We must also leave open the possibility that the man will not be tempted to draw out any coin whatsoever. The odds against the marked coin being drawn out are thus 5999 to 1. The odds against Silverdale returning my affection are 6000 to 1. As Butler rightly points out, probability is the only guide to conduct, which is, we know from Matthew Arnold, three-fourths of life. Am I to risk ruining three-fourths of my life, in defiance of the unerring dogmas of the Doctrine of Chances? No, father, do not exact this sacrifice from me. Ask me anything you please, and I will grant it—oh! so gladly—but do not, oh, do not ask me to marry the man I love!"

The millionaire stroked her hair, and soothed her in piteous silence. He had made his pile in pig-iron, and had not science enough to grapple with the situation.

"Do you mean to say," he said at last, "that because you love a man, he can't love you?"

"He can. But in all human probability he won't. Suppose you put on a fur waistcoat and went out into the street, determined to invite to dinner the first man in a straw hat, and supposing he replied that you had just forestalled him,

8

as he had gone out with a similar intention to look for the first man in a fur waistcoat.—What would you say?"

The millionaire hesitated. "Well, I shouldn't like to insult the man," he said slowly.

"You see!" cried Lillie triumphantly.

"Well, then, dear," said he, after much pondering, "the only thing for it is to marry a man you *don't* love."

"Father!" said Lillie in terrible tones.

The millionaire hung his head shamefacedly at the outrage his suggestion had put upon his daughter.

"Forgive me, Lillie," he said; "I shall never interfere again in your matrimonial concerns."

So Lillie wiped her eyes and founded the Old Maids' Club.

She said it was one of her matrimonial concerns, and so her father could not break his word, though an entire suite of rooms in his own Kensington mansion was set aside for the rooms of the Club. Not that he desired to interfere. Having read "The Bachelors' Club," he thought it was the surest way of getting her married.

The object of the Club was defined by the foundress as "the depolarization of the term 'Old Maid'; in other words, the dissipation of all those disagreeable associations which have gradually and most unjustly clustered about it; the restoration of the homely Saxon phrase to its pristine purity, and the elevation of the enviable class denoted by it to their due pedestal of privilege and homage."

The conditions of membership, drawn up by Lillie, were:

1. Every candidate must be under twenty-five. 2. Every candidate must be beautiful and wealthy, and undertake to continue so. 3. Every candidate must have refused at least one advantageous offer of marriage.

The rationale of these rules was obvious. Disappointed, soured failures were not wanted. There was no virtue in being an "Old Maid" when you had passed twenty-five. Such creatures are merely old maids—Old Maids (with capitals) were required to be in the flower of youth and the flush of beauty. Their anti-matrimonial motives must be above suspicion. They must despise and reject the married state, though they would be welcomed therein with open arms.

9

Only thus would people's minds be disabused of the old-fashioned notions about old maids.

The Old Maids were expected to obey an elaborate array of by-laws, and respect a series of recommendations.

According to the by-laws they were required:

1. To regard all men as brothers. 2. Not to keep cats, lap-dogs, parrots, pages, or other domestic pets. 3. Not to have less than one birthday per year. 4. To abjure medicine, art classes, and Catholicism. 5. Never to speak to a Curate. 6. Not to have any ideals or to take part in Woman's Rights Movements, Charity Concerts, or other Platform Demonstrations. 7. Not to wear caps, curls, or similar articles of attire. 8. Not to kiss females.

In addition to these there were the

GENERAL RECOMMENDATIONS:

Never refuse the last slice of bread, etc., lest you be accused of dreading celibacy. Never accept bits of wedding cake, lest you be suspected of putting them under your pillow. Do not express disapproval by a sniff. In travelling, choose smoking carriages; pack your umbrellas and parasols inside your trunk. Never distribute tracts. Always fondle children and show marked hostility to the household cat. Avoid eccentricities. Do not patronize Dorothy Restaurants or the establishments of the Aerated Bread Company. Never drink cocoa-nibs. In dress it is better to avoid Mittens, Crossovers, Fleecy Shawls, Elastic-side Boots, White Stockings, Black Silk Bodies, with Pendent Gold Chains, and Antique White Lace Collars. One-button White Kid Gloves are also inadvisable for afternoon concerts; nor should any glove be worn with fingers too long to pick up change at booking-offices. Parcels should not be wrapped in whitey-brown paper and not more than three should be carried at once. Watch Pockets should not be hung over the bed, sheets and mattresses should be left to the servants to air, and rooms should be kept in an untidy condition.

Refrain from manufacturing jam, household remedies, gossip or gooseberry wine. Never nurse a cold or a relative. It is advisable not to have a married sister, as she might decease and the temptation to marry her husband is such as no mere human being ought to be exposed to. For cognate reasons eschew friendship with cripples and hunchbacks (especially when they have mastered the violin in twelve lessons), men of no moral character, drunkards who wish to reform themselves, very ugly men, and husbands with wives in lunatic asylums. Cultivate rather the acquaintance of handsome young men (who have been duly vaccinated), for this species is too conceited to be dangerous.

On the same principle were the rules for admitting visitors:

1. No unmarried lady admitted. 2. No married gentlemen admitted.

If they admitted single ladies there would be no privilege in being a member, while if they did not admit single gentlemen, they might be taunted with being afraid that they were not fireproof. When Lillie had worked this out to her satisfaction she was greatly chagrined to find the two rules were the same as for "The Bachelors' Club." To show their club had no connection with the brother institution, she devised a series of counterblasts to their misogynic maxims. These were woven on all the antimacassars; the deadliest were:

The husband is the only creature entirely selfish. He is a low organism, consisting mainly of a digestive apparatus and a rude mouth. The lover holds the cloak; the husband drops it. Wedding dresses are webs. Women like clinging robes; men like clinging women. The lover will always help the beloved to be helpless. A man likes his wife to be just clever enough to comprehend his cleverness and just stupid enough to admire it. Women who catch husbands rarely recover. Marriage is a lottery; every wife does not become a widow. Wrinkles are woman's marriage lines; but when she gets them her husband will no longer be bound.

The woman who believes her husband loves her, is capable of believing that she loves him. A good man's love is the most intolerable of boredoms. A man often marries a woman because they have the same tastes and prefer himself to the rest of creation. If a woman could know what her lover really thought of her she would know what to think of him. Possession is nine points of the marriage law. It is impossible for a man to marry a clever woman. Marriages are made in heaven, but old maids go there.

Lillie also painted a cynical picture of dubious double-edged incisiveness. It was called "Latter-day Love," and represented the ill hap of Cupid, neglected and superfluous, his quiver full, his arrows rusty, shivering with the cold, amid contented couples passing him by with never an eye for the lugubrious legend, "Pity the Poor Blind."

The picture put the finishing touch to the rooms of the Club. When Lillie Dulcimer had hung it up, she looked round upon the antimacassars and felt a proud and happy girl.

The Old Maids' Club was now complete. Nothing was wanting except members.

Latter-Day Love.

CHAPTER II.

THE HONORARY TRIER.

Lord Silverdale was the first visitor to the Old Maids' Club. He found the fair President throned alone among the epigrammatic antimacassars. Lillie received him with dignity and informed him that he stood on holy ground. The young man was shocked to hear of the change in her condition. He, himself, had lately spent his time in plucking up courage to ask her to change it—and now he had been forestalled.

"But you must come in and see us often," said Lillie. "It occurs to me that the by-laws admit you."

"How many will you be?" murmured Silverdale, heartbroken.

"I don't know yet. I am waiting for the thing to get about. I have been in communication with the first candidate, and expect her any moment. She is a celebrated actress."

"And who elects her?"

"I, of course!" said Lillie, with an imperial flash in her passionate brown eyes. She was a brunette, and her face sometimes looked like a handsome thunder-cloud. "I am the President and the Committee and the Oldest Old Maid. Isn't one of the rules that candidates shall not believe in Women's Rights? None of the members will have any voice whatever."

"Well, if your actress is a comic opera star, she *won't* have any voice whatever."

"Lord Silverdale," said Lillie sharply, "I hate puns. They spoiled the Bachelors' Club."

His lordship, who was the greatest punster of the peers, and the peer of the greatest punsters, muttered savagely that he would like to spoil the Old Maids' Club. Lillie punned herself sometimes, but he dared not tell her of it.

"And what will be the subscription?" he said aloud.

"There will be none. I supply the premises."

"Ah, that will never do! Half the pleasure of belonging to a club is the feeling that you have not paid your subscription. And how about grub?"

"Grub! We are not men. We do not fulfil missions by eating."

"Unjust creature! Men sometimes fulfil missions by being eaten."

13

"Well, papa will supply buns, lemonade and ices. Turple the magnificent, will always be within call to hand round the things."

"May I send you in a hundred-weight of chocolate creams?"

"Certainly. Why should weddings have a monopoly of presents? This is not the only way in which you can be of service to me, if you will."

"Only discover it for me, my dear Miss Dulcimer. Where there's a way there's a will."

"Well, I should like you to act as Trier."

"Eh! I beg your pardon?"

"Don't apologize; to try the candidates who wish to be Old Maids."

"Try them! No, no! I'm afraid I should be prejudiced against bringing them in innocent."

"Don't be silly. You know what I mean. I could not tell so well as you whether they possessed the true apostolic spirit. You are a man—your instinct would be truer than mine. Whenever a new candidate applies, I want you to come up and see her."

"Really, Miss Dulcimer, I—I can't tell by looking at her!"

"No, but you can by her looking at you."

"You exaggerate my insight."

"Not at all. It is most important that something of the kind should be done. By the rules, all the Old Maids must be young and beautiful. And it requires a high degree of will and intelligence——"

"To be both!"

"For such to give themselves body and soul to the cause. Every Old Maid is double-faced till she has been proved single-hearted."

"And must I talk to them?"

"In plain English——"

"It's the only language I speak plainly."

"Wait till I finish, boy! In plain English, you must flirt with them."

"Flirt?" said Silverdale, aghast. "What! With young and beautiful girls?"

"I know it is hard, Lord Silverdale, but you will do it for my sake!" They were sitting on an ottoman, and the lovely face which looked pleadingly up into his was very near. The young man got up and walked up and down.

"Hang it!" he murmured disconsolately. "Can't you try them on Turple the magnificent. Or why not get a music-master or a professor of painting?"

"Music-masters touch the wrong chord, and professors of painting are mostly old masters. You are young and polished and can flirt with tact and taste."

"Thank you," said the poor young peer, making a wry face. "And therefore I'm to be a flirtation machine."

"An electric battery if you like. I don't desire to mince my words. There's no gain in not calling a spade a spade."

"And less in people calling a battery a rake."

"Is that a joke? I thought you clubmen enjoyed being called rakes."

"That is all most of us do enjoy. Take it from me that the last thing a rake does is to sow wild oats."

"I know enough of agriculture not to be indebted to you for the information. But I certainly thought you were a rake," said the little girl, looking up at him with limpid brown eyes.

"You flatter me," he said with a mock bow; "you are young enough to know better."

"But you have seen Society (and theatres) in a dozen capitals!"

"I have been behind the scenes of both," he answered simply. "That is the thing to keep a man steady."

"I thought it turned a man's head," she said musingly.

"It does. Only one begins manhood with his head screwed the wrong way on. Homœopathy is the sole curative principle in morals. Excuse this sudden discharge of copy-book mottoes. I sometimes go off that way, but you mustn't take me for a Maxim gun. I am not such a bore, I hope."

Lillie flew off at a feminine tangent.

"All of which only proves the wisdom of my choice in selecting you."

"What! To pepper them with pellets of platitude?" he said, dropping despairingly into an arm-chair.

"No. With eyeshot. Take care!"

"What's the matter?"

"You're sitting on an epigram."

"Take care! You're sitting on an epigram."

The young man started up as if stung, and removed the antimacassar, without, however, seeing the point.

"I hope you don't mind my inquiring whether you have any morals," said Lillie.

"I have as many as Æsop. The strictest investigation courted. References given and exchanged," said the peer lightly.

"Do be serious. You know I have an insatiable curiosity to know everything about everything—to feel all sensations, think all thoughts. That is the note of my being." The brown eyes had an eager, wistful look.

"Oh, yes—a note of interrogation."

"O that I were a man! What *do* men think?"

"What do *you* think? Men are human beings first and masculine afterwards. And I think everybody is like a suburban Assembly Hall—to-day a temperance lecture, to-morrow a dance, next day an oratorio, then a farcical comedy, and on Sunday a religious service. But about this appointment?"

"Well, let us settle it one way or another," Lillie said. "Here is my proposal ——"

"I have an alternative proposal," he said desperately.

"I cannot listen to any other. Will you, or will you not, become Honorary Trier of the Old Maids' Club?"

"I'll try," he said at last.

"Yes or no?"

"Shall you be present at the trials?"

"Certainly, but I shall cultivate myopia."

"It's a short-sighted policy, Miss Dulcimer. Still, sustained by your presence, I feel I could flirt with the most beautiful and charming girl in the world. I could do it, even unsustained by the presence of the other girl."

"Oh, no! You must not flirt with me. I am the only Old Maid with whom flirtation is absolutely taboo."

"Then I consent," said Silverdale with apparent irrelevance. And seating himself on the piano stool, after carefully removing an epigram from the top of the instrument, he picked out "The Last Rose of Summer" with a facile forefinger.

"Don't!" said Lillie. "Stick to your lute."

Thus admonished, the nobleman took down Lillie's banjo, which was hanging on the wall, and struck a few passionate chords.

"Do you know," he said, "I always look on the banjo as the American among musical instruments. It is the guitar with a twang. Wasn't it invented in the States? Anyhow it is the most appropriate instrument to which to sing you my Fin de Siècle Love Song."

"For Heaven's sake, don't use that poor overworked phrase!"

"Why not? It has only a few years to live. List to my sonnet."

So saying, he strummed the strings and sang in an aristocratic baritone:

AD CHLOEN.—A Valedictory.

O Chloe, you are very, very dear,
      And far above your rivals in the town,
Who all in vain essay to beat you down,
      Embittered by your haughtiness austere.
Too high you are for lowly me, I fear.
      You would not stoop to pick up e'en a crown,
Nor cede the slightest lowering of a gown,
      Though in men's eyes far fairer to appear.

With this my message, kindly current go,
      At half-penny per word—it should be less—
To Chloe, telegraphical address
      (Thus written to economize two *d*)
Of Messrs. Robinson, De Vere & Co.,
      Costumers, 90, Ludgate Hill, E. C.

Lillie laughed. "My actress's name is something like Chloe. It is Clorinda —Clorinda Bell. She tells me she is very celebrated."

"Oh, yes, I've heard of her," he said.

"There is a sneer in your tones. Have you heard anything to her disadvantage?"

"Only that she is virtuous and in Society."

"The very woman for an Old Maid! She is beautiful, too."

"Is she? I thought she was one of those actresses who reserve their beauty for the stage."

"Oh, no. She always wears it. Here is her photograph. Isn't that a lovely face?"

"It is a lovely photograph. Does she hope to achieve recognition by it, I wonder?"

"Sceptic!"

"I doubt all charms but yours."

"Well, you shall see her."

"All right, but mention her name clearly when you introduce me. Women are such changing creatures—to-day pretty, to-morrow plain, yesterday ugly. I have to be reintroduced to most of my female acquaintances three times a week. May I wait to see Clorinda?"

"No, not to-day. She has to undergo the Preliminary Exam. Perhaps she may not even matriculate. Where you come in is at the graduation stage."

"I see. To pass them as Bachelors—I mean Old Maids. I say, how will you get them to wear stuff gowns?"

The bell rang loudly. "That may be she. Good-bye, Lord Silverdale. Remember you are Honorary Trier of the Old Maids' Club, and don't forget those chocolate creams."

CHAPTER III.

THE MAN IN THE IRONED MASK.

The episode that turned Clorinda Bell's thoughts in the direction of Old Maidenhood was not wanting in strangeness. She was an actress of whom everybody spoke well, excepting actresses. This was because she was so respectable. Respectability is all very well for persons who possess no other ability; but bohemians rightly feel that genius should be above that sort of thing. Clorinda never went anywhere without her mother. This lady—a portly taciturn dame, whose hair had felt the snows of sixty winters—was as much a part of her as a thorn is of a rose. She accompanied her always—except when she was singing—and loomed like some more substantial shadow before or behind her at balls and receptions, at concerts and operas, private views and church bazaars. Her mother was always with her behind the scenes. She helped her to make up and to unmake. She became the St. Peter of the dressing-room in her absence. At the Green Room Club they will tell you how a royal personage asking permission to come and congratulate her, received the answer: "I shall be most honored—in the presence of my mother."

There were those who wished Clorinda had been born an orphan.

But the graver sort held Miss Bell up as a typical harbinger of the new era, when actresses would keep mothers instead of dog-carts. There was no intrinsic reason, they said, why actresses should not be received at Court, and visit the homes of the poor. Clorinda was very charming. She was tall and fair as a lily, with dashes of color stolen from the rose and the daffodil, for her eyes had a sparkle and her cheeks a flush and her hair was usually golden. Not the least of her physical charms was the fact that she had numerous admirers. But it was understood that she kept them at a distance and that they worshipped there. The Society journals, to which Clorinda was indebted for considerable information about herself, often stated that she intended to enter a convent, as her higher nature found scant satisfaction in stage triumphs, and she had refused to exchange her hand either for a coronet or a pile of dollars. They frequently stated the opposite, but a Society journal cannot always be contradicting a contemporary. It must sometimes contradict itself, as a proof of impartiality. Clorinda let all these rumors surge about her unheeded, and her managers had to pay for the advertisement. The money came back to them, though, for Clorinda was a sure draw. She brought the odor of sanctity over the footlights, and people have almost as much curiosity to see a saint as a sinner—especially when the saint is beautiful.

Gentlemen in particular paid frequent pilgrimages to the shrine of the saint, and adored her from the ten-and-sixpenny pews. There was at this period a noteworthy figure in London dress circles and stalls, an inveterate first-nighter, whose identity was the subject of considerable speculation. He was a mystery in a swallow-tail coat. No one had ever seen him out of it. He seemed to go through life armed with a white breastplate, starched shot-proof and dazzling as a grenadier's cuirass. What wonder that a wit (who had become a dramatic critic through drink) called him. "The Man in the Ironed Mask." Between the acts he wore a cloak, a crush-hat and a cigarette. Nobody ever spoke to him nor did he ever reply. He could not be dumb, because he had been heard to murmur "Brava, bravissima," in a soft but incorrect foreign manner. He was very handsome, with a high, white forehead of the Goth order of architecture, and dark, Moorish eyes. Nobody even knew his name, for he went to the play quite anonymously. The pit took him for a critic, and the critics for a minor poet. He had appeared on the scene (or before it) only twelve months ago, but already he was a distinguished man. Even the actors and actresses had come to hear of him, and not a few had peeped at him between their speeches. He was certainly a sight for the "gods."

Latterly he had taken to frequenting the *Lymarket*, where Miss Clorinda Bell was "starring" for a season of legitimate drama. It was the only kind the scrupulous actress would play in. Whenever there was no first night on anywhere else, he went to see Clorinda. Only a few rivals and the company knew of his constancy to the entertainment. Clorinda was, it will be remembered, one of the company.

It was the *entr'acte* and the orchestra was playing a gavotte, to which the eighteenth-century figures on the drop scene were dancing. The Man in the Ironed Mask strolled in the lobby among the critics, overhearing the views they were not going to express in print. Clorinda Bell's mother was brushing her child's magnificent hair into a more tragical attitude in view of the fifth act. The little room was sacred to the "star," the desire of so many moths. Neither maid nor dresser entered it, for Mrs. Bell was as devoted to her daughter as her daughter to her, and tended her as zealously as if she were a stranger.

"Yes, but why doesn't he speak?" said Clorinda.

"You haven't given him a chance, darling," said her mother. "Nonsense—

there is the language of flowers. All my lovers commence by talking that."

"You get so many bouquets, dear. It may be—as you say his appearance is so distinguished—that he dislikes so commonplace a method."

"Well, if he doesn't want to throw his love at my feet, he might have tried to send it me in a billet-doux."

"That is also commonplace. Besides, he may know that all your letters are delivered to me, and opened by me. The fact has often enough appeared in print."

"Ah, yes, but genius will find out a way. You remember Lieutenant Campbell, who was so hit the moment he saw me as Perdita that he went across the road to the telegraph-office and wired, 'Meet me at supper, top floor, Piccadilly Restaurant, 11.15,' so that the doorkeeper sent the message direct to the prompter, who gave it me as I came off with Florizel and Camilla. That is the sort of man I admire!"

"But you soon tired of him, darling."

"Oh, mother! How can you say so? I loved him the whole run of the piece."

"Yes, dear, but it was only Shakespeare."

"Would you have love a Burlesque? 'A Winter's Tale' is long enough for any flirtation. Let me see, was it Campbell or Belfort who shot himself? I for ——oh! oh! that hairpin is irritating me, mother."

"There! There! Is that easier?"

"Thanks! There's only the Man in the Ironed Mask irritating me now. His dumb admiration provokes me."

"But you provoke his dumb admiration. And are you sure it is admiration?"

"People don't go to see Shakespeare seventeen times. I wonder who he is —an Italian count most likely. Ah, how his teeth flash beneath his moustache!"

"You make me feel quite curious about him. Do you think I could peep at him from the wing?"

"No, mother, you shall not be put to the inconvenience. It would give you a crick in your neck. If you desire to see him, I will send for him."

"Very well, dear," said the older woman submissively, for she was accustomed to the gratification of her daughter's whims.

So when the Man in the Ironed Mask resumed his seat, a programme girl slipped a note into his hand. He read it, his face impassive as his Ironed Mask. When the play was over, he sauntered round to the squalid court in which the stage door was located and stalked nonchalantly up the stairs. The doorkeeper was too impressed by his air not to take him for granted. He seemed to go on instinctively till he arrived at a door placarded, "Miss Clorinda Bell— Private."

He knocked, and the silvery accents he had been listening to all the evening bade him come in. The beautiful Clorinda, clad in diaphanous white and radiating perfumes, received him with an intoxicating smile.

"It is so kind of you to come and see me," she said.

He made a stately inclination. "The obligation is mine," he said. "I am greatly interested in the drama. This is the seventeenth time I have been to see you."

"I meant here," she said piqued, though the smile stayed on.

"Oh, but I understood——" His eyes wandered interrogatively about the room.

"Yes, I know my mother is out," she replied. "She is on the stage picking up the bouquets. I believe she sent you a note. I do not know why she wants to see you, but she will be back soon. If you do not mind being left alone with me——"

"Pray do not apologize, Miss Bell," he said considerately.

"It is so good of you to say so. Won't you sit down?"

The Man in the Ironed Mask sat down beside the dazzling Clorinda and stared expectantly at the door. There was a tense silence. His cloak hung negligently upon his shoulders. He held his crush hat calmly in his hand.

Clorinda was highly chagrined. She felt as if she could slap his face and kiss the place to make it well.

"Did you like the play?" she said, at last.

He elevated his dark eyebrows. "Is it not obvious?"

"Not entirely. You might come to see the players."

"Quite so, quite so."

He leaned his handsome head on his arm and looked pensively at the floor. It was some moments before he broke the silence again. But it was only by rising to his feet. He walked towards the door.

"I am sorry I cannot stay any longer," he said.

"Oh, no! You mustn't go without seeing my mother. She will be terribly disappointed."

"Not less so than myself at missing her. Good-night, Miss Bell." He made his prim, courtly bow.

"Oh, but you must see her! Come again to-morrow night, anyhow," exclaimed Clorinda desperately. And when his footsteps had died away down the stairs, she could not repress several tears of vexation. Then she looked hurriedly into a little mirror and marvelled silently.

"Is he gone already?" said her mother, entering after knocking cautiously at the door.

"Yes, he is insane."

"Madly in love with you?"

"Madly out of love with me."

He came again the next night, stolid and courteous. To Clorinda's infinite regret her mother had been taken ill and had gone home early in the carriage. It was raining hard. Clorinda would be reduced to a hansom. "They call it the London gondola," she said, "but it is least comfortable when there's most water. You have to be framed in like a cucumber in a hothouse."

"Indeed! Personally I never travel in hansoms. And from what you tell me I should not like to make the experiment to-night. Good-bye, Miss Bell; present my regrets to your mother."

"Deuce take the donkey! He might at least offer me a seat in his carriage," thought Clorinda. Aloud she said: "Under the circumstances may I venture to ask you to see my mother at the house? Here is our private address. Won't you come to tea to-morrow?"

He took the card, bowed silently and withdrew.

In such wise the courtship proceeded for some weeks, the invalid being confined to her room at teatime and occupied in picking up bouquets by night. He always came to tea in his cloak, and wore his Ironed Mask, and was extremely solicitous about Clorinda's mother. It became evident that so long as he had the ghost of an excuse for talking of the absent, he would never talk of Clorinda herself. At last she was reduced to intimating that she would be found at the matinée of a new piece next day (to be given at the theatre by a débutante) and that there would be plenty of room in her box. Clorinda was determined to eliminate her mother, who was now become an impediment instead of a pretext.

But when the afternoon came, she looked for him in vain. She chatted lightly with the acting-manager, who was lounging in the vestibule, but her eye was scanning the horizon feverishly.

25

"Is this woman going to be a success?" she asked.

"Oh, yes," said the acting-manager promptly.

"How do you know?"

"I just saw the flowers drive up."

"I just saw the flowers drive up."

Clorinda laughed. "What's the piece like?"

"I only saw one rehearsal. It seemed great twaddle. But the low com. has got a good catchword, so there's some chance of its going into the evening bills."

"Oh, by the way, have you seen anything of that—that—the man in the Ironed Mask, I think they call him?"

"Do you mean here—this afternoon?"

"Yes."

"No. Do you expect him?"

"Oh, no; but I was wondering if he would turn up. I hear he is so fond of this theatre."

"Bless your soul, he'd never be seen at a matinée."

"Why not?" asked Clorinda, her heart fluttering violently.

"Because he'd have to be in morning dress," said the actor-manager, laughing heartily.

To Clorinda his innocent merriment seemed the laughter of a mocking fiend. She turned away sick at heart. There was nothing for it but to propose outright at teatime. Clorinda did so, and was accepted without further difficulty.

"And now, dearest," she said, after she had been allowed to press the first kiss of troth upon his coy lips, "I should like to know who I am going to be?"

"Clorinda Bell, of course," he said. "That is the advantage actresses have. They need not take their husband's name in vain."

"Yes, but what am *I* to call you, dearest?"

"Dearest?" he echoed enigmatically. "Let me be dearest—for a little while."

She forbore to press him further. For the moment it was enough to have won him. The sweetness of that soothed her wounded vanity at his indifference to the prize coveted by men and convents. Enough that she was to be mated to a great man, whose speech and silence alike bore the stamp of individuality.

"Dearest be it," she answered, looking fondly into his Moorish eyes. "Dearest! Dearest!"

"Thank you, Clorinda. And now may I see your mother? I have never learnt what she has to say to me."

"What does it matter now, dearest?"

"More than ever," he said gravely, "now she is to be my mother-in-law."

Clorinda bit her lip at the dignified rebuke, and rang for his mother-in-law elect, who came from the sick room in her bonnet.

"Mother," she said, as the good dame sailed through the door, "let me introduce you to my future husband."

28

A Family Reunion.

The old lady's face lit up with surprise and excitement. She stood still for an instant, taking in the relationship so suddenly sprung upon her. Then she darted with open arms towards the Man in the Ironed Mask and strained his Mask to her bosom.

"My son! my son!" she cried, kissing him passionately. He blushed like a stormy sunset and tried to disengage himself.

"Do not crumple him, mother," said Clorinda pettishly. "Your zeal is overdone."

"But he is my long-lost Absalom! Think of the rapture of having him restored to me thus. O what a happy family we shall be! Bless you, Clorinda. Bless you, my children. When is the wedding to be?"

The Man in the Ironed Mask had regained his composure.

"Mother," he said sternly, "I am glad to see you looking so well. I always knew you would fall on your feet if I dropped you. I have no right to ask it— but as you seem to expect me to marry your daughter, a little information as to the circumstances under which you have supplied me with a sister would be not unwelcome.

"Stupid boy! Don't you understand that Miss Bell was good enough to engage me as mother and travelling companion when you left me to starve? Or rather, the impresario who brought her over from America engaged me, and Clorinda has been, oh, so good to me! My little drapery business failed three months after you left me to get a stranger to serve. I had no resource but —to go on the stage."

The old woman was babbling on, but the cold steel of Clorinda's gaze silenced her.

The outraged actress turned haughtily to the Man in the Ironed Mask.

"So *this* is your mother?" she said with infinite scorn.

"So this is *not* your mother!" he said with infinite indignation.

"Were you ever really simple enough to suspect me of having a mother?" she retorted contemptuously. "I had her on the hire system. Don't you know that a combination of maid and mother is the newest thing in actresses' wardrobes? It is safer then having a maid, and more comfortable than having a mother."

"But I *have* been a mother to you, Clorinda," the old dame pleaded.

"Oh, yes, you have always been a good, obedient woman. I am not finding fault with you, and I have no wish to part with you. I do find fault and I shall certainly part with your son."

"Nonsense," said the Man in the Ironed Mask. "The situation is essentially unchanged. She is still the mother of one of us, she can still become the mother-in-law of the other. Besides, Clorinda, that is the only way of keeping the secret in the family."

"You threaten?"

"Certainly. You are a humbug. So am I. United we stand. Separated, you fall."

"You fall, too."

"Not from such a height. I am still on the first rungs."

"Nor likely to get any higher."

"Indeed? Your experience of me should have taught you different. High as you are, I can raise you yet higher if you will only lift me up to you."

"How do you climb?" she said, his old ascendency reasserting itself.

"By standing still. Profound meditation on the philosophy of modern society has convinced me that the only way left for acquiring notoriety is to do nothing. Every other way has been exploited and is suspected. It is only a year since the discovery flashed upon me, it is only a year that I have been putting it in practice. And yet, mark the result! Already I am a known man. I had the *entrée* to no society; for half-a-guinea a night (frequently paid in paper money) I have mingled with the most exclusive. When there was no *premiere* anywhere, I went to see you—not from any admiration of you, but because the *Lymarket* is the haunt of the best society, and in addition, the virtue of Shakespeare and of yourself attracts there a highly respectable class of bishops whom I have not the opportunity of meeting elsewhere. By doing nothing I fascinated you—somebody was sure to be fascinated by it at last, as the dove flutters into the jaws of the lethargic serpent—by continuing to do nothing I completed my conquest. Had I met your advances, you would have repelled mine. My theories have been completely demonstrated, and but for the accident of our having a common mother——"

"Speak for yourself," said Clorinda haughtily.

"It is for myself that I am speaking. When we are one, I shall continue this policy of masterly inactivity of which I claim the invention, though it has long been known in the germ. Everybody knows for instance that not to trouble to answer letters is the surest way of acquiring the reputation of a busy man, that not to accept invitations is an infallible way of getting more, that not to care a jot about the feelings of the rest of the household, is an unfailing means of enforcing universal deference. But the glory still remains to him who first grasped this great law in its generalized form, however familiar one or two isolated cases of it may be to the world. 'Do nothing' is the last word of social science, as 'Nil admirari' was its first. Just as silence is less self-contradictory than speech, so is inaction a safer foundation of fame than action. Inaction is perfect. The moment you do anything you are in the region of incompleteness, of definiteness. Your work may be outdone—or undone. Your inventions may be improved upon, your victories annulled, yourpopular books ridiculed, your theories superseded, your paintings decried, the seamy side of your explanations shown up. Successful doing creates not only enemies but the material for their malice to work upon. Only by not having done anything to deserve success can you be sure of surviving the reaction which success always brings. To be is higher than to do. To be is calm, large, elemental; to do is trivial, artificial, fussy. To be has been the moth of the English aristocracy, it is the secret of their persistence. *Qui s'excuse s'accuse.* He who strives to justify his existence imperils it. To be is inexpugnable, to do is dangerous. The same principle rules in all departments of social life. What is a successful reception? A gathering at which everybody *is*. Nobody does anything. Nobody enjoys anything. There everybody *is*—if only for five minutes each, and whatever the crush and discomfort. You are there—and there you *are*, don't you know? What is a social lion? A man who *is* everywhere. What is social ambition? A desire to *be* in better people's drawing-rooms. What is it for which people barter health, happiness, even honor? To *be* on certain pieces of flooring inaccessible to the mass. What is the glory of doing compared with the glory of being? Let others elect to do, I elect to *be*."

"So long as you do not choose to be my husband——"

"It is husband or brother," he said, threateningly.

"Of course. I become your sister by rejecting you, do I not?"

"Don't trifle. You understand what I mean. I will let the world know that your mother is mine."

They stood looking at each other in silent defiance. At last Clorinda spoke:

"A compromise! let the world know that my mother is yours."

"I see. Pose as your brother!"

"Yes. That will help you up a good many rungs. I shall not deny I am your sister. My mother will certainly not deny that you are her son."

"Done! So long as my theories are not disproved. Conjugate the verb 'to be,' and you shall be successful. Let me see. How does it run? I am—your brother, thou art—my sister, she is—my mother,—we are—her children, you are—my womankind, they are—all spoofed."

So the man in the Ironed Mask turned out to be the brother of the great and good actress, Clorinda Bell. And several people had known it all along, for what but fraternal interest had taken him so often to the *Lymarket*? And when his identity leaked out, Society ran after him, and he gave the interviewers interesting details of his sister's early years. And everyone spoke of his mother, and of his solicitous attendance upon her. And in due course the tale of his virtues reached a romantic young heiress who wooed and won him. And so he continued *being*, till he was—no more. By his own request they buried him in an Ironed Mask, and put upon his tomb the profound inscription

"HERE LIES THE MAN WHO WAS."

———————

And this was why Clorinda, disgusted with men and lovers, and unable to marry her brother, caught at the notion of the Old Maids' Club and called upon Lillie.

It was almost as good a cover as a mother, and it was well to have something ready in case she lost her, as you cannot obtain a second mother even on the hire system. But Lord Silverdale's report consisted of one word, "Dangerous!"—and he rejoiced at the whim which enabled him thus to protect the impulsive little girl he loved.

Clorinda divined from Lillie's embarrassment next day that she was to be blackballed.

"I am afraid," she hastened to say, "that on second thoughts I must withdraw my candidature, as I could not make a practice of coming here without my mother."

Lillie referred to the rules. "Married women are admitted," she said simply. "I presume, therefore, your mother——"

"It's just like your presumption," interrupted Clorinda, and flouncing angrily out of the Club, she invited a journalist to tea.

Next day the *Moon* said she was going to join the Old Maids' Club.

CHAPTER IV.

THE CLUB GETS ADVERTISED.

"I see you have disregarded my ruling, Miss Dulcimer!" said Lord Silverdale, pointing to the paragraph in the *Moon*. "What is the use of my trying the candidates if you're going to admit the plucked?"

"I am surprised at you, Lord Silverdale. I thought you had more wisdom than to base a reproach on a *Moon* paragraph. You might have known it was not true."

"That is not my experience, Miss Dulcimer. I do not think a statement is necessarily false because it appears in the newspapers. There is hardly a paper in which I have not, at some time or other, come across a true piece of news. Even the *Moon* is not all made of green cheese."

"But you surely do not think I would accept Clorinda Bell after your warning. Not but that I am astonished. She assured me she was ice."

"Precisely. And so I marked her 'Dangerous.' Are there any more candidates to-day?"

"Heaps and heaps! From all parts of the kingdom letters have come from ladies anxious to become Old Maids. There is even one application from Paris. Ought I to entertain that?"

"Certainly. Candidates may hail from anywhere—excepting naturally the United States.

"But what, I wonder, has caused this tide of applications?"

"The *Moon*, of course. The fiction that Clorinda Bell intended to take the secular veil has attracted all these imitators. She has given the Club a good advertisement in endeavoring merely to give herself one."

"You suspect her, then, of being herself responsible for the statement that she was going to join the Club?"

"No. I am sure of it. Who but herself knew that she was not?"

"I can hardly imagine that she would employ such base arts."

"Higher arts are out of employment nowadays."

"Is there any way of finding out?"

"I am afraid not. She has no bosom friends. Stay—there is her mother!"

"Mothers do not tell their daughters' secrets. They do not know them."

"Well, there's her brother. I was introduced to him the other day at Mrs. Leo Hunter's. But he seems such a reticent chap. Only opens his mouth twice an hour, and then merely to show his teeth. Oh, I know! I'll get at the *Moon* man. My aunt, the philanthropist, who is quite a journalist (sends so many paragraphs round about herself, you know), will tell me who invents that sort of news, and I'll interview the beggar."

"Yes, won't it be fun to run her to earth?" said Lillie gleefully.

Silverdale took advantage of her good-humor.

"I hope the discovery of the baseness of your sex will turn you again to mine." There was a pleading tenderness in his eyes.

"What! to your baseness? I thought you were so good."

"I am no good without you," he said boldly.

"Oh, that is too rich! Suppose I had never been born?"

"I should have wished I hadn't."

"But you wouldn't have known *I* hadn't."

"You're getting too metaphysical for my limited understanding."

"Nonsense, you understand metaphysics as well as I do."

"Do not disparage yourself. You know I cannot endure metaphysics."

"Why not?"

"Because they are mostly made in Germany. And all Germans write as if their aim was to be misunderstood. Listen to my simple English lay."

"Another love-song to Chloe?"

"No, a really great poem, suggested by the number of papers and poems I have already seen this *Moon* paragraph in."

He took down the banjo, thrummed it, and sang:

THE GRAND PARAGRAPHIC TOUR.

I composed a little story
    About a cockatoo,
With no desire of glory,
    To see what would ensue.

It took the public liking
    From China to Peru.

The point of it was striking,
      Though perfectly untrue.

It began in a morning journal
      When gooseberries were due,
The subject seemed eternal,
      So many scribes it drew.

And in every evening column
      It made a great to-do,
Sub-editors so solemn
      Just adding thereunto.

In the London Correspondence
      'Twas written up anew,
And then a fog came on dense
      And hid me quite from view.

And some said they had heard it
      From keepers in the Zoo,
While others who averred it
      Had *seen* that cockatoo.

It lived, my little fable,
      I chuckled and I crew
As at my very table
      Friends twisted it askew.

It leapt across the Channel,
      A bounding kangaroo.
It did not shrink like flannel
      But gained in size and hue.

It appeared in French and Spanish
      With errors not a few,
In Russian, Greek and Danish,
      Inaccurately, too.

And waxing more romantic
      With every wind that blew,
It crossed the broad Atlantic
      And grew and grew and grew.

At last, like boomerang, it
      Sped back across the blue,
And tall and touched with twang, it
      Appeared whence first it flew.

An annual affliction,
> It tours the wide world through,
And I who bred the fiction
> Have come to think it true.

Life's burden it has doubled,
> For peace of mind it slew,
My dreams by it are troubled,
> My days are filled with rue.

Its horrors yearly thicken,
> It sticks to me like glue,
And sad and conscience-stricken
> I curse that cockatoo.

"That is what will happen with Clorinda Bell's membership of our club," continued the poet. "She will remain a member long after it has ceased to exist. Once a thing has appeared in print, you cannot destroy it. A published lie is immortal. Age cannot wither it, nor custom stale its infinite variety. It thrives by contradiction. Give me a cup of tea and I will go and interview the *Moon*-man at once."

The millionaire, hearing tea was on the tray, came in to join them, and Silverdale soon went off to his aunt, Lady Goody-Goody Twoshoes, and got the address of the man in the *Moon*.

"Lillie, what's this I see in the *Moon* about Clorinda Bell joining your Club?" asked the millionaire.

"An invention, father."

The millionaire looked disappointed.

"Will all your Old Maids be young?"

"Yes, papa. It is best to catch them young."

"I shall be dining at the Club sometimes," he announced irrelevantly.

"Oh, no, papa. You are not admissible during the sittings."

"Why? You let Lord Silverdale in."

"Yes, but he is not married."

"Oh!" and the millionaire went away with brighter brow.

The Millionaire.

The rest of the afternoon Lillie was busy conducting the Preliminary Examination of a surpassingly beautiful girl who answered to the name of "Princess," and would give no other name for the present, not even to Turple the magnificent.

"You got my letter, I suppose?" asked the Princess.

"Oh, yes," said the President. "I should have written to you."

"I thought it best to come and see you about it at once, as I have suddenly determined to go to Brighton, and I don't know when I may be back. I had not heard of your Club till the other day, when I saw in the *Moon* that Clorinda Bell was going to join it, and anything she joins must of course be strictly proper, so I haven't troubled to ask the Honorable Miss Primpole's advice—she lives with me, you know. An only orphan cannot be too careful!"

"You need not fear," said Lillie. "Miss Bell is not to be a member. We have refused her."

"Oh, indeed! Well, perhaps it is as well not to bring the scent of the footlights over the Club. It is hard upon Miss Bell, but if you were to admit her, I suppose other actresses would want to come in. There are so many of them that prefer to remain single."

"Are you sure *you* do?"

"Positive. My experience of lovers has been so harassing and peculiar that I shall never marry, and as my best friends cannot call me a wall-flower, I venture to think you will find me a valuable ally in your noble campaign against the degrading superstition that Old Maids are women who have not found husbands, just as widows are women who have lost them."

"I sincerely hope so," said Lillie enthusiastically. "You express my views very neatly. May I ask what are the peculiar experiences you speak of?"

"Certainly. Some months ago I amused myself by recording the strange episodes of my first loves, and in anticipation of your request I have brought the manuscript."

"Oh, please read it!" said Lillie excitedly.

"Of course I have not given the real names."

"No, I quite understand. Won't you have a chocolate cream before you commence?"

"Thank you. They look lovely. How awfully sweet!"

"Too sweet for you?" inquired Lillie anxiously.

"No, no. I mean they are just nice."

The Princess untied the pretty pink ribbon that enfolded the dainty, scented manuscript, and pausing only to munch an occasional chocolate cream, she read on till the shades of evening fell over the Old Maids' Club and the soft glow of the candles illuminated its dainty complexion.

CHAPTER V.

"THE PRINCESS OF PORTMAN SQUARE."

I am an only child. I was born with a silver spoon in my mouth, and although there was no royal crest on it, yet no princess could be more comfortable in the purple than I was in the ordinary trappings of babyhood. From the cradle upwards I was surrounded with love and luxury. My pet name "Princess" fitted me like a glove. I was the autocrat of the nursery and my power scarce diminished when I rose to the drawing-room. My parents were very obedient and did not even conceal from me that I was beautiful. In short they did their best to spoil me, though I cannot admit that they succeeded. I lost them both before I was sixteen. My poor mother died first and my poor father followed within a week; whether from grief or from a cold caught through standing bareheaded in the churchyard, or from employing the same doctor, I cannot precisely determine.

After the usual period of sorrow, I began to pick up a bit and to go out under the care of my duenna, a faded flower of the aristocracy whose declining years my guardian had soothed by quartering her on me. She was a gentle old spinster, the seventh daughter of a penniless peer, and although she has seen hard times and has almost been reduced to marriage, yet she has scant respect for my ten thousand a year. She has never lost the sense of condescension in living with me, and would be horrified to hear she is in receipt of a salary. It is to this sense of superiority on her part that I owe a good deal of the liberty I enjoy under her régime. She does not expect in me that rigid obedience to venerable forms and conventions which she. prescribes for herself; she regards it as a privilege of the higher gentlewoman to be bound hand and foot by fashionable etiquette, and so long as my liberty does not degenerate into license I am welcome to as much as I please of it. She has continued to call me "Princess," finding doubtless some faint reverberation of pleasure in the magnificent syllables. I should add that her name is the Honorable Miss Primpole and that she is not afraid of the butler.

Our town-house was situated in Portman Square and my parents tenanted it during the season. There is nothing very poetic about the Square, perhaps, not even in the summer, when the garden is in bloom, yet it was here that I first learnt to love. This dull parallelogram was the birthplace of a passion as spiritual and intangible as ever thrilled maiden's heart. I fell in love with a Voice.

It was a rich, baritone Voice, with a compass of two and a half octaves, rising from full bass organ-notes to sweet, flute-like tenor tones. It was a glorious Voice, now resonant with martial ecstasy, now faint with mystic rapture. Its vibrations were charged with inexpressible emotion, and it sang of love and death and high heroic themes. I heard it first a few months after my father's funeral. It was night. I had been indoors all day, torpid and miserable, but roused myself at last and took a few turns in the square. The air was warm and scented, a cloudless moon flooded the roadway with mellow light and sketched in the silhouettes of the trees in the background. I had reached the opposite side of the square for the second time when the Voice broke out. My heart stood still and I with it.

On the soft summer air the Voice rose and fell; it was accompanied on the piano, but it seemed in subtler harmony with the moonlight and the perfumed repose of the night. It came through an open window behind which the singer sat in the gloaming. With the first tremors of that Voice my soul forgot its weariness in a strange sweet trance that trembled on pain. The song seemed to draw out all the hidden longing of my maiden soul, as secret writing is made legible by fire. When the Voice ceased, a great blackness fell upon all things, the air grew bleak. I waited and waited but the Square remained silent. The footsteps of stray pedestrians, the occasional roll of a carriage alone fell on my anxious ear. I returned to my house, shivering as with cold. I had never loved before. I had read and reflected a great deal about love, and was absolutely ignorant of the subject. I did not know that I loved now—for that discover only came later when I found myself wandering nightly to the other side of the parallelogram, listening for the Voice. Rarely, very rarely, was my pilgrimage rewarded, but twice or thrice a week the Square became an enchanted garden, full of roses whose petals were music. Round that baritone Voice I had built up an ideal man—tall and straight-limbed and stalwart, fair- haired and blue-eyed and noble-featured, like the hero of a Northern Saga. His soul was vast as the sea, shaken with the storms of passion, dimpled with smiles of tenderness. His spirit was at once mighty and delicate, throbbing with elemental forces yet keen and swift to comprehend all subtleties of thought and feeling. I could not understand myself, yet I felt that he would understand me. He had the heart of a lion and of a little child; he was as merciful as he was strong, as pure as he was wise. To be with him were happiness, to feel his kiss ecstasy, to be gathered to his breast, delirium, But alas! he never knew that I was waiting under his window.

I made several abortive attempts to discover who he was or to see him. According to the Directory the house was occupied by Lady Westerton. I concluded that he was her elder son. That he might be her husband—or some other lady's—never even occurred to me. I do not know why I should have attached the Voice to a bachelor, any more than I can explain why he should be the eldest son, rather than the youngest. But romance has a logic of its own. From the topmost window of my house I could see Lady Westerton's house across the trees, but I never saw him leave or enter it. Once, a week went by without my hearing him sing. I did not know whether to think of him as a sick bird or as one flown to warmer climes. I tried to construct his life from his periods of song, I watched the lights in his window, my whole life circled round him. It was only when I grew pale and feverish and was forced by the doctors and my guardian to go yachting that my fancies gradually detached themselves from my blue-eyed hero. The sea-salt freshened my thoughts, I became a healthy-minded girl again, carolling joyously in my cabin and taking pleasure in listening to my own voice. I threw my novels overboard (metaphorically, that is) and set the Hon. Miss Primpole chatting instead, when the seascape palled upon me. She had a great fund of strictly respectable memories. Most people's recollections are of no use to anybody but the owner, but hers afforded entertainment for both of us. By the time I was back in London the Voice was no longer part even of my dreams, though it seemed to belong to them. But for accident it might have remained forever "a voice and nothing more." The accident happened at a musical-afternoon in Kensington. I was introduced to a tall, fair, handsome blue-eyed guardsman, Captain Athelstan by name. His conversation was charming and I took a lot of it, while Miss Primpole was busy flirting with a seductive Spaniard. You could not tell Miss Primpole was flirting except by looking at the man. In the course of the afternoon the hostess asked the captain to sing. As he went to the piano my heart began to flutter with a strange foreboding. He had no music with him, but plunged at once into the promontory chords. My agitation increased tenfold. He was playing the prelude to one of the Voice's songs—a strange, haunting song with a Schubert atmosphere, a song which I had looked for in vain among the classics. At once he was transfigured to my eyes, all my sleeping romantic fancies woke to delicious life, and in the instant in which I waited, with bated breath, for the outbreak of the Voice at the well-known turn of the melody, it was borne in upon me that this was the only man I had ever loved or would ever love. My Saga hero! my Berserker, my Norse giant!

Miss Primpole was flirting with a seductive Spaniard.

When the Voice started it was not *my* Voice. It was a thin, throaty tenor. Compared with the Voice of Portman Square, it was as a tinkling rivulet to a rushing full-volumed river. I sank back on the lounge, hiding my emotions behind my fan.

When the song was finished, he made his way through the "Bravas" to my side.

"Sweetly pretty!" I murmured.

"The song or the singing?" he asked with a smile.

"The song," I answered frankly. "Is it yours?"

"No, but the singing is!"

His good-humor was so delightful that I forgave his not having my Voice.

"What is its name?"

"It is anonymous—like the composer."

"Who is he?"

"I must not tell."

"Can you give me a copy of the song?"

He became embarrassed.

"I would with pleasure, if it were mine. But the fact is—I—I—had no right to sing it at all, and the composer would be awfully vexed if he knew."

"Original composer?"

"He is, indeed. He cannot bear to think of his songs being sung in public."

"Dear me! What a terrible mystery you are making of it," I laughed.

"O r-really there is no abracadabra about it. You misunderstand me. But I deserve it all for breaking faith and exploiting his lovely song so as to drown my beastly singing."

"You need not reproach yourself," I said. "I have heard it before."

He started perceptibly. "Impossible," he gasped.

"Thank you," I said freezingly.

"But how?"

"A little bird sang it me."

"It is you who are making the mystery now."

"Tit for tat. But I will discover yours."

"Not unless you are a witch!"

"A what?"

"A witch."

"I am," I said enigmatically. "So you see it's of no use hiding anything from me. Come, tell me all, or I will belabor you with my broomstick."

"If you know, why should I tell you?"

"I want to see if you can tell the truth."

"No, I can't." We both laughed. "See what a cruel dilemma you place me in!" he said beseechingly.

"Tell me, at least, why he won't publish his songs. Is he too modest, too timid?"

"Neither. He loves art for art's sake—that is all."

"I don't understand."

"He writes to please himself. To create music is his highest pleasure. He can't see what it has got to do with anybody else."

"But surely he wants the world to enjoy his work?"

"Why? That would be art for the world's sake, art for fame's sake, art for money's sake!"

"What an extraordinary view!"

"Why so? The true artist—the man to whom creation is rapture—surely he is his own world. Unless he is in need of money, why should he concern himself with the outside universe? My friend cannot understand why Schopenhauer should have troubled himself to chisel epigrams or Leopardi lyrics to tell people that life was not worth living. Had either been a true artist, he would have gone on living his own worthless life, unruffled by the applause of the mob. My friend can understand a poet translating into inspired song the sacred secrets of his soul, but he cannot understand his scattering them broad-cast through the country, still less taking a royalty on them. He says it is selling your soul in the market-place, and almost as degrading as going on the stage."

"And do you agree with him?"

"Not entirely, otherwise I should never have yielded to the temptation to sing his song to-night. Fortunately he will never hear of it. He never goes into society, and I am his only friend."

"Dear me!" I said sarcastically. "Is he as careful to conceal his body as his soul?"

His face grew grave. "He has an affliction," he said in low tones.

"Oh, forgive me!" I said remorsefully. Tears came into my eyes as the vision of the Norse giant gave away to that of an English hunchback. My adoring worship was transformed to an adoring matronly tenderness. Divinely-gifted sufferer, if I cannot lean on thy strength, thou shalt lean on mine! So ran my thought till the mist cleared from my eyes and I saw again the glorious Saga-hero at my side, and grew strangely confused and distraught.

"There is nothing to forgive," answered Captain Athelstan. "You did not know him."

"You forget I am a witch. But I do not know him—it is true. I do not even know his name. Yet within a week I undertake to become a friend of his."

He shook his head. "You do not know him."

"I admitted that," I answered pertly. "Give me a week, and he shall not only know me, he shall abjure those sublime principles of his at my request."

The spirit of mischief moved me to throw down the challenge. Or was it some deeper impulse?

He smiled sceptically.

"Of course if you know somebody who will introduce you," he began.

"Nobody shall introduce me," I interrupted.

"Well, he'll never speak to you first."

"You mean it would be unmaidenly for me to speak to him first. Well, I will bind myself to do nothing of which Mrs. Grundy would disapprove. And yet the result shall be as I say."

"Then I shall admit you are indeed a witch."

"You don't believe in my power, that is. Well, what will you wager?"

"If you achieve your impossibility, you will deserve anything."

"Will you back your incredulity with a pair of gloves?"

"With a hundred."

"Thank you. I am not a Briareus. Let us say one pair then."

"So be it."

"But no countermining. Promise me not to communicate with your mysterious friend in the interval."

"I promise."

"But how shall I know the result?"

I pondered. "I will write—no, that would be hardly proper. Meet me in the Royal Academy, Room Six, at the 'Portrait of a Gentleman,' about noon to-morrow week."

47

"A week is a long time!" he sighed.

I arched my eyebrows. "A week a long time for such a task!" I exclaimed.

Next day I called at the house of the Voice. A gorgeous creature in plush opened the door.

"I want to see—to see—gracious! I've forgotten his name," I said in patent chagrin. I clucked my tongue, puckered my lips, tapped the step with my parasol, then smiled pitifully at the creature in plush. He turned out to be only human, for a responsive sympathetic smile flickered across his pompous face. "You know—the singer," I said, as if with a sudden inspiration.

"Oh. Lord Arthur!" he said.

"Yes, of course," I cried, with a little trill of laughter. "How stupid of me! Please tell him I want to see him on an important matter."

"He—he's very busy, I'm afraid, miss."

"Oh, but he'll see me," I said confidently.

"Yes, miss; who shall I say, miss?"

"The Princess."

He made a startled obeisance, and ushered me into a little room on the right of the hall. In a few moments he returned and said—"His lordship will be down in a second, your highness."

Sixty minutes seemed to go to that second, so racked was I with curiosity. At last I heard a step outside and a hand on the door, and at that moment a horrible thought flashed into my mind. What certainty was there my singer was a hunchback? Suppose his affliction were something more loathly. What if he had a monstrous wen! For the instant after his entry I was afraid to look up. When I did, I saw a short, dark-haired young man, with proper limbs and refined features. But his face wore a blank expression, and I wondered why I had not divined before that my musician was blind!

He bowed and advanced towards me. He came straight in my direction so that I saw he *could* see. The blank expression gave place to one of inquiry.

"I have ventured to call upon your lordship in reference to a Charity Concert," I said sweetly; "I am one of your neighbors, living just across the square, and as the good work is to be done in this district, I dared to hope that I could persuade you to take part in it."

I happened to catch sight of my face in the glass of a chiffonier as I spoke, and it was as pure and candid and beautiful as the face of one of Guido's angels. When I ceased, I looked up at Lord Arthur's. It was spasmodically agitated, the mouth was working wildly. A nervous dread seized me.

After what seemed an endless interval, he uttered an explosive "Put!" following it up by "f-f-f-f-f-f-f-f-or two g-g-g-g-g-g-g-g——"

"It is very kind of you," I interrupted mercifully. "But I did not propose to ask you for a subscription. I wanted to enlist your services as a performer. But I fear I have made a mistake. I understood you sang." Inwardly I was furious with the stupid creature in plush for having misled me into such an unpleasant situation.

"I d-d-d-o s-s-s-s-s——" he answered.

As he stood there hissing, the truth flashed upon me at last. I had heard that the most dreadful stammerers enunciate as easily as anybody else when they sing, because the measured swing of the time keeps them steady. My heart sank as I thought of the Voice so mutilated! Poor young peer! Was this to be the end of all my beautiful visions?

As cheerfully as I could I cut short his sibilations. "Oh, that's all right, then," I said. "Then I may put you down for a couple of items."

He shook his head, and held up his hands deprecatingly.

"Anything but that!" he stammered; "Make me a patron, a committee-man, anything! I do not sing in public."

While he was saying this I thought long and deeply. The affliction was after all less terrible than I had a right to expect, and I knew from the advertisement columns that it was easily curable. Demosthenes, I remembered, had stoned it to death. I felt my love reviving, as I looked into his troubled face, instinct with the double aristocracy of rank and genius. At the worst the singing Voice was unaffected by the disability, and as for the conversational, well there was consolation in the prospect of having the last word while one's husband was still having the first. *En attendant*, I could have wished him to sing his replies instead of speaking them, for not only should I thus enjoy his Voice but the interchange of ideas would proceed less tardily. However that would have made him into an operatic personage, and I did not want him to look so ridiculous as all that.

It would be tedious to recount our interview at the length it extended to. Suffice it to say that I gained my point. Without letting out that I knew of his theories of art for art's sake, I yet artfully pleaded that whatever one's views, charity alters cases, inverts everything, justifies anything. "For instance," I said with charming *naïveté*, "I would not have dared to call on you but in its sacred name." He agreed to sing two songs—nay, two of his own songs. I was to write to him particulars of time and place. He saw me to the door. I held out my hand and he took it, and we looked at each other, smiling brightly.

"B-but I d-d-d-don't know your n-n-name," he said suddenly. "P-p-p-rincess what?"

He spoke more fluently, now he had regained his composure.

"Princess," I answered, my eyes gleaming merrily. "That is all. The Honorable Miss Primpole will give me a character, if you require one." He laughed—his laugh was like the Voice—and followed me with his eyes as I glided away.

I had won my gloves—and in a day. I thought remorsefully of the poor Saga hero destined to wait a week in suspense as to the result. But it was too late to remedy this, and the organization of the Charity Concert needed all my thoughts. I was in for it now, and I resolved to carry it through. But it was not so easy as I had lightly assumed. Getting the artists, of course, was nothing—there are always so many professionals out of work or anxious to be brought out, and so many amateurs in search of amusement. I could have filled the Albert Hall with entertainers. Nor did I anticipate any difficulty in disposing of the tickets. If you are at all popular in society you can get a good deal of unpopularity by forcing them on your friends. No, the real difficulty about this Charity Concert was the discovery of an object in aid of which to give it. In my innocence I had imagined that the world was simply bustling with unexploited opportunities for well-doing. Alas! I soon found that philanthropy was an over-crowded profession. There was not a single nook or corner of the universe but had been ransacked by these restless free-lances; not a gap, not a cranny but had been filled up. In vain I explored the map, in the hopes of lighting on some undiscovered hunting-ground in far Cathay or where the khamsin sweeps the Afric deserts. I found that the wants of the most benighted savages were carefully attended to, and that, even when they had none, they were thoughtfully supplied with them. Anxiously I scanned the newspapers in search of a calamity, the sufferers by which I might relieve, but only one happened during that week, and that was snatched from between my very fingers by a lady who had just been through the Divorce Court. In my despair I bethought myself of the preacher I sat under. He was a very handsome man, and published his sermons by request.

I went to him and I said: "How is the church?"

"It is all right, thank you," he said.

"Doesn't it want anything done to it?"

"No, it is in perfect repair. My congregation is so very good."

I groaned aloud. "But isn't there any improvement that you would like?"

"The last of the gargoyles was put up last week. Mediæval architecture is always so picturesque. I have had the entire structure made mediæval, you know."

"But isn't the outside in need of renovation?"

"What! When I have just had it made mediæval!"

"But the interior—there must be something defective somewhere!"

"Not to my knowledge."

"But think! think!" I cried desperately. "The aisles—transept—nave—lectern—pews—chancel—pulpit—apse—porch—altar-cloths—organ—spires—is there nothing in need of anything?"

He shook his head.

"Wouldn't you like a colored window to somebody?"

"All the windows are taken up. My congregation is so very good."

"A memorial brass then?"

He mused.

"There is only one of my flock who has done anything memorable lately."

My heart gave a great leap of joy. "Then why do you neglect him?" I asked indignantly. "If we do not perpetuate the memory of virtue——"

"He's alive," he interrupted.

I bit my lips in vexation.

"I think you need a few more choristers," I murmured.

"Oh no, we are sending some away."

"The Sunday School Fund—how is that?"

"I am looking about for a good investment for the surplus. Do you know of any? A good mortgage, perhaps?"

"Is there none on the church?" I cried with a flicker of hope.

"Heaven forbid!"

I cudgelled my brains frantically. "What do you think of a lightning-rod!"

"A premier necessity. I never preach in a building unprotected by one."

I made one last wild search.

"How about a reredos?"

He looked at me in awful, pained silence.

I saw I had stumbled. "I—I mean a new wing," I stammered.

"I am afraid you are not well this morning," said the preacher, patting my hand soothingly. "Won't you come and talk it over, whatever it is, another time?"

"No, no," I cried excitedly. "It must be settled at once. I have it. A new peal of bells!"

"What is the matter with the bells?" he asked anxiously. "There isn't a single one cracked."

I saw his dubiety, and profited by it. I learnt afterwards it was due to his having no ear of his own.

"Cracked! Perhaps not," I replied in contemptuous accents. "But they deserve to be. No wonder the newspapers keep correspondences going on the subject."

"Yes, but what correspondents object to is the bells ringing at all."

"I don't wonder," I said. "I don't say your bells are worse than the majority, or that I haven't got a specially sensitive ear for music, but I know that when I hear their harsh clanging, I—well I don't feel inclined to go to church and that's the truth. I am quite sure if you had a really musical set of chimes, it would increase the spirituality of the neighborhood."

"How so?" he asked sceptically.

"It would keep down swearing on Sunday."

"Oh!" He pondered a moment, then said: "But that would be a great expense."

"Indeed? I thought bells were cheap."

"Certainly. Area bells, hand-bells, sleigh-bells. But Church-bells are very costly. There are only a few foundries in the kingdom. But why are you so concerned about my church?"

"Because I am giving a Charity Concert, and I should like to devote the proceeds to something."

"A very exemplary desire. But I fear one bell is the most you could get out of a Charity Concert."

I looked disappointed. "What a pity! It would have been such a nice precedent to improve the tone of the Church. The 'constant readers' would have had to cease their letters."

"No, no, impossible. A 'constant reader' seems to be so called because he is a constant writer."

"But there might have been leaders about it."

"Hardly sensational enough for that! Stay I have an idea. In the beautiful Ages of Faith, when a Church-bell was being cast, the pious used to bring silver vessels to be fused with the bell-metal in the furnace, so as to give the bell a finer tone. A mediæval practice is always so poetical. Perhaps I could revive it. My congregation is so very good."

"Good!" I echoed, clapping my hands. "But a Concert will not suffice— we shall need a Bazaar," said the preacher.

"Oh, but I must have a Concert!"

"Certainly Bazaars include Concerts."

How the Duchess wanted to appear.

That was how the Great Church Bazaar originated and how the Rev. Melitos Smith came to resurrect the beautiful mediæval custom which brought him so much kudos and extracted such touching sentiments from hardened journalists. The Bazaar lasted a week, and raised a number of ladies in the social scale, and married off three of my girl-friends, and cut me off the visiting list of the Duchess of Dash. She was pining for a chance of coming out in a comic opera chanson, but this being a Church Bazaar I couldn't allow her to kick up her heels. Everything could be bought at that Bazaar, from photographs of the Rev. Melitos Smith to impracticable mouse-traps, from bread-and-cheese to kisses. There were endless side-shows, and six gipsy girls scattered about the rooms, so that you could have your fortune told in six different ways. I should not like to say how much that Bazaar cost me when the bill for the Bells came in, but then Lord Arthur sang daily in the Concert Hall, and I could also deduct the price of the pair of gloves Captain Athelstan gave me. For the Captain honorably stood the loss of his wager, nay, more, cheerfully accepted his defeat, and there on the spot—before the "Portrait of another Gentleman"—offered to enlist in the Bazaar. And very useful he proved, too. We had to be together, organizing it, nearly all day and I don't know what I should have done without him. I don't know what his Regiment did without him, but then I have never been able to find out when our gallant officers do their work. They seem always to be saving it up for a rainy day.

I was never more surprised in my life than when, on the last night of the Bazaar-boom, amid the buzz of a brisk wind-up, Lord Arthur and Captain Athelstan came into the little presidential sanctum, which had been run up for me, and requested a special interview.

"I can give you five minutes," I said, for I felt my finger was on the pulse of the Bazaar, and my time correspondingly important.

They looked grateful, then embarrassed. Captain Athelstan opened his mouth and closed it.

"*You* had better tell her," he said, nervously, to Lord Arthur.

"N-n-no, y-y-y-y——"

"What is it, Captain Athelstan?" I interrupted, pointedly, for I had only five minutes.

"Princess, we both love you," began the Captain, blushing like a hobbledehoy, and rushing *in medias res*. I allowed them to call me Princess, because it was not my Christian name.

"Is this the time—when I am busy feeling the pulse of the Bazaar?"

"You gave us five minutes," pleaded the Captain, determined to do or die, now he was in the thick of it.

"Go on," I said, "I will forgive you everything—even your love of me—if you are only brief."

"We both love you. We are great friends. We have no secrets. We told each other. We are doubtful if you love either—or which. We have come together."

He fired off the short, sharp sentences as from a six-barrelled revolver.

"Captain Athelstan—Lord Arthur," I said. "I am deeply touched by the honor you have done your friendship and me. I will be equally frank—and brief—with you. I cannot choose either of you, because I love you both. Like every girl, I formed an ideal of a lover. I have been fortunate in finding my ideal in the flesh. I have been unfortunate in finding it in two pieces. Fate has bisected it, and given the form to one and the voice to the other. My ideal looks like you, Captain Athelstan, and sings like you, Lord Arthur. It is a stupid position, I know, and I feel like the donkey between two bundles of hay. But under the circumstances I have no choice."

They looked at each other half-rapturously, half-despairingly.

"Then what's to be done?" cried the Captain.

"I don't know," I said, hopelessly. "Love seems not only blind, but a blind alley, this time."

"D-do you m-m-ean," asked Lord Arthur, "'how happy could I be with either, were t'other dear charmer away?'"

I was glad he sang it, because it precipitated matters.

"That is the precise position," I admitted.

"Oh, then, Arthur, my boy, I congratulate you," said the Captain, huskily.

"N-n-no, I'll g-g-go away," said the singer.

They wrangled for full ten minutes, but the position remained a block.

Bazaar proposal of Marriage.

"Gentlemen," I interposed, "if either of you had consented to accept the other's sacrifice, the problem would have been solved; only I should have taken the other. But two self-sacrifices are as bad as none."

"Then let us toss up for you, Princess," said the Captain, impulsively.

"Oh, no!" I cried, with a shudder. "Submit my life to the chances of head or tail! It would make me feel like a murderess, with you for gentlemen of the jury."

A painful silence fell upon the sanctum. Unwitting of the tragedy playing within, all the fun of the fair went on without.

"Listen," I said, at last. "I will be the wife of him who wins me. Chance shall not decide, but prowess. Like the princesses of old, I will set you a task. Whoever accomplishes it shall win my hand."

"Agreed," they said eagerly, though not simultaneously.

"Ay, but what shall it be?" I murmured.

"Why not a competition?" suggested the Captain.

"Very well, a competition—provided you promise to fight fair, and not play into each other's hands."

They promised, and together we excogitated and rejected all sorts of competitions. The difficulty was to find something in which each would have a fair chance. At length we arranged that they should play a game of chess, the winner to be mated. They agreed it would be a real "match game." The five minutes had by this time lasted half an hour, so I dismissed them, and hastened to feel the pulse of the Bazaar, which was getting more and more feverish as the break-up drew nigh.

They played the game in Lord Arthur's study. Lord Arthur was white and the Captain black. Everything was fair and above board. But they played rather slowly. Every evening I sent the butler over to make inquiries.

"The Princess's compliments," he was told to say, "and how is it to-day?"

"It is getting on," they told him, and he came back with a glad face. He was a kind soul despite his calves, and he thought there was a child dying.

Once a week I used to go over and look at it. Ostensibly I called in connection with the Bazaar accounts. I could not see any difference in the position from one week's end to another. There seemed to be a clump of pawns in the middle, with all the other pieces looking idly on; there was no thoroughfare anywhere.

They told me it always came like that when you played cautiously. They said it was a French opening. I could not see any opening anywhere; it certainly was not the English way of fighting. Picture my suspense during those horrible weeks.

"Is this the way all match-games are played?" I said once.

"N-n-o," admitted Lord Arthur. "We for-g-g-ot to p-p-p-ut a t-t-t-t-time-limit."

"What's the time-limit?" I asked the Captain, wishing my singer could learn to put one to his sentences.

"So many moves must be made in an hour—usually fifteen. Otherwise the younger champion would always win, merely by outliving the elder. We forgot to include that condition."

At length our butler brought back word that "it couldn't last much longer." His face was grave and he gave the message in low tones.

"What a blessing. It's been lingering long enough! I wish they would polish it off," I murmured fretfully. After that I frequently caught him looking at me as if I were Lucrezia Borgia.

The end came suddenly. The butler went across to make the usual inquiry. He returned, with a foolish face of horror and whispered, "It is all over. It has been drawn by perpetual check!"

"Great Heavens!" I cried. My consternation was so manifest that he forgave the utterance of a peevish moment. I put on my nicest hat at once and went over. We held a council of war afresh.

"Let's go by who catches the biggest trout," suggested the Captain.

"No," I said. "I will not be angled for. Besides, the biggest is not grammatical. It should be the bigger."

Thus reproved, the Captain grew silent and we came to a deadlock once more. I gave up the hunt at last.

"I think the best plan will be for you both to go away and travel. Go round the world, see fresh faces, try to forget me. One of you will succeed."

"But suppose we both succeed?" asked the Captain.

"That would be more awkward than ever," I admitted.

"And if neither succeed?" asked Lord Arthur at some length.

"I should say neither succeeds," I remarked severely. "Neither takes a singular verb."

"Pardon me," said Lord Arthur with some spirit. "The plurality is merely apparent. 'Succeed' is subjunctive after if."

"Ah, true," I said. "Then suppose you go round the world and I give my hand to whoever comes back and proposes to me first."

"Something like the man in Jules Verne!" cried the Captain. "Glorious!"

"Except that it can be done quicker now," I said.

Lord Arthur fell in joyously with the idea, which was a godsend to me, for the worry of having about you two men whom you love and who love you cannot be easily conceived by those who have not been through it. They, too, were pining away and felt the journey would do them good. Captain Athelstan applied for three months' furlough. He was to put a girdle round the earth from West to East, Lord Arthur from East to West. It was thought this would work fairly—as whatever advantages one outgoing route had over the other would be lost on the return. Each drew up his scheme and prepared his equipment. The starting-point was to be my house, and consequently this was also the goal. After forty-eight days had passed (the minimum time possible) I was to remain at home day and night, awaiting the telegram which was to be sent the moment either touched English soil again. On the receipt of the telegram I was to take up my position at the front window on the ground floor, with a white rose in my hair to show I was still unwon, and to wait there day and night for the arrival of my offer of marriage, which I was not to have the option of refusing. During the race they were not to write to me.

The long-looked-for day of their departure duly arrived. Two hansoms were drawn up side by side, in front of the house. A white rose in my hair, I sat at the window. A parting smile, a wave of my handkerchief, and my lovers were off. In an instant they were out of sight. For a month they were out of mind, too. After the exhausting emotions I had undergone this period of my life was truly halcyon. I banished my lovers from my memory and enjoyed what was left of the season and of my girlish freedom. In two months I should be an affianced wife and it behoved me to make the best of my short span of spinsterhood. The season waned, fashion drifted to Cowes, I was left alone in empty London. Then my thoughts went back to the two travellers. As day followed day, my anxiety and curiosity mounted proportionately. The forty-eight days went by, but there was no wire. They passed slowly—oh, so slowly —into fifty, while I waited, waited, from dawn to midnight, with ears pricked up, for that double rat-tat which came not or which came about something else. The sands of September dribbled out, and my fate still hung in the balance. I went about the house like an unquiet spirit. In imagination I was seeing those two men sweeping towards me—one from the East of the world, one from the West. And there I stood, rooted to the spot, while from either side a man was speeding inevitably towards me, across oceans and continents, through canals and tunnels, along deserts or rivers, pressing into his service every human and animal force and every blind energy that man had tamed. To my fevered imagination I seemed to be between the jaws of a leviathan, which were closing upon me at a terrific rate, yet which took days to snap together, so wide were they apart, so gigantic was the monster. Which of the jaws would touch me first?

The fifties mounted into the sixties, but there was no telegram. The tension became intolerable. Again and again I felt tempted to fly, but a lingering sense of honor kept me to my post. On the sixty-first day my patience was rewarded. Sitting at my window one morning I saw a telegraph-boy sauntering along. He reached the gate. He paused. I rushed to the door and down the steps, seized the envelope and tore it frantically open.

*"Coming, but suppose all over.—*Arthur.*"*

I leaned on the gate, half fainting. When I went to my room, I read the wire again and noted it had been handed in at Liverpool. In four or five hours at most I should cease to belong to myself. I communicated the news to the Honorable Miss Primpole who congratulated me cordially. She made no secret of her joy that the nobleman had won. For my part I was still torn with conflicting emotions. Now that I knew it was to be the one, I hankered after the other. Yet in the heart of the storm there was peace in the thought that the long suspense was over. I ordered a magnificent repast to be laid for the home-coming voyager, which would also serve to celebrate our nuptials. The Honorable Miss Primpole consented to grace the board and the butler to surrender the choicest vintages garnered in my father's cellar.

Two hours and a half dragged by; then there came another wire—I opened it with some curiosity, but as my eye caught the words I almost swooned with excitement. It ran:

*"Arrived, but presume too late.—*Athelstan.*"*

With misty vision I strove to read the place of despatch. It was Dover. A great wave of hope surged in my bosom. My Saga-hero might yet arrive in time. Half frenziedly I turned over the leaves of Bradshaw. No, after sending that wire, he would just have missed the train to Victoria! Cruel! Cruel! But stay! there was another route. He might have booked for Charing Cross. Yes! Heaven be praised, if he did that, he would just catch a train. And of course he would do that—surely he would have planned out every possibility while crossing the Channel, have arranged for all—my Captain, my blue-eyed Berserker! But then Lord Arthur had had two and a half hours' start.—I turned to Liverpool and essayed to discover whether that was sufficient to balance the difference of the two distances from London. Alas! my head swam before I had travelled two stations. There were no less than four routes to Euston, to St. Pancras, to King's Cross, to Paddington! Still I made out that if he had kept his head very clear, and been very, very fortunate, he might just get level with the Captain. But then on a longer route the chances of accidental delays were more numerous. On the whole the odds were decidedly in favor of the Captain. But one thing was certain—that they would both arrive in time for supper. I ordered an additional cover to be laid, then I threw myself upon a couch and tried to read. But I could not. Terrible as was the strain, my thoughts refused to be distracted. The minutes crawled along—

gradually peace came back as I concluded that only by a miracle could Lord Arthur win. At last I jumped up with a start, for the shades of evening were falling and my toilette was yet to make. I dressed myself in a dainty robe of white, trimmed with sprays of wild flowers, and I stuck the white rose in my hair—the symbol that I was yet unasked in wedlock, the white star of hope to the way-worn wanderer! I did my best to be the fairest sight the travellers should have seen in all the world.

The Honorable Miss Primpole started when she saw me. "What have you been doing to yourself, Princess?" she said. "You're lovelier than I ever dreamed."

And indeed the crisis had lent a flush to my cheek and a flash to my eye which I would not willingly repay. My bosom rose and fell with excitement. In half an hour I should be in my Saga-hero's arms! I went down to the ground-floor front and seated myself at the open window and gazed at the Square and the fiery streaks of sunset in the sky. The Honorable Miss Primpole lay upon an ottoman, less excited. Every now and again she asked,

"Do you see anything, Princess?"

"Nothing," I answered.

Of course she did not take my answer literally. Several times cabs and carriages rattled past the window, but with no visible intention of drawing up. Duskier, duskier grew the September evening, as I sat peering into the twilight.

"Do you see anything, Princess?"

"Nothing."

A moment after a hansom came dashing into sight—a head protruded from it. I uttered a cry and leant forward, straining my eyes. Captain Athelstan. Yes! No! No! Yes! No! *No!* Will it be believed that (such is the heart of woman) I felt a sensation of relief on finding the issue still postponed? For in the moment when the Captain seemed to flash upon my vision—it was borne in upon me like a chilling blast that I had lost my Voice. Never would that glorious music swell for me as I sat alone with my husband in the gloaming.

The streaks of sunset faded into gray ashes.

"Do you see anything, Princess?"

"Nothing."

Even as I spoke I heard the gallop of hoofs in the quiet Square, and, half paralyzed by the unexpected vision, I saw Lord Arthur dashing furiously up on horseback—Lord Arthur, bronzed and bearded and travel-stained, but Lord

Arthur beyond a doubt. He took off his hat and waved it frantically in the air when he caught sight of my white figure, with the white rose of promise nestling in my hair. My poor Saga-hero!

F.H Townsend 92

At the winning Post.

He reined in his beautiful steed before my window and commenced his proposal breathlessly.

"*W-w-w——*"

Even Mr. Gladstone, if he had been racing as madly as Lord Arthur might well have been flustered in his speech. The poor singer could not get out the first word, try as he would. At last it came out like a soda-water cork and 'you' with it. But at the 'be' there was—O dire to tell!—another stoppage.

"*B-b-b-b-b*——"

"Fire! Fire! Hooray!" The dull roar of an advancing crowd burst suddenly upon our ears, mingled with the piercing exultation of small boys. The thunderous clatter of the fire-engine seemed to rock the soil of the Square.

But neither of us took eyes off the other.

"*Be!*" It was out at last. The end was near. In another second I should say "Yes."

"Fire! Fire!" shrieked the small boys.

"*M-m-m-y*——"

Lord Arthur's gallant steed shifted uneasily. The fire-engine was thundering down upon it.

"*W-w-w*——"

"*Will you be*——" The clarion notes of the Captain rang out above the clatter of the fire-engine from which he madly jumped.

"*Wife?*" }
"*Mine?*" } the two travellers exclaimed together.

"Dead heat," I murmured, and fell back in a dead faint. My overwrought nerves could stand no more.

Nevertheless it was a gay supper-party; the air was thick with travellers' tales, and the butler did not spare the champagne. We could not help being tickled by the quaint termination of the colossal globe-trotting competition, and we soothed Lord Arthur's susceptibilities by insisting that if he had only remembered the shorter proposal formula employed by his rival, he would have won by a word. It was a pure fluke that the Captain was able to tie, for he had not thought of telegraphing for a horse, but had taken a hansom at the station, and only exchanged to the fire-engine when he heard people shouting there was a fire in Seymour Street. Lord Arthur obliged five times during the evening, and the Honorable Miss Primpole relaxed more than ever before and accompanied him on the banjo. Before we parted, I had been persuaded by my lovers to give them one last trial. That night three months I was to give another magnificent repast, to which they were both to be invited. During the interval each was to do his best to become famous, and at the supper-party I was to choose the one who was the more widely known throughout the length and breadth of the kingdom. They were to place before me what proofs and arguments they pleased, and I was to decide whose name had penetrated to the greater number of people. There was to be no appeal from my decision, nor any limitation to what the candidates might do to force themselves upon the universal consciousness, so long as they did not merely advertise themselves at so much a column or poster. They could safely be trusted not to do anything infamous in the attempt to become famous, and so there was no need to impose conditions. I had a secret hope that Lord Arthur might thus be induced to bring his talents before the world and get over his objection to the degradation of public appearances. My hope was more than justified.

"Ba, ba, ba, boodle-dee."

I grieve to say neither strove to benefit his kind. His lordship went on the music-hall stage, made up as a costermonger, and devoted his wonderful voice and his musical genius to singing a cockney ballad with a chorus consisting merely of the words "Ba, ba, ba, boodle-dee" repeated sixteen times. It caught on like a first-class epidemic. "Ba, ba, ba, boodle-dee" microbes floated in every breeze. The cholera-chorus raged from Piccadilly to Land's End, from Kensington to John o'Groats. The swarthy miners hewed the coal to it. It dropped from passing balloons, the sailors manned the capstan to it, and the sound of it superseded fog-horns. Duchesses danced to it, and squalid infants cried for it. Divines with difficulty kept it out of their sermons, philosophers drew weighty lessons from it, critics traced its history, and as it didn't mean anything the greatest Puritans hummed it inaccurately. "Ba, ba, ba, boodle-dee," sang Lord Arthur nightly at six halls and three theatres, incidentally clearing off all the debts on the family estates, and, like a flock of sheep, the great British public took up the bleat, and in every hall and drawing-room blossomed the big pearl buttons of the cockney costermonger.

But Captain Athelstan came to the front far more easily, if less profitably. He sent a testimonial to the Perfect Cure Elixir. The Elixir was accustomed to testimonials from the suffering millions. The spelling generally had to be corrected before they were fit for publication. It also received testimonials which were useless, such as: "I took only one bottle of your Elixir and I got fourteen days." But a testimonial from a Captain of the Guards was a gold-mine. The Captain's was the best name the Elixir had ever had, and he had enjoyed more diseases than it had hitherto professed to cure. Astonished by its own success the Elixir resolved to make a big spurt and kill off all its rivals. For the next few months Captain Athelstan was rammed down the throats of all England. He came with the morning milk in all the daily papers, he arrived by the first post in a circular, he stared at people from every dead wall when they went out to business, he was with them at lunch, in little plaques and placards in every restaurant, he nodded at them in every bar, rode with them in every train and tram-car, either on the wall or on the back of the ticket, joined them at dinner in the evening papers and supplied the pipe lights after the meal. You took up a magazine and found he had slipped between the sheets, you went to bed and his diseased figure haunted your dreams. Life lost its sweetness, literature its charm. The loathsome phantasm of the complexly- afflicted Captain got between you and the sunshine. Stiff examination papers (compiled from the Captain) were set at every breakfast-table, and you were sternly interrogated as to whether you felt an all-gone sensation at the tip of your nose, and you were earnestly adjured to look at your old diseases. You began to read an eloquent description of the Alps, and lo! there was the Captain perched on top. You started a thrilling story of the sea, and the Captain bobbed up from the bottom; you began a poetical allegory concerning the Valley of the Shadow, and you found the Captain had been living there all his life—till he came upon the Elixir. A little innocent child remarked, "Pater, it is almost bath-time," and you felt for your handkerchief in view of a touching domestic idyl, but the Captain froze your tears. "Why have sunstroke in India?" you were asked, and the Captain supplied the answer. Something came like a thief in the night. It was the Captain. You were startled to see that there was "A Blight Over All Creation," but it turned out to be only the Captain. Everything abutted on the Captain—Shakespeare and the musical glasses, the Venus of Milo and the Mikado, Day and Night and all the seasons, the potato harvest and the Durham Coal Strike, the advantages of early rising, and the American Copyright Act. He was at the bottom of every passage, he lurked in every avenue, he was at the end of every perspective. The whole world was familiar with his physical symptoms, and his sad history. The exploits of Julius Cæsar were but a blur in the common mind, but everybody knew that the Captain's skin grew Gobelin blue, that the whites of his eyes turned green, and his tongue stuck in his cheek, and that the rest of his organism behaved with corresponding gruesomeness. Everybody knew how they dropped off, "petrified by my breath," and how his sympathetic friends told him in large capitals

"You will never get better, Captain,"

and how his weeping mother, anxious to soothe his last hours, remarked in reply to a request for another box of somebody else's pills,

"The only box you'll ever want will be a Coffin,"

and how

"He thought it was only Cholera,"

but how one dose of the Elixir (which new-born babies clamored for in preference to their mother's milk) had baffled all their prognostications and made him a celebrity for life. In private the Captain said that he really had these ailments, though he only discovered the fact when he read the advertisements of the Elixir. But the Mess had an inkling that it was all done for a wager, and christened him "The Perfect Cure." To me he justified himself on the ground that he had scrupulously described himself as having his tongue in his cheek, and that he really suffered from love-sickness, which was worse than all the ills the Elixir cured.

I need scarcely say that I was shocked by my lovers' practical methods of acquiring that renown for which so many gifted souls have yearned in vain, though I must admit that both gentlemen retained sufficient sense of decorum to be revolted by the other's course of action. They remonstrated with each other gently but firmly. The result was that their friendship snapped and a week before the close of the competition they crossed the Channel to fight a duel. I got to hear of it in time and wired to Boulogne that if they killed each other I would marry neither, that if only one survived I would never marry my lover's murderer, and that a duel excited so much gossip that, if both survived, they would be equally famous and the competition again a failure.

These simple considerations prevented any mishap. The Captain returned to his Regiment and Lord Arthur went on to the Riviera to while away the few remaining days and to get extra advertisement out of not appearing at his halls through indisposition. At Monte Carlo he accidentally broke the bank, and explained his system to the interviewers. To my chagrin, for I was tired of see-sawing, this brought him level with the Captain again. I had been prepared to adjudicate in favour of the latter, on the ground that although "Ba, ba, ba, boodle-dee" was better known than the Patent Cure Elixir, yet the originator of the song remained unknown to many to whom the Captain was a household word, and this in despite of the extra attention secured to Lord Arthur by his rank. The second supper-party was again sicklied over with the pale cast of thought.

"No more competitions!" I said. "You seem destined to tie with each other instead of with me. I will return to my original idea. I will give you a task which it is not likely both will perform. I will marry the man who asks me, provided he comes, neither walking nor riding, neither sailing nor driving, neither skating nor sliding nor flying, neither by boat nor by balloon nor by bicycle, neither by swimming nor by floating nor by anybody carrying or dragging or pushing him, neither by any movement of hand or foot nor by any extraordinary method whatever. Till this is achieved neither of you must look upon my face again."

"They looked aghast when I set the task. They went away and I have not seen them from that day to this. I shall never marry now. So I may as well devote myself to the cause of the Old Maids you are so nobly championing." She rolled up the MS.

"But," said Lillie excitedly, breaking in for the first time, "what is the way you want them to come?"

The Princess laughed a silvery laugh.

"No way. Don't you understand? It was a roundabout way of saying I was tired of them."

"Oh!" said Lillie.

"You see, I got the idea from a fairy-tale," said the Princess. "There, the doer evaded the conditions by being dragged at a horse's tail—I have guarded against this, so that now the thing is impossible." Again her mischievous laughter rang out through the misanthropic room.

Lillie smiled, too. She felt certain Lord Silverdale would find no flaw in the Princess's armor, and she was exultant at so auspicious an accession. For the sake of formality, however, she told her that she would communicate her election by letter.

The next day a telegram came to the Club.

"*Compelled to withdraw candidature. Feat accomplished.* Princess, Hotel Metropole, Brighton."

Equally aghast and excited, Lillie wired back, "*How?*" and prepaid the reply.

"*Lover happened to be here. Came up in lift as I was waiting to go down.*"

Still intensely piqued by curiosity and vexation, Lillie telegraphed.

"*Which?*"

"*Leave you to guess,*" answered the electric current.

CHAPTER VI.

THE GRAMMAR OF LOVE.

The *Moon*-man's name was Wilkins, and he did nine-tenths of the interviews in that model of the new journalism. Wilkins was the man to catch the weasel asleep, hit off his features with a kodak, and badger him the moment he awoke as to why he popped. Wilkins lived in a flat in Chancery Lane, and had his whiskey and his feet on the table when Silverdale turned the handle of the door in the gloaming.

"What do you want?" said Wilkins gruffly.

"I have come to ask you a few questions," said Silverdale politely.

"But I don't know you, sir," said Wilkins stiffly. "Don't you see I'm busy?"

"It is true I am a stranger, but remember, sir, I shall not be so when I leave. I just want to interview you about that paragraph in the *Moon*, stating——"

"Look here!" roared Wilkins, letting his feet slide from the table with a crash. "Let me tell you, sir, I have no time to listen to your impertinence. My leisure is scant and valuable. I am a hard-worked man. I can't be pestered with questions from inquisitive busybodies. What next, sir? What I write in the *Moon* is my business and nobody else's. Damn it all, sir, is there to be nothing private? Are you going to poke and pry into the concerns of the very journalist? No, sir, you have wasted your time as well as mine. We never allow the public to go behind what appears in our paper."

"But this is a mere private curiosity—what you tell me shall never be published."

"If it could be, I wouldn't tell it you. I never waste copy."

"Tell me—I am willing to pay for the information—who wrote the paragraph about Clorinda Bell and the Old Maids' Club."

"Go to the devil!" roared Wilkins.

"I thought you would know more than he," said Silverdale, and left. Wilkins came downstairs on his heels, in a huff, and walked towards Ludgate Hill. Silverdale thought he would have another shot, and followed him unseen. The two men jumped into a train, and after an endless-seeming journey arrived at the Crystal Palace. A monster balloon was going off from the grounds. Herr Nickeldorf, the great aeronaut, was making in solitude an experimental night excursion to Calais, as if anxious to meet his fate by moonlight alone. Wilkins rushed up to Nickeldorf, who was standing among the ropes giving directions.

"Go avay!" said Nickeldorf, when he saw him. "I hafe nodings to say to you. You makes me *schwitzen*." He jumped into the car and bade the men let go.

Ordinarily Wilkins would have been satisfied with this ample material for half a column, but he was still in a bad temper, and, as the car was sailing slowly upwards, he jumped in, and the aeronaut gave himself up for pumped. In an instant, moved by an irresistible impulse, Silverdale gave a great leap and stood by the *Moon*-man's side. The balloon shot up and the roar of the crowd became a faint murmur as the planet flew from beneath their feet.

"Good-evening, Mr. Wilkins," said Lord Silverdale. "I should just like to interview you about——"

"You jackanapes!" cried the *Moon*-man, pale with anger, "If you don't go away at once, I'll kick you down stairs."

Go away, or I'll kick you Down Stairs.

"My dear Mr. Wilkins," suavely replied Lord Silverdale, "I will willingly go down, provided you accompany me. I am sure Herr Nickeldorf is anxious to drop both of us."

"*Wirklich*," replied the aeronaut

"Well, lend us a parachute," said Silverdale.

"No, danks. Beobles never return barachutes."

"Well, we won't go without one. I forgot to bring mine with me. I didn't know I was going to have such a high old time."

"By what right, sir," said Mr. Wilkins, who had been struggling with an attack of speechlessness, "do you persecute me like this? *You* are not a member of the Fourth Estate."

"No, I belong merely to the Second."

"Eh? What? A Peer!"

"I am Lord Silverdale."

"No, indeed! Lord Silverdale!"

"Lord Silverdale!" echoed the aeronaut, letting two sand-bags fall into the clouds. Most people lose their ballast in the presence of the aristocracy.

"Oh, I am so glad! I have long been anxious to meet your lordship," said the *Moon*-man, taking out his notebook. "What is your lordship's opinion of the best fifty books for the working man's library?"

"I have not yet written fifty books."

"Ah!" said the *Moon*-man, carefully noting down the reply. "And when is your lordship's next book coming out?"

"I cannot say."

"Thank you," said the *Moon*-man, writing it down. "Will it be poetry or prose?"

"That is as the critics shall decide."

"Is it true that your lordship has been converted to Catholicism?"

"I believe not."

"Then how does your lordship account for the rumor?"

"I have an indirect connection with a sort of new nunnery, which it is proposed to found—the Old Maids' Club."

"Oh, yes, the one that Clorinda Bell is going to join."

"Nonsense! who told you she was going to join?"

The *Moon*-man winced perceptibly at the question, as he replied indignantly: "Herself!"

"Thank you. That's what I wanted to know. You may contradict it on the authority of the president. She only said so to get an advertisement."

"Then why give her two by contradicting it?"

"That is the woman's cleverness. Let her have the advertisement, rather than that her name should be connected with Miss Dulcimer's."

"Very well. Tell me something, please, about the Club."

"It is not organized yet. It is to consist of young and beautiful women, vowed to celibacy to remove the reproach of the term 'Old Maid.'"

"It is a noble idea!" said the *Moon*-man, enthusiastically. "Oh, what a humanitarian time we are having!"

"Lord Silverdale," said Herr Nickeldorf, who had been listening with all his ears, "I hafe to you give de hospitality of my balloon. Vill you, in return, take *mein frau* into de Old Maids' Club?"

"As a visitor? With pleasure, as she is a married woman."

"*Nein, nein.* I mean as an old maid. *Ich habe sic nicht nöthig.* I do not require her any longer."

"Ah, then, I am afraid we can't. You see she *isn't* an old

maid!" "But she haf been."

"Ah, yes, but we do not recognize past services."

"Oh, *warum* wasn't the Club founded before I married?" groaned the old German. "*Himmel*, vat a terrible mistake! It is to her I owe it that I am de most celebrated aeronaut in *der ganzeu welt*. It is the only profession in wich I escape her *gewiss*. She haf de *kopf* too veak to rise mit me. Ah, when I come oop here, it is *Himmel*."

"Rather taking an unfair rise out of your partner, isn't it?" queried the *Moon*-man with a sickly smile.

"And vat vould you haf done in—*was sagt man*—in my shoes?"

The *Moon*-man winced.

"Not put them on."

"You are not yourself married?"

The *Moon*-man winced.

"No, I'm only engaged."

"*Mein herr*," said the old German solemnly, "I haf nodings but drouble from you. You make to me mein life von burden. But I cannot see you going to de altar widout putting out de hand to safe you. It was stupid to yourself engage at all—but, now dat you haf committed de mistake, shtick to it!"

"How do you mean?"

"Keep yourself engaged. Do not change your gondition any more."

"What do you say, Lord Silverdale?" said the *Moon*-man, anxiously.

"I am hardly an authority. You see I have so rarely been married. It depends on the character of your betrothed. Does she long to be of service in the world?"

The *Moon*-man winced.

"Yes, that's why she fell in love with me. Thought a *Moon*-man must be all noble sentiment like the *Moon* itself!"

"She is, then, young," said Silverdale, musingly. "Is she also beautiful?"

The *Moon*-man winced.

"Bewitching. Why does your lordship ask?"

"Because her services might be valuable as an Old Maid."

"Oh, if you could only get Diana to see it in that light!"

"You seem anxious to be rid of her."

"I do. I confess it. It has been growing on me for some time. You see hers is a soul perpetually seeking more light. She is always asking questions. This thirst for information would be made only more raging by marriage. You know what Stevenson says:—'To marry is to domesticate the Recording Angel.' At present my occupations keep me away from her—but she answers my letters with as many queries as a 'Constant Reader.' She wants to know all I say, do, or feel, and I never see her without having to submit to a string of inquiries. It's like having to fill up a census paper once a week. If I don't see her for a fortnight she wants to know how I am the moment we meet. If this is so before marriage, what will it be after, when her opportunities of buttonholing me will be necessarily more frequent?"

"But I see nothing to complain of in that!" said Lord Silverdale. "Tender solicitude for one's betrothed is the usual thing with those really in love. You wouldn't like her to be indifferent to what you were doing, saying, feeling?"

The *Moon*-man winced.

"No, that's just the dilemma of it, Lord Silverdale. I am afraid your lordship does not catch my drift. You see, with another man, it wouldn't matter; as your lordship says, he would be glad of it. But to me all that sort of thing's 'shop.' And I hate 'shop.' It's hard enough to be out interviewing all day, without being reminded of its when you get home and want to put your slippers on the fender and your feet inside them and be happy. No, if there's one thing in this world I can't put up with, it's 'shop' after business hours. I want to forget that I get my gold in exchange for notes of interrogation. I shudder to be reminded that there are such things in the world as questions—I tremble if I hear a person invert the subject and predicate of a sentence. I can hardly bear to read poetry because the frequent inversions make the lines look as if they were going to be inquisitive. Now you understand why I was so discourteous to your lordship, and I trust that you will pardon the curt expression of my hyper-sensitive feelings. Now, too, you understand why I shrink from the prospect of marriage, to the brink of which I once bounded so heedlessly. No, it is evident a life of solitude must be my portion. If I am ever to steep my wearied spirit in forgetfulness of my daily grind, if my nervous system is to be preserved from premature break-down, I must have no one about me who has a right of interrogation, and my housekeeper must prepare my meals without even the preliminary 'Chop or Steak, sir?' My home-life must be restful, peaceful, balsamic—it must exhale a papaverous aroma of categorical proposition."

"But is there no way of getting a wife with a gift of categorical conversation?"

"Please say, 'There is no way, etc.,' for unless you yourself speak categorically, the sentences grate upon my ear. I can ask questions myself, without experiencing the slightest inconvenience, but the moment I am myself interrogated, every nerve in me quivers with torture. No, I am afraid it is impossible to find a woman who will eschew the interrogative form of proposition, and limit herself to the affirmative and negative varieties; who will, for mere love of me, invariably place the verb after the noun, and unalterably give the subject the precedence over the predicate. Often and often, when my Diana, in all her dazzling charms, looks up pleadingly into my face, I feel towards her as Ahasuerus felt towards the suppliant Queen Esther, and I yearn to stretch out my reporter's pencil towards her, and to say: 'Ask me what you will—even if it be half my income—so long as you do not ask me a question.'"

"But isn't there—I mean there is—such a thing obtainable as a dumb wife?"

"Mutes are for funerals, and not for marriages. Besides, then, everybody would be asking me why I married her. No, the more I think of it, the more I see the futility of my dream of matrimonial felicity. Why, a question lies at the very threshold of marriage—'Wilt thou have this woman to be thy wedded wife?'—and to put up the banns is to loose upon yourself an interviewer in a white-tie! No, leave me to my unhappy destiny. I must dree my weird. And anything your lordship can do in the way of enabling me to dree it by soliciting my Diana into the Old Maids' Club, shall be received with the warmest thanksgiving and will allow me to remain your lordship's most grateful and obedient servant, Daniel Wilkins."

"Enough!" said Lord Silverdale, deeply moved, "I will send her a circular. But do you really think you would be happy if you lost her?"

"If," said the *Moon*-man moodily. "It would require a great many 'ifs' to make me happy. As I once wrote:

If cash were always present,
    And business always paid;
If skies were always pleasant,
    And pipes were never laid;
If toothache emigrated,
    Dyspepsia disappeared,
And babies were cremated,
    And boys and girls were speared;
If shirts were always creamy,
    And buttons never broke;
If eyes were always beamy,
    And all could see a joke;
If ladies never fumbled
    At railway pigeon holes;
New villas never crumbled,
    And lawyers boasted souls;
If beer was never swallowed,
    And cooks were never drunk,
And trades were never followed,
    And thoughts were never thunk;
If sorrow never troubled,
    And pleasure never cloyed,
And animals were doubled,
    And humans all destroyed;
Then—if there were no papers,
    And more words rhymed with "giving"—
Existence would be capers,
    And life be worth the living.

Your lordship might give me a poem in exchange," concluded the *Moon-man* conceitedly. "An advance quote from your next volume, say."

"Very well," and the peer good-naturedly began to recite the first fytte of an old English romance.

Ye white moon sailed o'er ye dark-blue vault,
And safely steered mid ye fleet of starres,
And threw down smiles to ye antient salt,
While Venus flyrtede with wynkynge Mars.
Along ye sea-washed slipperie slabbes
Ye whelkes were stretchynge their weary limbs,
While prior to going to bedde ye crabbes
Were softlie chaunting their evenynge hymnes."

At this point a sudden shock threw both bards off their feet, inverting them in a manner most disagreeable to the *Moon*-man. While they were dropping into poetry, the balloon had been dropping into a wood, and the aeronaut had thrown his grapnel into the branches of a tree.

"What's the matter?" they cried.

"Change here for London!" said the Herr, phlegmatically, "unless you want to go mit me to Calais. In five more minutes I shall be crossing de Channel."

"No, no, put us down," said the *Moon*-man. "I never *could* cross the Channel. Oh, when are they going to make that tunnel?" Thereupon he lowered himself into the tree, and Lord Silverdale followed his example.

Coming Down from the Clouds.

"*Guten nacht!*" said the Herr. "Folkestone should be someveres about. Fordunately, de moon is out, and you may be able to find it!"

"I say!" shrieked the *Moon*-man, as the balloon began to free itself on its upward flight, "How far off is it?"

"I vill not be—*was heist es?*—interviewed. *Guten nacht.*"

Soon the great sphere was no bigger than a star in the heavens.

"This is a nice go," said the *Moon*-man, when they had climbed down.

"Oh, don't trouble. I know the Southeast coast well. There is sure to be a town within a four mile radius."

"Then let us take a hansom," said the *Moon*-man.

"Wilkins, are you—I mean you are—losing your head," said Lord Silverdale. And linking the interviewer's arm in his, he fared forth into the darkness.

"Do you know what I thought," said Wilkins, as they undressed in the lonely roadside inn (for ballooning makes us acquainted with strange bedfellows), "when I was sliding down the trunk with you on the branches above?"

"No—what did you—I mean you did think what?"

"Well, I'm a bit superstitious, and I saw in the situation a forecast of my future. That tree typifies my genealogical tree, for when I have grown rich and prosperous by my trade, there will be a peer perched somewhere on the upper branches. Debrett will discover him."

"Indeed I hope so," said the peer fervently, "for in the happy time when you shall have retired from business you will be able to make Diana happy."

CHAPTER VII.

THE IDYL OF TREPOLPEN.

"No, we can't have Diana," the President said, when Lord Silverdale reported the matter. "That is, not if the *Moon*-man breaks off the engagement. According to the rules, the candidate must have herself discarded an advantageous marriage, and that Miss Diana will give up Mr. Wilkins is extremely questionable."

"Like everything connected with the *Moon*-man's bride. However, my aerial expedition has not been fruitless; if I have not brought you a member from the clouds, at least we know how right I was to pluck Clorinda Bell."

"Yes, and how right I was to appoint you Honorary Trier!" said Lillie. "I have several more candidates for you, chosen from my last batch of applications. While you were in the clouds, I was working. I have already interviewed them. They fulfil all the conditions. It only remains for you to do your part."

"Have they given good reasons for their refusal to marry their lovers?"

"Excellent reasons. Reasons so strange as to bear the stamp of truth. Here is the first reduced to writing. It is compounded of what Miss Ellaline Rand said to me and of what she left unsaid. Read it, while I put another of these love stories into shape. I am so glad I founded the Old Maids' Club. It has enlarged my experience incalculably."

Lord Silverdale took the manuscript and read.

When John Beveridge went to nurse his misanthropy in the obscure fishing village of Trepolpen, he had not bargained for the presence of Ellaline Rand. And yet there she was, living in a queer little cottage on the very top of the steep hill which constituted Trepolpen, and sloped down to a pebbly beach where the dark nets dried and the trawl boats were drawn up. The people she was staying with were children of the soil and the sea—the man, a rugged old fish-dealer who had been a smuggler in his time; the woman, a chirpy grandame whose eyes were still good enough to allow her to weave lace by lamplight. The season was early June, and the glittering smile on the broad face of the Atlantic made the roar of the breakers sound like stentorian laughter. There was always a whiff of fish—a blend of mackerel and crabs and mullet—striking up from the beach, but the salt in the air kept the odoriferous atoms fairly fresh. Everything in Trepolpen was delightfully archaic, and even the far-away suggestions of antiquity about the prevailing piscine flavor seemed in poetic keeping with the spirit of the primitive little spot.

In a village of one street it is impossible not to live in it, unless you are a coastguard, and then you don't live in the village. This was why John Beveridge was a neighbor of Ellaline's. He lived much lower down, where the laugh of the Atlantic was louder and the scent of the fish was stronger, and before he knew of Ellaline's existence he used to go down hill (which is easy), smoke his pipe and chat with the trawlers, and lie on his back in the sun. After they had met, he grew less lazy and used to take exercise by walking up to the top of the hill. Probably by this time the sea-breezes had given him strength. Sometimes he met Ellaline coming down; which was accident. Then he would turn and walk down with her; which was design. The manner of their first meeting was novel, but in such a place it could not be long delayed. Beveridge had obeyed a call from the boatmen to come and help them drag in the seine. He was tugging with all his might at the section of the netting, for the fishers seemed to be in luck and the fish unfortunate. Suddenly he heard the pit-pat of light feet running down the hill, and the next moment two little white hands peeping out of white cuffs were gripping the net at the side of his own fleshy brown ones. For some thirty seconds he was content to divine the apparition from the hands. There was a flutter of sweet expectation about his heart, a stirring of the sense of romance.

The day was divine. The sky was a brooding blue; the sea was a rippling play of light on which the seine-boat danced lightly. One little brown sail was visible far out in the bay, the sea-gulls hovering about it. It seemed to Beveridge that the scene had only been waiting for those gentle little hands, whose assistance in the operation of landing the spoil was such a delicious farce. They could be no native lass's, these soft fingers with their pink little nails like pretty sea-pearls. They were fingers that spoke (in their mute digital dialect) of the crayon and the violin-bow, rather than of the local harmonium. There was something, too, about the coquettish cuffs, irresistibly at variance with the village Wesleyanism. Gradually, as the net came in, Beveridge let his eyes steal towards her face. The prevision of romance became a certainty. It was a charming little face, as symmetrically proportioned to the hands as the face of a watch is. The nose was retroussé and piquant, but the eyes contradicted it, being demure and dreamy. There was a little Cupid's bow of a mouth, and between the half-parted rosy lips a gleam of white teeth clenched with the exertion of hauling in the seine. A simple sailor's hat crowned a fluff of flaxen hair, and her dress was of airy muslin.

She was so absorbed in the glee of hauling in the fish that it was some moments before she seemed to notice that her neighbor's eyes were fixed upon her, and that they were not set in the rugged tan of the local masculine face. A little blush leapt into the rather pale cheeks and went out again like a tiny spurt of rosy flame. Then she strained more desperately than ever at the net. It was soon ashore, with its wild and whirling mixture of mackerel, soles, dabs, squids, turbot—John Beveridge was not certain but what his heart was already among the things fluttering there in the net at her feet.

While the trawlers were sorting out the fish, spreading some on the beach and packing the mackerel in baskets, Ellaline looked on, patently interested in everything but her fellow amateur. After all, despite his shaggy coat and the clay pipe in his mouth, he was of the town, towny; some solicitor, artist, stockbroker, doctor, on a holiday; perhaps, considering the time of year, only a clerk. What she had come to Trepolpen for was something more primitive. And he! Surely he had seen and loved pretty women enough, not to stir an inch nearer this dainty vision. For what but to forget the wiles and treacheries of women of the town had he buried himself here? And yet was it the unexpectedness, was it that while bringing back the atmosphere of great cities she yet seemed a creature of the woods and waters, he felt himself drawn to her? He wanted to talk to her, to learn who she was and what she was doing here, but he did not know how to begin, though he had the gift of many tongues. Not that he deemed an introduction necessary—in Trepolpen, where not to give everybody you met "good-morning" was to court a reputation for surliness. And it would have been easy enough to open on the weather, or the marine harvest they had both helped to gather in. But somehow John Beveridge learnt embarrassment in the presence of this muslined mermaiden, who seemed half of the world and half of the sea. And so, amid the bustle of the beach, the minutes slipped away, and Beveridge spoke no word but leaned against the cliff, content to drowse in the light of the sun and Ellaline.

The dealers came down to the beach—men and women—among them a hale, grizzly old fellow who clasped Ellaline's hand in his huge, gnarled fist. The auction began. John Beveridge joined the crowd at a point behind the strangely assorted couple. Of a sudden Ellaline turned to him with her great limpid eyes looking candidly into his, and said, "Some of those poor mackerel are not quite dead yet—I wonder if they suffer." John Beveridge was taken aback. The last vestiges of his wonted assurance were swept away before her sweet simplicity.

"I—I—really—I don't know—I've never thought about it," he stammered.

"Men never do," said Ellaline with a gentle reproachful look. "They think only of their own pain. I do hope fish have no feelings."

"They are cold-blooded," he reminded her, beginning to recover himself.

"Ah!" she said musingly. "But what right have we to take away their lives? They must be—oh so happy!—in the beautiful wide ocean! I am sorry I had a hand in destroying them. I shall never do it again."

"You have very little to reproach yourself with," he said, smiling.

"Ah! now you are laughing at me. I know I'm not big and strong, and that my muscles could have been dispensed with. But the will was there, the intention was there," she said with her serious air.

"Oh, of course, you are a piscicide in intention," he admitted. "But you will enjoy the mackerel all the same."

"No, I won't," she said with a charming little shake of the head, "I won't eat any."

"What! you will nevermore eat fish?"

"Never," she said emphatically. "I love fish, but I won't eat 'em! only tinned things, like sardines. Oh, what a little stupid I am! Don't laugh at me again, please. I forgot the sardines must be caught first, before they are tinned, mustn't they?"

"Not necessarily," he said. "It often suffices if sprats are caught."

She laughed. Her laugh was a low musical ripple, like one of the little sunlit waves translated into sound.

"Twenty-two shillings!" cried the owner of a lot.

"I'll give 'ee eleven!" said Ellaline's companion, and the girl turned her head to listen to the violent chaffering that ensued, and when she went away she only gave John Beveridge a nod and a smile. But he followed her with his eyes as she toiled up the hill, growing ever smaller and daintier against the horizon. The second time he met her was at the Cove, a little way from the village, where great foliage-crowned cliffs came crescent-wise round a space of shining sand, girdled at its outer margin by tumbling green, foam-crested surges. Huge mammoth-like boulders stood about, bathing their feet in the incoming tide, the cormorants perching cautiously down the precipitous half-worn path that led to the sands. There was a point at which the landward margin of the shore beneath first revealed itself to the descending pedestrian, and it was a point so slippery that it was thoughtless of Fate to have included Ellaline in the area of vision. She was lying, sheltered by a blue sunshade, on the golden sand, with her head on the base of the cliff, abstractedly tearing a long serpentine weed to dark green ribbons, and gazing out dreamily into the throbbing depths of sea and sky. There was an open book before her, but she did not seem to be reading. John Beveridge saved himself by grasping a stinging bush, and he stole down gently towards her, forgetting to swear.

He came to her with footsteps muffled by the soft sand, and stood looking down at her, admiring the beauty of the delicate flushed young face and the flaxen hair against the sober background of the aged cliff with its mellow subtly-fused tints.

"Thinking of the little fishes—or of the gods?" he said at last in a loud pleasant voice.

Ellaline gave a little shriek.

"Oh, where did you spring from?" she said, half raising herself.

"Not from the clouds," he said.

"Of course not. I was *not* thinking of the gods," said Ellaline.

He laughed. "I am not even a Perseus," he said, "for the tide though coming in is not yet dangerous enough to be likened to the sea-monster, though you might very well pass for Andromeda."

Ellaline blushed and rose to her feet, adjusting a wrap round her shoulders. "I do not know," she said with dignity, "what I have done to encourage such a comparison."

John Beveridge saw he had slipped. This time there was not even a stinging bush to cling to.

"You are beautiful, that is all I meant," he said apologetically.

"Is it worth while saying such commonplace things?" she said a little mollified.

It was an ambiguous remark. From her it could only mean that he had been guilty of compliment.

"I am very sorry. A thousand pardons. But, pray, do not let me drive you away. You seemed so happy here. I will go back." He made a half turn.

"Yes, I was happy," she said simply. "In my foolish little way I thought I had discovered this spot—as if anything so beautiful could have escaped the attention of those who have been near it all their lives."

Her words caused him a sudden pang of anxious jealousy. Must they not be true of herself?

"And you, too, seemed to have discovered it," she went on. "Doubtless you know all the coast well, for you were here before me. Do you know," she said, looking up at his face with her candid gray eyes, "this is the first time in my life I have seen the sea, so you must not laugh if I seem ignorant, but oh! how I love to lie and hear it roar, tossing its mane like some great wild animal that I have tamed and that will not harm me."

"There are other wild animals that you may tame, here by the sea," he said.

She considered for a moment gravely.

"That is rather pretty," she announced. "I shall re-remember that. But please do not tell me again I am beautiful." She sat down on the sand, with her back to the cliff, re-adjusting her parasol.

"Very well. I sit reproved," he replied, taking up his position by her side. "What book is that you are reading?"

She handed him the little paper-covered, airily-printed volume, suggesting summer in every leaf.

"Ah, it is *The Cherub That Sits Up Aloft*!" he said, with a shade of superciliousness blent with amusement.

"Yes, have you read it?" she asked.

"No," he said, "I have heard of it. It's by that new woman who came out last year and calls herself Andrew Dibdin, isn't it?"

"Yes," said Ellaline. "It's made an enormous hit, don't you know."

"Oh, yes, I know," he said, laughing. "It's a lot of sentimental rot, isn't it? Do you like it?"

"I think it is sweetly pretty," she said, a teardrop of vexation gathering on her eyelid. "If you haven't read it, why should you abuse it?"

"Oh, one can't read everything," he said. "But one gets to pick up enough about a book to know whether he cares to read it. Of course, I am aware it is about a little baby on board a ship that makes charming inarticulate orations and is worshipped by everybody, from the captain to the little stowaway, and is regarded by the sailors as the sweet little cherub that sits up aloft, etc., and that there is a sensational description of a storm at sea—which is Clarke Russell and water, or rather Clarke Russell and more water."

"Ah, I see you're a cynic," said Ellaline. "I don't like cynics."

"No, indeed, I am not," he pleaded. "It is false, not true, sentiment I object to."

"And how do you know this is false sentiment?" she asked in honest indignation. "When you haven't read it?"

"What does it matter?" he murmured, overwhelmed by her sense of duty. She was evidently unaccustomed to the light flippancies of elegant conversation.

"Oh, nothing. To some people nothing matters. Will you promise to read the book if I lend it you?"

"Of course I will," he said, delighted at the establishment of so permanent a link. "Only I don't want to deprive you of it—I can wait till you have finished with it."

"I have finished. I have read it over and over again. Take it." She handed it to him. Their finger-tips met.

"I recant already," he said. "It must have something pure and good in it to take captive a soul like yours."

And indeed the glamour of Ellaline was over every page of it. As he read, he found tears of tenderness in his eyes, when otherwise they might have sprung from laughter. He adored the little cherub who sat up aloft on the officers' table and softened these crusty sea-dogs whose hearts were become as ship's-biscuits. He could not tell what had come over himself, that his own sere heart should be so quick again to the beauties of homely virtue and duty, to the engaging simplicity and pathos of childhood, to the purity of womanhood. Was it that Ellaline was all these things incarnate?

He avowed his error and his conversion, and gradually they came to meet often in the solitary creek, as was but right for the only two intellectual people in Trepolpen. Sometimes, too, they wandered further afield, amid the ferny lanes. But the Cove was their favorite trysting place, and there lying with his head in her lap, he would talk to her of books and men and one woman.

Talked to her of books and men and one woman.

He found her tastes were not limited to *The Cherub That Sits Up Aloft*, for she liked Meredith. "Really," he said, "if you had not been yourself, I should have doubted whether your admiration was genuine."

"Yes, his women are so real. But I do not pretend to care for the style."

"Style!" he said, "I call it a five-barred fence. To me style is everything. Style alone is literature, whether it be the man or not."

"Oh, then you are of the school of Addiper?"

"Ah, have you heard of that? I am. I admire Addiper and agree with him. Form is everything—literature is only a matter of form. And a book is only a form of matter."

"I see," she said, smiling. "But I adore Addiper myself, though I regret the future seems likely to be his. I have read all he has written. Every line is so lucid. The form is exquisite. But as for the matter——!"

"No matter!" summed up John Beveridge, laughing heartily.

"I am so glad you agree with me sometimes," said Ellaline. "Because it shows you don't think I am so very stupid after all."

"Of course I don't—except when you get so enthusiastic about literary people and rave about Dibdin and Addiper and Blackwin and the rest. If you mixed with them, my little girl, as I have done, you would soon lose your rosy illusions. Although perhaps you are better with them."

"Ah, then you're not a novelist yourself?" she said anxiously.

"No, I am not. What makes you ask?"

"Nothing. Only sometimes, from your conversation, I suspected you might be."

"Thank you, Ellaline," he said, "for a very dubious compliment. No, I am afraid I must forego that claim upon your admiration. Unless I tell a lie and become a novelist by doing so. But then wouldn't it be the truth?"

"Are you, then, a painter or a musician?"

He shook his head. "No, I do not get my living by art."

"Not of any kind?"

"Not of any kind."

"How *do* you get it?" she asked simply, a candid light shining in the great gray eyes.

"My father was a successful saddle-maker. He is dead."

"Oh!" she said.

"Leather has made me, from childhood up—it has chastised, supported, educated me, and given me the *entrée* everywhere. So you see I cannot hold a candle to your demigods."

"Ah, but there is nothing like leather," said Ellaline, and stroked the head in her lap reassuringly.

The assurance permeated John Beveridge's frame like a pleasant cordial. All that was hard and leathery in him seemed to be soaked soft. Here, at last, was a woman who loved him for himself—an innocent, trusting woman in whose weakness a man might find strength. Her pure lips were like the wayside well at which the wearied wanderer from great stony cities might drink and be refreshed. And yet, delightful as her love would be in his droughty life, he felt that his could not prove less delightful to her. That he, John Beveridge, with the roses thrusting themselves into his eyes, should stoop to pick the simple little daisy at his feet, could not fail to fill her with an admiring gratitude that would add the last charm to her passion for him.

But it was not till a week afterwards that the formal proposal, so long impending, broke. They were resting in a lane and discussing everything they didn't want to discuss, the unspoken playing with subtle sweetness about the spoken.

"Have you read Mr. Gladstone's latest?" she asked at last.

"No," he said; "has Mr. Gladstone ever a latest?"

"Oh, yes, take him day by day, like an evening paper. I'm referring to his article on 'Ancient Beliefs in a Future State.'"

"What's that—the belief of old maids that they'll get married?"

"Now you are blasphemous," she cried with a pretty pout.

"How? Are old maids a sacred subject?"

"Everything old should be sacred to us," she said simply. "But you know that is not what I mean."

"Then why do you say it?" he asked.

"Oh, what a tease you are!" she cried. "I shan't be sorry to be quit of you. Your flippancy is quite dreadful."

"Why, do you believe in a future state?" he said.

"Of course I do. If we had only one life, it would not be worth living."

"But nine times one life *would* be worth living. Is that the logic? If so, happy cats! I wonder," he added irrelevantly, "why the number nine always goes with cats—nine lives, nine tails, nine muses?"

Ellaline made a *moue* and shrank petulantly away from him. "I will not discuss our future state, unless you are prepared to do it seriously," she said.

"I am," he replied with sudden determination. "Let us enter it together. I am tired of the life I've been leading, and I love you."

"What!" she said in a little horrified whisper. "You want us to commit suicide together?"

"No, no—matrimony. I cannot do it alone—I have never had the courage to do it at all. With you at my side, I should go forward, facing the hereafter cheerfully, with faith and trust."

"I—I—am—afraid—I——" she stammered.

"Why should you be afraid?" he interrupted. "Have you no faith and trust in me?"

"Oh, yes," she said with a frank smile, "if I had not confidence in you, I should not be here with you."

"You angel!" he said, his eyes growing wet under her clear, limpid gaze. "But you love me a little, too?"

"I do not," she said, shaking her head demurely.

John Beveridge groaned. After so decisive an avowal from the essence of candor, what remained to be said? Nothing but to bid her and his hopes farewell—the latter at once, the former as soon as she was escorted back to Trepolpen. His affection had grown so ripe, he could not exchange it for the green fruit of friendship. And yet, was this to be the end of all that sweet idyllic interlude, a jarring note and then silence for evermore?

"But could you never learn to love me?"

She laughed her girlish, ringing laugh.

"I am not so backward as all that," she said. "I mastered it in a dozen lessons."

He stared at her, a wild hope kindling in his eyes. "Did I hear aright?" he asked in a horse tone.

She nodded, still smiling.

"Then I did not hear aright before?"

"Oh, yes, you did. I said I did not love you a little. I love you a great deal."

There were tears in the gray eyes now, but they smiled on. He caught her in his arms and the Devonshire lane was transformed to Eden. How exquisite this angelic frankness, when the words pleased! How delicious the frankness of her caress when words were *de trop*!

But at last she spoke again. "And now that I know you love me for myself, I will tell you a secret." The little hands that had first clasped his attention were laid on his shoulders, the dreamy face looked up tenderly and proudly into his. "They say a woman cannot keep a secret," she said. "But you will never believe that again, when I tell you mine?"

"I never believed it," he said earnestly. "Consider how every woman keeps the great secret of her age."

"Ah, that is not what I am going to tell you," she said archly. "It is another of the great secrets of my age. You remember that book you liked so much —*The Cherub That Sits Up Aloft*?"

"Yes!" he said wonderingly.

"Well, I wrote it!"

"You!" he exclaimed, startled. His image of her seemed a pillar of sand upon which the simoom had burst. This fresh, simple maiden a complex literary being, a slave of the midnight lamp.

"Yes, I—I am Andrew Dibdin—the authoress who drew tears from your eyes."

"You, Andrew Dibdin!" he repeated mechanically.

She nodded her head with a proud and happy smile. "I knew you would be pleased—but I wanted you to love me, not my book."

"I love both," he exclaimed. The new conceptions had fitted themselves into the old. He saw now what the charm of the little novel was—the book was Ellaline between covers. He wondered he had not seen it before. The grace, the purity, the pathos, the sweet candor, the recollections of a childhood spent on the great waters in the company of kindly mariners—all had flowed out at the point of her pen. She had put herself into her work. He felt a subtle jealousy of the people who bought her on the bookstalls for a shilling—or even for ninepence at the booksellers'. He wanted to have her all to himself. He experienced a mad desire to buy up the edition. But there would be a new one. He realized the feelings of Othello. Oh, if he could but arrest her circulation!

"If you knew how happy it made me to hear you say you love my book!" she replied. "At first I hated you because you sneered at it. All my friends love my books—and I wanted you to be a friend of mine."

"I am more than that," he said exultantly. "And I want to love all your books. What else have you written?"

"Only two others," she said apologetically. "You see I have only been in literature six months and I only write straight from the heart."

"Yes, indeed!" he said. "You wear your heart upon your leaves."

Jealous as he was of her readers, he felt that there was balm in Gilead. She was not a hack-writer, turning out books for the market of malice aforethought; not the complex being he had figured in the first moment of consternation, the literary quack with finger on the pulse of the public. She did but write as the birds carolled—not the slave, but the genius of the midnight lamp.

"But I must not wear my heart out," she replied, laughingly. "So I came down here for a month to get fresh material. I am writing a novel of Cornish peasant life—I want to photograph the people with all their lights and shades, all their faiths and superstitions, all their ways of speech and thought—the first thorough study ever made of a fast-fading phase of Old English life. You see, I didn't know what to do; I feared the public would be tired of my sailor-stories and I thought I'd locate my next story on land. Accident determined its environment. I learnt, by chance, that we had some poor relatives in Trepolpen, whom my people had dropped, and so I thought I'd pick them up again, and turn them into 'copy,' and I welcomed the opportunity of making at the same time the acquaintance of the sea, which, as I think I told you, I have never seen before. You see I was poor myself till *The Cherub That Sits Up Aloft* showered down the gold, and, being a Cockney, had never been able to afford a trip to the seaside."

"My poor Ellaline!" he said, kissing her candid lips. She was such an inveterate truth-teller that he could only respect and admire and adore—though she fell from heaven. Her candor infected him. He felt an overwhelming paroxysm of veracity.

The mask could be dropped now. Did she not love John Beveridge?

"Now I see why you rave so over literary people!" he said. "You are dipped in ink yourself."

"Yes," she said with a happy smile, "there is nobody I admire so much as our great writers."

"But you would not love me more, if I were a great writer?" he said anxiously.

"No, certainly not. I couldn't," she said decisively.

He stooped and kissed her gratefully. "Thank you for that, my sweet Ellaline. And now I think I can safely confess that I am Addiper."

She gave a little shriek. Her face turned white. "Addiper!" she breathed.

"Yes, dearest, it is my *nom de guerre*. I am Addiper, the writer you admire so much, the man with whose school, you were pleased to say, the future lies."

"Addiper!" she said again. "Impossible! why you said you did not get your living by art of any kind."

"Of course I don't!" he said. "Books like mine—all style, no sentiment, morals or theology—never pay. Fortunately I am able to publish them at my own expense. I write only for writers. That is why you like me. Successful writers are those who write for readers, just as popular painters are those who paint for spectators."

The poor little face was ashen gray now. The surprise was too much for the fragile little beauty. "Then you really are Addiper!" she said in low, slow tones.

"Yes, dearest," he said not without a touch of pride. "I am Addiper—and in you, love, I have found a fresh fount of inspiration. You shall be the guiding star of my work, my rare Ellaline, my pearl, my beryl. Ah, this is a great turning-point in my life. To-day I enter into my third manner."

"This is not one of your teasing jokes?" she said appealingly, her piteous eyes looking up into his.

"No, my Ellaline. Do you think I would hoax you thus—to dash you to earth again?"

"Then," she said slowly and painfully, "then I can never marry you. We must say 'good-bye.'"

Her lover gazed at her in dazed silence. The butterflies floated in the summer air, a bee buzzed about a wayside flower, from afar came the tinkle of a brook. A deep peace was on all things—only in the hearts of the two littérateurs was pain and consternation.

The Confession of Ellaline.

"You can never marry me!" repeated John Beveridge at last. "And why not?"

"I have told you. Because you are Addiper."

"But that is no reason."

"Is it not?" she said. "I thought Addiper would have a subtler apprehension."

"But what is it you object to in me?"

"To your genius, of course."

"To my genius!"

"Yes, no mock modesty. Between augurs it won't do. Every author must know very well he stands apart from the world, or he would not set himself to paint it. I know quite well I am not as other women. What is the use of paltering with one's consciousness!"

Still the same delicious candor shone in the gray eyes. John Beveridge, not at all grasping his dismissal, felt an unreasoning impulse to kiss them.

"Well, supposing I am a genius," he said instead. "Where's the harm?"

"No harm till you propose to yoke me with it! I never will marry a genius."

"Oh, don't be so absurd, Ellaline!" he said. "You've been reading the foolish nonsense about the geniuses necessarily making bad husbands. No doubt in some prominent instances geniuses have not been working models of the domestic virtues, but on the other hand there are scores of instances to the contrary. And blockheads make quite as bad husbands as your Shelleys and your Byrons. Besides it was only in the past that geniuses were blackguards; to-day it is the correct thing to be correct. Respectability nowadays adds chastity to the studies from the nude; marital fidelity enhances the force of poems of passion: and philanthropy adds the last touch to tragic acting. So why should I suffer for the sins of my predecessors? If I may judge myself by my present sensations, what I am gifted with is a genius for domesticity. Do not sacrifice me, dearest, to an unproved and unscientific generalization."

"It is not of that I am thinking," Ellaline replied, shaking her head sadly. "In my opinion the woman who refused Shakespeare merely on the ground that he wrote Shakespeare's works, should be sent to Coventry as a coward. No, do not fancy I am that. I may not be strong, but I have courage enough to marry you if that were all. It is not because I am afraid you would make me unhappy."

"Ah, there is something you are hiding from me," he said anxiously, impressed by the gravity and sincerity of her tones.

"No, there is nothing. I cannot marry you, because you are a genius."

He saw what she meant now. She had been reading the modern works on genius and insanity.

"Ah, you think me mad!" he cried.

"Mad—when you love me?" she said, with a melancholy smile.

"You know what I mean. You think that 'great wits to madness nearly are allied,' that sane as I appear, there is in me a hidden vein of madness. And yet, if anything, the generalization connecting genius with insanity is more unsound than that connecting it with domestic infelicity. It would require a genius to really prove such a connection, and as he would, on his own theory, be a lunatic, what becomes of his theory?"

"Your argument involves a fallacy," replied Ellaline quietly. "It does not follow that if a man is a lunatic everything he says or does has the taint of madness. A genius who held that genius meant insanity might be sane just on this one point."

"Or insane just on the one point. Seriously, Ellaline," said John Beveridge, beginning to lose his temper, "you don't mean to say that you believe that genius is really 'a psychical neurosis of the epileptoid order.' If you do you must be mad yourself, that's all I can say."

"Of course I should have to admit I am mad myself if I held the theory that genius meant insanity. But I don't."

"You don't!" he said, staring blankly at her. "You don't believe I'm insane, and you don't believe I'll make a bad husband—I should be insane if I did, my sweet little Ellaline. And you still wish to cry off?"

"I must."

"Then you no longer love me!"

"Oh, I beg of you, do not say that! You do not know how hard it is for me to give you up—do not make our parting harder."

"Ellaline, in heaven's name vex me no further. What is this terrible mystery? Why can you no longer think of me?"

"If you only thought of me a little you would guess. But men are so selfish. If it were only you that had genius the thing would be simple. But you forget that I, too——" She paused; a little modest blush completed the sentence.

"Yes, I know you are a genius, my rare Ellaline. But what then?" he cried. "I only love you the more for it."

"Yes, but if we marry," said Ellaline, "we two geniuses, look what will happen."

He stared at her afresh—she met his gaze unflinchingly. "What new scientific bogie have you been conjuring up." he murmured.

"Oh, I wish you would drive science out of your head," she replied pettishly. "What have I to do with science? Really, if you go on so stupidly I shall believe you're not a genius after all."

"And then you will marry me?" he said eagerly.

"Don't be so stupid! To speak plainly, for you seem as dull as a clod- hopper to-day, I cannot afford to marry a genius, and a recognized genius to boot. I am only a struggling young authoress, with a considerable following, it is true, but still without an unquestioned position. The high-class organs that review you all to yourself still take me as one of a batch and are not always as complimentary as they might be. The moment I marry you and my rushlight is hidden in your bushel, out it goes. I become absorbed simply in you, a little satellite circling round your planetary glory. I shall have no independent existence—the fame I have toiled and struggled for will be eclipsed in yours. 'Mrs. Addiper—the wife of the celebrated writer, scribbles a little herself, don't you know! Wonder what he could see in her!' That's how people will talk of me. When I go into a room we shall be announced, 'Mr. and Mrs. Addiper'—and everybody will rush round you and hang on your words, and I shall be talked to only by the way of getting you at second-hand, as a medium through which your personality is partially radiated. And parties will be given 'To meet Mr. Addiper,' and I shall accompany you for the same reason that your dress-coat will—because it is the etiquette."

"But, Ellaline——" he protested.

"Let me finish. I could not even afford to marry you, if my literary position were equal to yours. Such a union would do nothing to enhance my reputation. No woman of genius should marry a man of genius—were she even the greater of the two she would become merged in him, even as she would take his name. The man I must marry, the man I have been waiting to fall in love with and be loved by, is a plain honest gentleman, unknown to fame and innocent of all aspiration but that of making me happy. He must devote his life to mine, sink himself in me, sacrifice himself on the altar of my fame, live only for the enhancement of my reputation. Such a man I thought I had found in you—but you deceived me. I thought here is a man who loves me only for myself, but whose love will increase tenfold when he learns that I stand on a pedestal of glory, and who will rejoice at the privilege of passing the rest of his days uplifting that pedestal to the gaze of the world, a man who will say of me what I can hardly say of myself, who will drive the bargains with my publishers, wrap me up against the knowledge of malicious criticisms, conduct my correspondence, receive inconvenient callers, arrange my interviews, and send incessant paragraphs to the papers about me, commencing Mrs. John Beveridge (Andrew Dibdin), varied by Andrew Dibdin (Mrs. John Beveridge). Here is a man who will be a living gratuitous advertisement, inserted daily in the great sheets of the times, a steadfast column of eulogy, a pillar of praise. Here is a man who will be as much a halo as a husband. When I enter a drawing-room with him (so ran my innocent, maiden dream) there will be a thrill of excitement, everybody will cluster round me, he will efface himself or be effaced, and, even if he finds anybody to talk to, it is about me he will talk. Invitations to our own 'At Homes' will be eagerly sought for—not for his sake, but for mine. All that is famous in literature and art will crowd our salon—not for his sake, but for mine. And while I shall be the cynosure of every eye, it will be his to note down the names of the illustrious gazers in society paragraphs beginning Mrs. John Beveridge (Andrew Dibdin), alternating with Andrew Dibdin (Mrs. John Beveridge). And am I to give up all this, merely because I love you?"

So ran my Innocent Maiden Dream.

"Yes, why not!" he said passionately. "What is fame, reputation, weighed against love? What is it to be on the World's lips, if the lips we love are to be taken away?"

"How pretty!" she said with simple admiration. "If you will not claim the phrase, I should like to give it to my next heroine."

"Claim it!" he said bitterly. "I do not want any phrases. I want you."

"Do you not see it is impossible? If you could become obscure again, it might be. You say fame is nothing weighed against love. Come now, would you give up your genius, your reputation, just to marry me?"

He was silent.

"Come!" she repeated. "I have been frank with you, have I not!"

"You have," he admitted, with a melancholy grimace.

"Well, be equally frank with me. Would you sacrifice these things to your love for me?"

"I could not if I would."

"But would you, if you could?"

He did not answer.

"Of course you wouldn't," she said. "I know you as I know myself."

"What is the use of thinking of what can never be!" he said impatiently.

"Just so. That is what I say. I can never give you my hand; so give me yours and we'll turn homewards."

He gave her his hand and she jumped lightly to her feet. Then he got up and shook himself, and looked still in a sort of daze, at the gentle face and the dainty figure.

He seized her passionately by the arms.

"And must this be the end?" he cried hoarsely.

"Finis," she said decisively, though the renewed pallor of her face showed what it cost her to complete the idyl.

"An unhappy ending?" he said in hopeless interrogation.

"It is not my style," she said simply, "but, after all, this is only real life."

He burst forth in a torrent of half reproachful regrets—he, Addiper, the chaste, the severe, the self-contained.

"And you the sweet, innocent girl who won the heart I no longer hoped to feel living, you would coldly abandon the love for whose existence you are responsible! You, who were to be so fresh and pure an influence on my work, are content to deprive literature of those masterpieces our union would have called into being! Oh, but you cannot unshackle yourself thus from my life— for good or evil your meeting with me determined my third manner. Hitherto I thought it was for good; now I fear it will be for evil."

"You seem to have forgotten *all* your manners," she said, annoyed. "And if our meeting was for evil, at least our parting shall be for good."

John Beveridge and Ellaline Rand spake no more, but walked home in silence through the country lanes on which the sunlight seemed to lie cold. The past was but a dream—not for these two the simple emotions which cross with joy or sorrow the web of common life. At the cottage near the top of the hill, where the sounds and scents of the sea were faintest, they parted. The idyl of Trepolpen was ended.

And John Beveridge went downhill.

CHAPTER VIII.

MORE ABOUT THE CHERUB.

The trial interview between Lord Silverdale and Ellaline Rand took place in the rooms of the Old Maids' Club in the presence of the President. Lillie, encouraged by the rush of candidates, occupied herself in embroidering another epigrammatic antimacassar—"It is man who is vain of woman's dress." She had deliberately placed herself out of earshot. To Miss Rand, Lord Silverdale was a casual visitor with whom she had drifted into conversation, yet she behaved as prettily as if she knew she was undergoing the *viva-voce* portion of the examination for entranceship.

There are two classes of flirts—those who love to flirt, and those who flirt to love. There is little to be said against the latter, for they are merely experimenting. They intend to fall in love, but they can hardly compass it without preliminary acquaintance, and by giving themselves a wide and varied selection, are more likely to discover the fitting object of affection. It is easy to confound both classes of flirts together, and heartbroken lovers generally do so, when they do not use a stronger expression. But so far as Lord Silverdale could tell, there was nothing in Miss Rand's behavior to justify him in relegating her to either class, or to make him doubt the genuineness of the anti-hymeneal feelings provoked by her disappointment in Trepolpen. Her manner was simple and artless—she gushed, indeed, but charmingly, like a daintily sculptured figure on a marble fountain in a fair pleasaunce. You could be as little offended by her gush, as by her candid confessions of her own talents. The Lord had given her a good conceit of herself, and given it her so gracefully, that it was one of her chiefest charms. She spoke with his lordship of Shakespeare and others of her profession, and mentioned that she was about to establish a paper called *The Cherub*, after her popular story *The Cherub That Sits Up Aloft*.

"I want to get into closer touch with my readers," she explained, helping herself charmingly to the chocolate creams. "In a book, you cannot get into direct *rapport* with your public. Your characters are your rivals and distract attention from the personality of the author. In a journal I shall be able to chat with them freely, open my heart to them and gather them to it. There is a legitimate curiosity to learn all about me—the same curiosity that I feel about other authors. Why should I allow myself to be viewed in the refracting medium of alien ink? Let me sketch myself to my readers, tell them what I eat and drink, and how I write, and when, what clothes I wear and how much I pay for them, what I think of this or that book of mine, of this or that character of my creation, what my friends think of me, and what I think of my friends. All the features of the paper will combine to make my face. I shall occupy all the stories, and every column will have me at the top. In this way I hope, not only to gratify my yearnings for sympathy, but to stimulate the circulation of my books. Nay more, with the eye of my admirers thus encouragingly upon me, I shall work more zealously. You see, Lord Silverdale, we authors are a race apart—without the public hanging upon our words, we are like butterflies in a London fog, or actors playing to an empty auditorium."

"I have noticed that," said Lord Silverdale dryly, "before authors succeed, it takes them a year to write a book, after they succeed it takes them only a month."

"You see I am right," said Ellaline eagerly. "That's what the sun of public sympathy does. It ripens work quickly."

"Yes, and when the sun is very burning, it sometimes takes the authors no time at all."

"Ah, now you are laughing at me. You are speaking of 'ghosts.'"

"Yes. Ghost stories are published all the year round—not merely at Christmas. Don't think I'm finding fault. I look upon an author who keeps his ghost, as I do on a tradesmen who keeps his carriage. It is a sign he has succeeded."

"Oh, but it's very wicked, giving the public underweight like that!" said Ellaline in her sweet, serious way. "How can anybody write as well as yourself? But why I mentioned about *The Cherub* is because it has just struck me the paper might become the organ of the Old Maids' Club, for I should make a point of speaking freely of my aims and aspirations in joining it. I presume you know all about Miss Dulcimer's scheme?"

"Oh, yes! But I don't think it feasible."

"You don't?" she said, with a little tremor of astonishment in her voice. "And why not?" She looked anxiously into his eyes for the reply.

"The candidates are too charming to remain single," he explained, smiling.

She smiled back a little at him, those sweet gray eyes still looking into his.

"*You* are not a literary man?" she said irrelevantly.

"I am afraid I must plead guilty to trying to be," he said. "The evidence is down in black and white."

The smile died away and for an instant Ellaline's brow went into black for it. She accepted an ice from Turple the magnificent, but took her leave shortly afterwards, Lillie promising to write to her.

"Well?" said the President when she was left alone with the Honorary Trier.

That functionary looked dubious. "Up till the very last she seemed single-hearted in her zeal. Then she asked whether *I* was a literary man. You know her story. What do you conclude?"

"I can hardly come to a conclusion. Do you think there is still a danger of her marrying to get someone to advertise her?"

"I think it depends on *The Cherub*. If *The Cherub* is born and lives, it will be a more effectual advertising medium than even a husband, and may replace him. A paper of your own can puff you rather better than a husband of your own, it has a larger circulation and more opportunities. An authoress-editress, her worth is far above rubies! Her correspondents praise her in the gates and her staff shall rise up and call her blessed. It may well be that she will arrive at that stage at which a husband is an incubus and marriage a manacle. In that day the honor of the Club will be safe in her hands."

"What do you suggest then?" said Lillie anxiously.

"That you wait till she is delivered of *The Cherub* before deciding."

"Very well," she replied resignedly. "Only I hope we shall be able to admit her. Her conception of the use of man is so sublime!"

Lord Silverdale smiled. "Ah, if the truth were known," he said, "I daresay it would be that pretty women regard man merely as a beast of draught and burden, a creature to draw their checks and carry their cloaks."

Lillie answered, "And men look on pretty women either as home pets or as drawing-room decorations."

Silverdale said further, "I do not look on you as either."

To which, Lillie, "Why do you say such obvious things? It is unworthy of you. Have you anything worthy of you in your pocket to-day?"

"Nothing of your hearing. Just a little poem about another Cherub."

AN ANCIENT PASSION.

Mine is no passion of to-day,
 Upblazing like a rocket,
To-morrow doomed to die away
 And leave you out of pocket.

Nor is she one who snared my love
  By just the woman's graces:
I loved her when, a sucking dove,
  She cooed and made grimaces.

And when the pretty darling cried,
  I often stooped and kissed her,
Though cold and faint her lips replied,
  As though she were my sister.

I loved her long but loved her still
  When she discarded long-clothes,
Yet here if she had had her will
  Would this romantic song close.

For, though we wandered hand in hand,
  Companions close and chronic,
She always made me understand
  Her motives were Platonic.

She said me "Nay" with merry mien,
  Not weeping like the cayman,
When she was Mab, the Fairy Queen,
  And I Tom King, highwayman.

'Twas at a Children's Fancy Ball,
  I got that first rejection,
It did not kill my love at all
  But heightened its complexion.

My love to tell, when she grew up,
  Necessitates italics.
Her hair was like the buttercup
  (Corolla not the calyx).

Her form was slim, her eye was bright,
  Her mouth a jewel-casket,
Her hand it was so soft and white
  I often used to ask it.

And so from year to year I wooed,
  My passion growing fiercer,
Though she in modest maiden mood
  Addressed me as "My *dear* sir."

At twenty she was still as coy,
  Her heart was like Diana's.

The future held for me no joy,
  Save smoking choice Havanas.

At last my perseverance woke
  A sweet responsivepassion,
And of her love for me she spoke
  In woman's wordless fashion.

I told her, when her speech was done,
  The task would be above her
To make a happy man of one
  Who long had ceased to love her.

Lillie put on an innocently analytical frown. "I think you behaved very badly," she exclaimed. "You might have waited a little longer."

"Do you think so? Then I will go and leave you to your labors," said Lord Silverdale with his wonted irrelevancy.

Lillie sat for a long time with pen in hand, thinking without writing. As a change from writing without thinking this was perhaps a relief.

Rejected Addresses.

"A penny for your thoughts," said the millionaire, stealing in upon her reflections.

Lillie started.

"I am not Ellaline Rand," she said smiling. "Wait till *The Cherub* comes out, and you will get hers at that price."

"Was Ellaline the girl who has just gone?"

"Did you see her? I thought you were gardening."

"So I was, but I happened to go into the dining-room for a moment and saw her from the window. I suppose she will be here often."

"I suppose so," said Lillie dubiously.

The millionaire rubbed his hands.

"Miss Eustasia Pallas," announced Turple the magnificent.

"A new candidate, probably," said the President.

"Father, you must go and play in the garden."

The millionaire left the room meekly.

CHAPTER IX.

OF WIVES AND THEIR MISTRESSES.

"No, no," said Miss Eustasia Pallas. "You misapprehend me. It is not because it would be necessary to have a husband and a home of one's own, that I object to marriage, but because it would be impossible to do without servants. While a girl lives at home, she can cultivate her soul while her mother attends to the *ménage*. But after marriage, the higher life is impossible. You must have servants. You cannot do your own dirty work— not merely because it is dirty, but because it is the thief of time. You can hardly get literature, music, and religion adequately into your life even with the whole day at your disposal; but if you had to make your own bed, too, I am afraid you wouldn't find time to lie on it."

"Then why object to servants?" inquired Lillie.

"Because servants are the asphyxiators of the soul. But for them I should long since have married."

"I do not quite follow you. Surely if you had servants to relieve you of all the grosser duties, the spiritual could then claim your individual attention."

"Ah, that is a pretty theory. It sounds very plausible. In practice, alas! it does not work. Like the servants. I have kept my eyes open almost from the first day of my life. I have observed my mother's household and other people's—I speak of the great middle-classes, mainly—and my unalterable conviction is, that every faithful wife who aspires to be housekeeper too, becomes the servant of her servants. They rule not only her but all her thoughts. Her life circles round them. She can talk of nothing else. Whether she visits, or is visited, servants are the staple of her conversation. Their curious habits and customs, their love-affairs, their laches, their impertinences, these gradually become the whole food of thought, ousting every higher aim and idea. I have watched a girl—my bosom-friend at Girton —deteriorate from a maiden to a wife, from a wife to a bondswoman. First she talked Shelley, then Charley, then Mary Ann. Gradually her soul shrank. She lost her character. She became a mere parasite on the servant's kitchen, a slave to the cook's drink and the housemaid's followers. Those who knew my mother before she was married speak of her as a bright, bonny girl, all enthusiasm and energy, interesting herself in all the life of her day and even taking a side in politics. But when I knew her, she was haggard and narrow. She never read, nor sang, nor played, nor went to the Academy. The greatest historical occurrences left her sympathies untouched. She did not even care whether Australia or England conquered at cricket, or whether Browning lived or died. You could not get her to discuss Whistler or the relations of Greek drama to Gaiety Burlesque, or any other subject that interests ordinary human beings. She did not want a vote. She did not want any alteration in the divorce laws. She did not want Russia to be a free country or the Empire to be federated. She did not want darkest England to be supplied with lamps. She did not want the working classes to lead better and nobler lives. She did not want to preserve the Commons or to abolish the House of Lords. She did not want to do good or even to be happy. All she wanted was a cook or a housemaid or a coachman, as the case might be, and she was perpetually asking all her acquaintance if they knew of a good one, or had heard of the outrageous behavior of the last.

"In her early married days, my father's income was not a twentieth of what it is to-day, and so she was fairly happy, with only one servant to tyrannize over her. But she always had hard mistresses, even in those comparatively easy years. Poor mother! One scene remains vividly stamped upon my mind. We had a girl named Selina who would not get up in the morning. We had nothing to complain of in the time of her going to bed—I think she went about nine—but the earliest she ever rose was eight, and my father always had to catch the eight-twenty train to the City, so you may imagine how much breakfast he got. My mother spoke to Selina about it nearly every day and Selina admitted the indictment. She said she could not help it, she seemed to dream such long dreams and never wake up in the middle. My mother had had such difficulty in getting Selina that she hesitated to send her away and start hunting for a new Selina, but the case seemed hopeless. The winter came on and we took to sending Selina to bed at six o'clock, that my father might be sure of a hot cup of coffee before leaving home in the morning. But she said the mornings were so cold and dark it was impossible to get out of bed, though she tried very hard and did her best. I think she spent only nine hours out of bed on the average. My father gave up the hope of breakfast. He used to leave by an earlier train and get something at a restaurant. This grieved my mother very much—she calculated it cost her a bonnet a month. She became determined to convert Selina from the error of her ways. She told me she was going to appeal to Selina's higher nature. Reprimand had failed, but the soul that cannot be coerced can be touched. That was in the days when my mother still read poetry and was semi-independent. One bleak bitter dawn my mother rose shivering, dressed herself and went down into the kitchen, to the entire disconcertion of the chronology of the black-beetles. She made the fire and put the kettle on to boil and swept the kitchen. She also swept the breakfast- room and lighted the fire and laid the breakfast. Then she sat down, put on a saintly expression and waited for Selina.

"An hour went by, but Selina did not make her appearance. The first half-hour passed quickly because my mother was busy thinking out the exact phrases in which to touch her higher nature. It required tact—a single clumsy turn of language—and she might offend Selina instead of elevating her. It was really quite a literary effort, the adequate expression of my mother's conception of the dignity and pathos of the situation, in fact it was that most difficult branch of literature, the dramatic, for my mother constructed the entire dialogue, speaking for Selina as well as for herself. Like all leading ladies, especially when they write their own plays, my mother allotted herself the 'tag,' and the last words of the dialogue were:—

"'There! there! my good girl! Dry your eyes. The past shall be forgotten. From to-morrow a new life shall begin. Come, Selina! drink that nice hot cup of tea—don't cry and let it get cold. That's right.

"The second half-hour was rather slower, my mother listening eagerly for Selina's footsteps, and pricking up her ears at every sound. The mice ran about the wainscoting, the kettle sang blithely, the little flames leaped in the grate, the kitchen and the breakfast-room were cheerful and cosy and redolent of the goodly savors of breakfast. A pile of hot toast lay upon a plate. Only Selina was wanting.

"All at once my mother heard the hall-door bang, and running to the window she saw a figure going out into the gray freezing fog. It was my father hurrying to catch his train. In the excitement of the experiment my mother had forgotten to tell him that for this morning at least, breakfast could be had at home. He might have had such beautiful tea and coffee, such lovely toast, such exquisite eggs, and there he was hastening along in the raw air on an empty stomach. My mother rapped on the panes with her knuckles but my father was late and did not hear. Her own soul a little ruffled, my mother sat down again in the kitchen and waited for Selina. Gradually she forgot her chagrin, after all it was the last time my father would ever have to depart breakfastless. She went over the dialogue again, polishing it up and adding little touches.

"I think it was past nine when Selina left her bedroom, unwashed and rubbing her eyes. By that time my mother had thrice resisted the temptation to go up and shake her, and it was coming on a fourth time when she heard Selina's massive footstep on the stair. Instantly my mother's irritation ceased. She reassumed her look of sublime martyrdom. She had spread a nice white cloth on the kitchen table and Selina's breakfast stood appetizingly upon it. Tears came into her eyes as she thought of how Selina would be shaken to her depths by the sight.

"Selina threw open the kitchen door with a peevish push, for she disliked having to get up early in these cold, dark winter mornings and vented her irritation even upon insensitive woodwork. But when she saw the deep red glow of the fire, instead of the dusky chillness of the normal morning kitchen, she uttered a cry of joy, and rushing forwards warmed her hands eagerly at the flame.

"'Oh, thank you, missus,' she said with genuine gratitude.

"Selina did not seem at all surprised. But my mother did. She became confused and nervous. She forgot her words, as if from an attack of stage-fright. There was no prompter and so for a moment my mother remained speechless.

"Selina, having warmed her hands sufficiently, drew her chair to the table and lifted the cosy from the tea-pot.

"'Why, you've let it get cold,' she said reproachfully, feeling the side of the pot.

"This was more than my mother could stand.

"'It's you that have let it get cold,' she cried hotly.

"Now this was pure impromptu 'gag,' and my mother would have done better to confine herself to the rehearsed dialogue.

"'Oh, missus!' cried Selina. 'How can you say that? Why, this is the first moment I've come down.'

"'Yes,' said my mother, gladly seizing the opportunity of slipping back into the text. 'Somebody had to do the work, Selina. In this world no work can go undone. If those whose duty it is do not do it, it must fall on the shoulders of other people. That is why I got up at seven this morning instead of you and have tidied up the place and made the master's breakfast.'

"'That was real good of you!' exclaimed Selina, with impulsive admiration.

"My mother began to feel that the elaborate set piece was going off in a damp sort of way, but she kept up her courage and her saintly expression and continued,

"'It was freezing when I got out of my warm bed, and before I could get the fire alight here I almost perished with cold. I shouldn't be surprised if I have laid the seeds of consumption.'

"'Ah,' said Selina with satisfaction. 'Now you see what I have had to put up with.' She took another piece of toast.

"Selina's failure to give the cues extremely disconcerted my mother.

Instead of being able to make the high moral remarks she had intended, she was forced to invent *repartées* on the spur of the moment. The ethical quality of these improvisations was distinctly inferior.

"'But you are paid for it, I'm not,' she retorted sharply.

"'I know. That is why I say it is so good of you,' replied Selina, with inextinguishable admiration. 'But you'll reap the benefit of it. Now that I've had my breakfast without any trouble I shall be able to go about my work a deal better. It's such a struggle to get up, I assure you, missus, it tires me out for the day. Might I have another egg?'

"My mother savagely pushed her another egg.

"'I'm thinking it would be a good plan,' said Selina, meditatively opening the egg with her fingers, 'if you would get up instead of me every morning. But perhaps that was what you were thinking of.'

"'Oh, you would like me to, would you?' said my mother.

"'I should be very grateful, I should indeed,' said Selina earnestly. 'And I'm sure the work would be better done. There don't seem to be a speck of dust anywhere,'—she rubbed her dirty thumb admiringly along the dresser —'and I'm sure the tea and toast are lots nicer than any I've ever made.'

"My mother waved her hand deprecatingly, but Selina continued:

"'Oh yes, you know they are. You've often told me I was no use at all in the kitchen. I don't need to be told of my shortcomings, missus. All you say of me is quite true. You would be ever so much more satisfied if you cooked everything yourself. I'm sure you would.'

"'And what would *you* do under this beautiful scheme?' inquired my mother with withering sarcasm.

"'I haven't thought of that yet,' said Selina simply. 'But no doubt, if I looked around carefully, I should find something to occupy me. I couldn't be long out of work, I feel sure.'

"Well, that was how mother's attempt to elevate Selina by moral means came to be a fiasco. The next time she tried to elevate her, it was by physical means. My mother left the suburb, and moved to a London flat very near the sky. She had given up hopes of improving Selina's matutinal habits, and made the breakfast hour later through my father having now no train to catch, but she thought she would cure her of followers. Selina's flirtations were not confined to our tradespeople and the local constabulary. She would exchange remarks about the weather with the most casual pedestrian in trousers. My mother thought she would remove her from danger by raising her high above all earthly temptations. We made the tradesmen send up their goods by lift and the only person she could flirt with was the old lift attendant. My father grumbled a good deal in the early days because the lift was always at the other extreme when he wanted it, but Selina's moral welfare came before all other considerations.

"By and by they began to renovate the exterior of the adjoining mansion. They put up a scaffolding, which grew higher and higher as the work advanced, and men swarmed upon it. At first my mother contemplated them with equanimity because they were British working-men and we were nearest heaven. But as the months went by, they began to get nearer and nearer. There came a time when Selina's smile was distinctly visible to the man engaged on the section of the scaffolding immediately below. That smile encouraged him. It seemed to say 'Excelsior.' He was a veritable Don Juan, that laborer. At every flat he flirted with the maid in possession. By counting the storeys in our mansion you could calculate the number of his *amours*. With every rise he left a love-passage behind him. He was a typical man—always looking higher, and, when he had raised himself to a more elevated position, spurning yesterday's love from beneath his feet. He seemed to mount on broken hearts. And now he was aspiring to the highest of all—Selina. Oh it is cruel! My mother had secluded Selina like a virgin Princess in an enchanted inaccessible tower and yet here was the Prince calmly scaling the tower, without any possibility of interference. Long before he had reached the top the consumption of Bass in our flat went up by leaps and bounds. Selina, my mother ultimately discovered, used to lower the beer by strings. It appeared, moreover, that she had two strings to her bow, for a swain in a slouch hat had been likewise climbing the height, at an insidious angle which had screened him from my mother's observation hitherto. Neither of these men did much work, but it made them very thirsty.

Lowering the Beer.

"That destroyed the last vestige of my mother's faith in Selina's soul. Like all disappointed women, she became crabbed and cynical. When my father's rising fortunes brought her more and more under the dominion of servants, the exposure and out-manœuvring of her taskmasters came to be the only pleasure of her life. She spent a great deal of time in the police-courts—the constant prosecution she suffered from, curtailed the last relics of her leisure. Everybody has heard of the law's delay, but few know how much time prosecutors have to lose, hanging about the Court waiting for their case to be called. When a servant robbed her, my mother rarely got off with less than seven days. The moment she had engaged a servant, she became morbidly suspicious of him or her. Often, when she had dressed for dinner, it would suddenly strike her that if she ransacked a certain cupboard something or other would be discovered, and off she would go to spoil her spotless silks. She had a mania for 'Spring cleanings' once a month, so as to keep the drones busy. Often I would bring a friend home, only to find the dining-room in the hall and the drawing-room on the landing. And yet to the end she retained a certain guileless, girlish simplicity—a fresh fund of hope which was not without a charm and pathos of its own. To the very last she believed that, faultless, flawless servants existed somewhere and she didn't intend to be happy till she got them; so that it was said of her by my sister's intended that she passed her life on the doorstep, either receiving an angel or expelling a fiend. It showed what a fine trustful nature had been turned to gall. She is at rest now, poor mother, her life's long slavery ended by the soft touch of all- merciful Death. Let us hope that she has opened her sorrow-stricken eyes on a brighter land, where earthly distinctions are annulled and the poor heavy- laden mistress may mix on equal terms with the radiant parlor-maid and the buxom cook."

The tears were in Lillie's eyes as Miss Eustasia Pallas concluded her affecting recital.

"But don't you think," said the President, conquering her emotion, "that with such an awful example in your memory, you could never yourself sink into such a serfage, even if you married?"

"I dare not trust myself," said Eustasia. "I have seen the fall of too many other women. Why should I expect immunity from the general fate? I think myself strong—but who can fathom her own weakness. Why, I have actually been talking servants to you all the time. Think how continuous is the temptation, how subtle. Were it not better to possess my soul in peace and to cultivate it nobly and wisely and become a shining light of the higher spinsterhood?"

Eustasia passed the preliminary examination and also the viva voce, and Lillie was again in high feather. But before the election was formally confirmed, she was chagrined to receive the following letter.

Drew up the Advertisement.

"My dear Miss Dulcimer.

"I have good news for you. Knowing your anxiety to find for me a way out of my matrimonial dilemma, I am pleased to be able to inform you that it has been found by my friend and literary adviser, Percy Swinshel Spatt, the well known philosopher and idealist. I met him writing down his thoughts in Bond Street. In the course of a dialogue upon the Beautiful, I put my puzzle to him and he solved it in a moment. 'Why *must* you keep a servant?' he asked, for it is his habit to question every statement he does not make. 'Why not rather keep a mistress?

Become a servant yourself and all your difficulties vanish.' It was like a flash of lightning. 'Yes,' I said, when I had recovered from the dazzle, 'but that would mean separation from my husband.' 'Why?' he replied with his usual habit. 'In many houses they prefer to take married couples.' 'Ah, but where should I find a man of like mind, a man to whom leisure for the cultivation of his soul was the one great necessity of life?' 'It is a curious coincidence, Eustasia,' he replied, 'that I was just myself contemplating keeping a master and retiring into a hermitage below stairs, to devote myself to philosophical contemplation. As a butler or a footman in a really aristocratic establishment, my duties would be nominal, and the other servants and my employers would attend to all my wants. Abstract speculation would naturally indue me with the grave silence and dignity which seem to be the chief duties of these superior creatures. It is possible, Eustasia, that I am not the first to perceive the advantages of this way of living and that plush is but the disguise of the philosopher. As for you, Eustasia, you could become a parlor-maid. Thus we should live together peacefully, with no sordid housekeeping cares, no squalid interests in rates or taxes, devoted heart and soul to the higher life.' 'You light up for me perspectives of Paradise,' I cried enthusiastically. 'Then let us get the key of the garden at once,' he replied rapturously, and turning over a new leaf of his philosophical note-book, he set to work then and there to draw up the advertisement: 'Wanted—by a young married couple, etc.' Of course we had to be a little previous, because I could not consent to marry him unless we had a situation to go to. We were only putting what the Greek grammars call a proleptic construction upon the situation. Well, it seems good servants are so scarce we got a place at once—the exact thing we were looking for. We are concealing our real names (lest the profession be overrun by jealous friends from Newnham and Girton and Oxford and Cambridge) so that I was able to give Percy a character and Percy to give me a character. We are going into our place next Monday afternoon, so, to avoid obtaining the situation by false pretences, we shall have to go before the Registrar on the Monday morning. Our honeymoon will be spent in the delightful and unexploited retreat of the back kitchen.

"Yours, in the higher sisterhood,

"EUSTASIA PALLAS."

CHAPTER X.

THE GOOD YOUNG MEN WHO LIVED.

"It is, indeed, a happy solution," said Lord Silverdale enviously. "To spend your life in the service of other men, yet to save it for yourself! It reconciles all ideals."

"Well, you can very easily try it," said Lillie. "I have just heard from the Princess of Portman Square—she is reorganizing her household in view of her nuptials. Shall I write you a recommendation?"

"No, but I will read you an Address to an Egyptian Tipcat," replied his lordship, with the irrelevancy which was growing upon him. "You know the recent excavations have shown that the little Egyptians used to play 'pussy-cat' five thousand years ago."

ADDRESS TO AN EGYPTIAN TIP-CAT.

And thou has flown about—how strange a story—
    Full five and forty centuries ago,
Ere Fayoum, fired with military glory,
    Received from Gurod, with purpureal show,
    The sea-born captives of the spear and bow;
And thou has blacked, perhaps, the very finest eye
That sparkled in the Twelfth Egyptian Dynasty.

The sight of thee brings visions panoramic
    Of manlier games, as *Faro, Pyramids.*
What hands, now tinct with substances balsamic,
    Have set thee leaping like the sportive kids,
    What time the passers-by did close their lids?
Did the stern Priesthood strive thy cult to smother,
Or wast thou worshipped, like thy purring brother?

Where is the youth by whom thou wast created
    And tipped profusely? Doth he frisk in glee
In Aahlu, or lives he, transmigrated,
    The lower life Osiris did decree,
    Of fowl, or fly, or fish, or fox, or flea?
Or, fallen deeper, is he politician,
Stumping the land, his country's quack physician?

Thou Sphynx in wood, unchanged, serene, immortal,
    How many States and Temples have decayed

And generations passed the mystic portal
>Whilst thou, still young, hast gone on being played?
>Say, when thy popularity shall fade?
And art thou—here's my last, if not my stiffest—
As good a bouncer as the hieroglyphist?

"Why, did the hieroglyphists use to brag?" asked Lillie.

"Shamefully. You can no more believe in their statements than in epitaphs. There seems something peculiarly mendacious about stone as a recording medium. Only it must be admitted on behalf of the hieroglyphists that it may be the Egyptologists who are the braggers. There never was an ancient inscription which is not capable of being taken in a dozen different ways, like a party-leader's speech. Every word has six possible meanings and half a dozen probable ones. The *savants* only pretend to understand the stones."

So saying Lord Silverdale took his departure. On the doorstep he met a young lady carrying a brown paper parcel. She smiled so sweetly at him that he raised his hat and wondered where he had met her.

But it was only another candidate. She faced Turple the magnificent and smiled on, unawed. Turple ended by relaxing his muscles a whit, then ashamed of himself he announced gruffly, "Miss Mary Friscoe."

After the preliminary formalities, and after having duly assured herself that there was no male ear within earshot, Miss Friscoe delivered herself of the following candid confession.

"I am a pretty girl, as you can see. I wear sweet frocks and smiles, and my eyes are of Heaven's own blue. Men are fond of gazing into them. Men are so artistic. They admire the beautiful and tell her so. Women are so different. I have overheard my girl friends call me 'that silly little flirt.'

"I hold that any woman can twist any man round her little finger or his arm round her waist, therefore I consider it no conceit to say I have attracted considerable attention. If I had accepted all the offers I received, my marriages could easily have filled a column of *The Times*. I know there are women who think that men are coarse, unsentimental creatures, given over to slang, tobacco, billiards, betting, brandies and sodas, smoking-room stories, flirtations with barmaids, dress and general depravity. But the women who say or write that are soured creatures, who have never been loved, have never fathomed the depth and purity of men's souls.

"I have been loved. I have been loved much and often, and I speak as one who knows. Man is the most maligned animal in creation. He is the least gross and carnal of creatures, the most exquisitely pure and refined in thought and deed; the most capable of disinterested devotion, self-sacrifice, chivalry, tenderness. Every man is his own Bayard.

"If men had their deserts we women—heartless, frivolous, venal creatures that we are—would go down on our knees to them, and beg them to marry us. I am a woman and again I speak as one who knows. For I am not a bad specimen of my sex. Even my best friends admit I am only silly. I am really a very generous and kind-hearted little thing. I never keep my tailor waiting longer than a year, I have made quite a number of penwipers for the poor, and I have never told an unnecessary lie in my life. I give a great deal of affection to my mother and even a little assistance in the household. I do not smoke scented cigarettes. I read travels and biographies as well as novels, play the guitar rather well, attend a Drawing Class, rise long before noon, am good-tempered, wear my ball-dresses more than once, turn winter dresses into spring frocks by stripping off the fur and putting on galon, and diversify my gowns by changing the sleeves. In short, I am a superior, thoroughly domesticated girl. And yet I have never met a man who has not had the advantage of me in all the virtues.

"There was George Holly,—I regret I cannot mention my lovers in chronological order, but my memories are so vague, they all seem to fuse into one another. Perhaps it is because there is a lack of distinctiveness about men —a monotonous goodness which has its charm but is extremely confusing. One thing I do remember though, about George—at least, I think it was George. His moustache was rather bristly, and the little curled tips used to tickle one's nose comically. I was very disappointed in George, I had heard such a lot of talk about him; but when I got to really know him I found he was not a bit like it. How I came to really know him was like this. 'Mary,' he said, as we sat on the stairs, high up, so as not to be in the way of the waiters. 'Won't you say "yes" and make me the happiest man alive? Never man loved as I love now. Answer me. Do not torture me with suspense.' I was silent; speechless with happiness to think that I had won this true manly heart. I looked down at my fan. My lips were forming the affirmative monosyllable, when George continued passionately,

"'Ah, Mary, speak! Mary, the only woman I ever loved.'

"I turned pale with emotion. Tears came into my eyes.

"'Is this true?' I articulated. 'Am I really the only woman you ever loved?'

"'By my hopes of a hereafter, yes!' George was a bit slangy in his general conversation. The shallow world never knew the poetry he could rise to. 'This is the first time I have known what it is to love, Mary, my sweet, my own.'

"'No, not your own,' I interrupted coldly, for my heart was like ice within me. 'I belong to myself, and I intend to. Will you give me your arm into the ballroom—Mr. Daythorpe must be looking for me everywhere.'

"It sounds very wicked to say it, I know, but I cannot delay my confession longer. I love, I adore, I doat on wicked men, men who love not wisely but too well. When I learnt history at school I could always answer questions about the reign of Charles II., it was such a deliciously wicked period. I love Burns, Lord Byron, De Musset, Lovelace—all the nice naughty men of history or fiction. I like Ouida's guardsman, whose love is a tornado, and Charlotte Bronte's Rochester, and Byron's Don Juan. I hate, I detest milksops. And a good man always seems to me a milksop. It is a flaw—a terrible flaw in my composition, I know—but I cannot help it. It makes me miserable, but what can I do? Nature will out.

"That was how I came to find George out, to discover he was not the terrible cavalier, the abandoned squire of dames the world said he was. His reputation was purely bogus. The gossips might buzz, but I had it on the highest authority. I was the first woman he had ever loved. What pleasure is there in such a conquest? It grieved me to break his heart, but I had no option.

"Daythorpe was another fellow who taught me the same lesson of the purity and high emotions of his cruelly libelled sex. He, too, when driven into a corner (far from the madding crowd) confessed that I was the only woman he had ever loved. I have tried them all—poets and musicians, barristers and business-men. They all had suffered from the same incapacity for affection till they met me. It was quite pathetic to discover how truly all men were brothers. The only difference was that while some added I was the only woman they ever could love, others insisted that never man had loved before as they did now. The latter lovers always remind me of advertisers offering a superior article to anything in the trade. Nowhere could I meet the man I longed for—the man who had lived and loved. Once I felt stirrings towards a handsome young widower, but he went out of his way to assure me he had never cared for his first wife. After that, of course, he had no chance.

Platonic Love.

"Unable to discover any but good young men, I resigned myself perforce to spinsterhood. I resolved to cultivate only Platonic relations. I told young men to come to me and tell me their troubles. I encouraged them to sit at my feet and confide in me while I held their hands to give them courage. But even so they would never confess anything worth hearing, and if they did love anybody it invariably turned out to be me and me only. Yes, I grieve to say these Platonic young men were just as good as the others; leaving out the audacity of their proposing to me when I had given them no encouragement. Here again I found men distressingly alike. They are constitutionally unable to be girls' chums, they are always hankering to convert the friendship into love. Time after time anticipations of a genuine comradeship were rudely dispelled by fatuous philandering. Yet I never ceased to be surprised, and I never lost hope. Such, I suppose, is the simple trustfulness of a girl's nature. In time I got to know when the explosion was coming, and this deadened the shock. I found it was usually preceded by suicidal remarks of a retrospective character. My comrades would tell me of their past lives, of the days when the world's oyster was yet unopened by them. In those dark days (tears of self- pity came into their eyes as they spoke of them) they were on the point of suicide— to a man. Only, one little thing always came to save them—their first brief, the acceptance of their first article, poem or song, the opportune deaths of aunts, the chance hearing of an organ-note rolling through the portal of a village church on a Sunday afternoon, a letter from an old schoolmaster. The obvious survival of the narrators rather spoiled the sensational thrill for me, but they themselves were always keenly touched by the story. And from suicide in the past to suicide in the future was an easy transition. Alas, I was the connecting link. They loved me—and unless I returned their love, that early suicide would prove to have been merely postponed. In the course of conversation it transpired that I was the first woman they had ever loved. I remember once rejecting on this account two such Platonic failures, within ten minutes of each other. One was a well-known caricaturist, and the other was the editor of a lady's paper. Each left me, declaring his heart was broken, that I had led him on shamelessly, that I was a heartless jilt and that he would go and kill himself. My brother Tom accidentally told me he saw them together about an hour afterwards at a bar in the Strand, asking each other what was their poison. So I learnt that they had spoken the truth. I had driven them to drink. And according to Tom the drink at this particular bar is superior to strychnine. He says men always take it in preference."

Driven to Drink.

"And have you then finally decided to abandon Platonics?" asked Lillie, when the flow of words came to an end.

"Finally."

"And you have decided to enroll in our ranks?"

Miss Mary Friscoe hesitated.

"Well about that part I'm not quite so certain. To tell the truth, there is one young man of my acquaintance who has never yet proposed. When I started for here in disgust at the goodness of mankind I forgot him, but in talking he has come back to my mind. I have a strong suspicion he is quite wicked. He is always painting actresses. Don't you think it would be unfair to him to take my vows without giving him a chance?"

"Well, yes," said Lillie musingly, "perhaps it would. You would feel easier afterwards. Otherwise you might always reproach yourself with the thought that you had perhaps turned away from a bad man's love. You might feel that the world was not so good as you had imagined in your girlish cynicism, and then you might regret having joined us."

"Quite so," said Miss Friscoe eagerly. "But he shall be the very last man I will listen to."

"When do you propose to be proposed to by him?"

"The sooner the better. This very day, if you like. I am going straight from here to my Drawing Class."

"Very well. Then you will come to-morrow and tell me your final decision?"

"To-morrow."

Miss Mary Friscoe arrived at the Drawing Class late. Her fellow students of both sexes were already at their easels and her entry distracted everybody. It was a motley gathering, working in motley media—charcoal, chalk, pencil, oil, water-color. One girl was modelling in clay, and one young gentleman, opera-glass in hand, was making enlarged colored copies of photographs. It was this young gentleman that Mary came out for to see. His name was Bertie Smythe. He was rich, but he would always be a poor artist. His ambition was to paint the nude.

There were lilies of the valley in the bosom of Mary's art-gown, and when she arrived she unfolded the brown paper parcel she carried and took therefrom a cardboard box containing a snow-white collar and spotless cuffs, which she proceeded to adjust upon her person. She then went to the drawing- board rack and stood helpless, unable to reach down her board, which was quite two inches above her head. There was a rush of embryo R.A.'S. Those who failed to hand her the board got down the cast and dusted it for her and fixed it up according to her minute and detailed directions, and adjusted her easel, and brought her a trestle, and lent her lead-pencils, and cut them for her, and gave her chunks of stale bread, for all which services she rewarded them with bewitching smiles and profuse thanks and a thousand apologies. It took her a long time getting to work on the charcoal cluster of plums which had occupied her ever since the commencement of the term, because she never ventured to commence without holding long confabulations with her fellow-students as to whether the light was falling in exactly the same way as last time. She got them to cock their heads on one side and survey the sketch, to retreat and look at it knowingly, to measure the visual angle with a stick of charcoal, or even to manipulate delicately the great work itself. Meantime she fluttered about it, chattering, alternately enraptured and dissatisfied, and when at last she started, it was by rubbing everything out.

The best position for drawing happened to be next to Bertie Smythe. That artist was now engaged in copying the portrait of an actress.

"Oh, Mr. Smythe," said Mary suddenly, in a confidential whisper. "I've got such a beautiful face for you to paint."

"I know you have!" flashed Bertie, in the same intimate tone.

"What a tease you are, twisting my words like that," said Mary, rapping him playfully on the knuckles with her mahl-stick. "You know what I mean quite well. It's a cousin of mine in the country."

"I see—it runs in the family," said Bertie.

"What runs in the family?" asked Mary.

"Beautiful faces, of course."

"Oh, that's too bad of you," said Mary pouting. "You know I don't like compliments." She rubbed a pellet of bread fretfully into her drawing.

"I don't pay compliments. I tell the truth," said Bertie, meeting her gaze unflinchingly.

"Oh, look at that funny little curl Miss Roberts is wearing to-night!"

"Bother Miss Roberts. When are you going to let me have *your* face to paint?"

"My cousin's, you mean," said Mary, rubbing away harder than ever.

"No, I don't. I mean yours."

"I never give away photographs to gentlemen."

"Well, sit to me then."

"Sit to you! Where?"

"In my studio."

"Good gracious! What are you talking about?"

"You."

"Oh, you are too tiresome. I shall never get this finished," grumbled Mary, concentrating herself so vigorously on the drawing that she absent-mindedly erased the last vestiges of it. She took up her plumb-line and held it in front of her cast and became absorbed in contemplating it.

"You haven't answered my question, Miss Friscoe," whispered Bertie pertinaciously.

"What question?"

"When are you going to lend me your face?"

"Look, there's Mr. Biskett going home already!"

"Hang Mr. Biskett! I say, Mary——" he began passionately.

"How are you getting on, Mr. Smythe?" came the creaking voice of Potts, the drawing-master, behind him.

"Pretty well, thank you; how's yourself?" mechanically replied Bertie, greatly flustered by his inopportune arrival.

Potts stared and Mary burst into a ringing laugh.

"Look at *my* drawing, Mr. Potts," she said. "It *will* come so funny."

"Why, there's nothing there," said Potts.

"Dear me, no more there is," said Mary. "I—I was entirely dissatisfied with it. You might just sketch it in for me."

Potts was accustomed to doing the work of most of the lady students. They used to let him do a little bit on each of his rounds till the thing was completed. He set to work on Mary's drawing, leaving her to finish being proposed to.

"And you really love me?" Mary was saying, while Potts was sketching the second plum.

"Can you doubt it?" Bertie whispered tremulously.

"Yes, I do doubt it. You have loved so many girls, you know. Oh, I have heard all about your conquests."

She thought it was best to take the bull by the horns, and her breath came thick and fast as she waited for the reply that would make or mar her life.

Bertie's face lit up with pleasure.

"Oh, but——" he began.

"Ah, yes, I know," she interrupted triumphantly. "What about that actress you are painting now?"

"Oh, well," said Bertie. "If you say 'yes,' I promise never to speak to her again."

"And you will give up your bad habits?" she continued joyfully.

"Every one. Even my cigarettes, if you say the word. My whole life shall be devoted to making you happy. You shall never hear a cross word from my lips."

Mary's face fell, her lip twitched. What was the use of marrying a milksop like that? Where would be the fun of a union without mutual recriminations and sweet reconciliations? She even began to doubt whether he was wicked after all.

"Did you ever really love that actress?" she whispered anxiously.

"No, of course I didn't," said Bertie soothingly. "To tell the truth, I have never spoken to her in my life. I bought her photo in the Burlington arcade and I only talk with the fellows about ballet girls in order, not to be behind the times. I never knew what love was till I met you. You are the only——"

Crash! bang! went his three-legged easel, upset by Mary's irrepressible movement of pique. The eyes of the class were on them in a moment, but only Mary knew that in that crash her last hope of happiness had fallen, too.

———————

"I do trust Miss Friscoe's last chance will not prove a blank again," said Lord Silverdale, when Lillie had told him of the poor girl's disappointments.

"Why?" asked the President.

"Because I shrink from the *viva voce* examination."

"Why?" asked the President.

"I am afraid I should be so dangerous."

"Why?" asked the President.

"Because *I have* loved before. I shall be desperately in love with another woman all through the interview."

"Oh, I am so sorry, but you are inadmissible," said Lillie, when Miss

Friscoe came to announce her willingness to join the Club.

"Why?" asked the candidate.

"Because you belong to an art-class. It is forbidden by our by-laws. How stupid of me not to think of it yesterday!"

"But I am ready to give it up."

"Oh, I couldn't dream of allowing that on any account," said the President. "I hear you draw so well."

So Mary never went before the Honorary Trier.

═══════════════════════════════

CHAPTER XI.

ADVENTURES IN SEARCH OF THE POLE.

"Oh, by the way, Miss Friscoe will not trouble you, you will be glad to hear," said Lillie, lightly.

"Indeed?" said Silverdale. "Then she has drawn a prize after all! I cannot say as much for the young man. I hardly think she is a credit to your sex. Somehow, she reminded me of a woman I used to know, and of some verses I wrote upon her."

("If he had given me a chance, and not gone on to read his poetry so quickly," wrote Lillie in her diary that night, "I might have told him that his inference about Miss Friscoe was incorrect. But it is such a trifle—it is not worth telling him now, especially as he practically intimated she would have been an undesirable member, and I only saved him the trouble of trying her.")

Lord Silverdale read his verses without the accompaniment of the banjo, an instrument too frivolous for the tragic muse.

LA FEMME QUE NE RIT PAS.

It was fair with a loveliness mystic,
    Like the faces that Raphael drew,
Enigmatic, intense, cabalistic,
    But surcharged with the light of the true:
Such a face, such a hauntingly magic
    Incarnation of wistful regret,
It was tenebrous, tender, and tragic,
    I dream of it yet.

And there lives in my charmed recollection,
    The sweet mouth with its lips cruelly curled,
As with bitter ironic rejection
    Of the gods of the frivolous world.
Yet not even disdain on her features
    Was enthroned, for a heavenly peace
Often linked her with bright seraph creatures
    Or statues of Greece.

I met her at dinners and dances,
    Or on yachts that by moonlight went trips,
And was thrilled by her marvellous glances,
    And the sneer or repose of her lips.

Never smile o'er her features did play light,
　　Never laughter illumined her eyes;
She grew to seem sundered from daylight
　　And sun-kindled skies.

Were they human at all, these dusk glories
　　Of eyes? And their owner, was she
A Swinburnian Lady Dolores,
　　Or a sprite from some shadowy sea?
A Cassandra at sea-trip and *soirée*,
　　Or Proserpina visiting earth?
Ah, what Harpy pursued her as quarry
　　To strangle so mirth?

Ah, but now I am wiser and sadder,
　　And my spirit can never again
At the sight of your fairness feel gladder,
　　O ladies, who coolly obtain
Our enamelled and painted complexion
　　On conditions (which really are "style,")
You must never by day risk detection
　　And nevermore smile.

"I don't see where the connection with Miss Friscoe comes in," said Lillie.

"No? Why simply if she acquired an enamelled complexion, it might be the salvation of her, don't you see? Like Henry I., she could never smile again."

Lillie smiled. Then producing a manuscript, she said: "I think you will be interested in this story of another of the candidates who applied during your expedition to the clouds. It is quite unique, and for amusement I have written it from the man's point of view."

"May I come in?" interrupted the millionaire, popping his head through the door. "Are there any Old Maids here?"

"Only me," said Lillie.

"Oh, then, I'll call another time."

"No, you may come in, father. Lord Silverdale and I have finished our business for the day. You can take that away with you and read it at your leisure, Lord Silverdale."

The millionaire came in, but without *empressement*.

That night Lord Silverdale, who was suffering from insomnia, took the manuscript to bed with him, but he could not sleep till he had finished it.

I, Anton Mendoza, bachelor, born thirty years ago by the grace of the Holy Virgin, on the *fête*-day of San Anton, patron of pigs and old maids, after sundry adventures by sea and land, found myself in the autumn of last year in the pestiferous atmosphere of London. I had picked up bad English and a good sum of money in South America, and by the aid of the two was enabled to thread my way through the mazes of the metropolis. I soon tired of the neighborhood of the Alhambra (in the proximity of which I had with mistaken patriotism established myself), for the wealthy quarters of all great cities have more affinities than differences, and after a few days of sight-seeing I resolved to fare forth in quest of the real sights of London. Mounting the box of the first omnibus that came along, I threw the reins of my fortunes into the hands of the driver, and drew a little blue ticket from the lottery of fate. I scanned the slip of paper curiously and learned therefrom that I was going fast to "The Angel," which I shrewdly divined to be a public-house, knowing that these islanders display no poetry and imagination save in connection with beer. My intuition was correct, and though it was the forenoon I alighted amid a double stream of pedestrians, the one branch flowing into "The Angel," and the other issuing therefrom. Extricating myself, I looked at my compass, and following the direction of the needle soon found myself in a network of unlovely streets. For an hour I paced forwards without chancing on aught of interest, save many weary organ-grinders, seemingly serenading their mistresses with upward glances at their chamber-windows, and I was commencing to fear that my blue ticket would prove a blank, when a savory odor of garlic struck on my nostrils and apprised me that my walk had given me an appetite. Glancing sideways I saw a door swinging, the same bearing in painted letters on the glass the words: "Menotti's Restaurant—Ici on parle Francais." It looked a queer little place, and the little back street into which I had strayed seemed hardly auspicious of cleanly fare. Still the jewel of good cookery harbors often in the plainest caskets, and I set the door swinging again and passed into a narrow room walled with cracked mirrors and furnished with a few little tables, a rusty waiter, and a proprietorial looking person perpetually bent over a speaking tube. As noon was barely arrived, I was not surprised to find the place all but empty. At the extreme end of the restaurant I caught a glimpse of a stout dark man with iron-gray whiskers. I thought I would go and lunch at the table of the solitary customer and scrape acquaintance, and thus perhaps achieve an adventure. But hardly had I seated myself opposite him than a shock traversed his face, the morsel he had just swallowed seemed to stick in his throat, he rose coughing violently, and clapping his palm over his mouth with the fingers spread out almost as if he wished to hide his face, turned his back quickly, seized his hat, threw half-a-crown to the waiter and scuttled from the establishment.

He scuttled from the Establishment.

I was considerably surprised at his abrupt departure, as if I had brought some infection with me. The momentary glimpse I had caught of his face had convinced me I had never seen it before, that it had no place in the photograph album of my brain, though now it would be fixed there forever. The nose hooked itself on to my memory at once. It must be that he had mistaken me for somebody else, somebody whom he had reason to fear. Perhaps he was a criminal and imagined me a detective. I called the proprietor and inquired of him in French who the man was and what was the matter with him. But he shook his head and answered: "That man there puzzles me. There is a mystery behind."

"Why, has he done anything strange before to-day?"

"No, not precisely."

"How then?"

"I will tell you. He comes here once a year."

"Once a year?" I repeated.

"No more. This has been going on for twelve years."

"What are you telling me there?" I murmured.

"It is true."

"But how have you remembered him from year to year?"

"I was struck by his face and his air the very first time. He seemed anxious, ill at ease, worried. He left his chop half eaten."

"Ha!" I murmured.

"Also he looks different from most of my clients. They are not of that type. Of course I forget him immediately—it is not my affair. But when he comes the second time I recall him on the instant, though a year has passed. Again he looks perturbed, restless. I say to myself: 'Aha, thou art not a happy man, there is something which preys on thy mind. However, thy money is good and to the devil with the rest.' So it goes on. After three or four visits I commence to look out for him, and I discover that it is only once a year he does me the honor to arrive. There are twelve years that I know him—I have seen him twelve times."

"And he has always this nervous air?"

"Not always. That varies. Sometimes he appears calm, sometimes even happy."

"Perhaps it is your fare," I said slily.

"Ah, no, monsieur, that does not vary. It is always of the first excellence."

"Does he always come on the same date?"

"No, monsieur. There is the puzzle. It is never exactly a year between his visits—sometimes it is more, sometimes it is less."

"There is, indeed, the puzzle," I agreed. "If it were always the same date, it would be a clue. Ah, an idea! He comes not always on the same date of the month, but he comes, perhaps, on the same day of the week, eh?"

Again the proprietor dashed me back into the depths of perplexity.

"No," he said, decisively. "Monday, Wednesday, Saturday,—it is all the same. The only thing that changes not is the man and his dress. Always the same broadcloth frock-coat and the same high hat and the same seals at the heavy watch-chain. He is a rich man, that sees itself."

I wrinkled my brow and tugged the ends of my moustache in the effort to find a solution. The proprietor tugged the ends of his own moustache in sympathetic silence.

"Does he always slink out if anybody sits down opposite to him?" I inquired again.

"On the contrary. He talks and chats quite freely with his neighbors when there are any. I have seen his countenance light up when a man has come to seat himself next to him."

"Then to-day is the first time he has behaved so strangely?"

"Absolutely."

Again I was silent. I looked at myself curiously in the cracked mirror.

"Do you see anything strange in my appearance?" I asked the proprietor.

"Nothing in the world," said the proprietor, shaking his head vigorously.

"Nothing in the world," echoed the waiter, emphatically.

"Then why does he object to me, when he doesn't object to anybody else?"

"Pardon," said the proprietor. "It is, after all, but rarely that a stranger sits at his table. He comes ordinarily so early for his lunch that my clients have not yet arrived, and I have only the honor to serve an accidental customer like yourself."

"Ah, then, there is some regularity about the time of day at least?"

"Ah, yes, there is that," said the proprietor, reflectively. "But even here there is no hard and fast line. He may be an hour earlier, he may be an hour later."

"What a droll of a man!" I said laughing, even as I wondered. "And you have not been able to discover anything about him, though he has given it you in twelve?"

"It is not my affair," he repeated, shrugging his shoulders.

"You know not his name even?"

"How should I know it?"

"Ah, very well, you shall see!" I said, buttoning up my coat resolutely and rising to my feet. "You shall see that I will find out everything in once. I, a stranger in London, who love the oceans and the forests better than the cities, I, who know only the secrets of Nature, behold, I will solve you this mystery of humanity."

"As monsieur pleases," replied the proprietor. "For me the only question is what monsieur will have for his lunch."

"I want no lunch," I cried. Then seeing his downcast face and remembering the man must be out of sight by this time and nothing was to be gained by haste, I ordered some broth and a veal and ham pie, and strode to the door to make sure there was no immediate chance of coming upon him. The little by-street was almost deserted, there was not a sign of my man. I returned to my seat and devoted myself to my inner man instead. Then I rebuttoned my coat afresh—though with less facility—and sauntered out joyously. Now at last I had found something to interest me in London. The confidence born of a good meal was strong in my bosom as I pushed those swinging doors open and cried "*Au revoir*," to my host, for I designed to return and to dazzle him with my exploits.

"*Au revoir*, monsieur, a thousand thanks," cried the proprietor, popping up from his speaking-tube. "But where are you going? Where do you hope to find this man?"

"I go not to find the man," I replied airily.

"*Comment!*" he exclaimed in his astonishment.

"I go to seek the woman," I said in imposing accents. And waving my hand amicably I sallied forth into the dingy little street.

But alas for human anticipations! The whole of that day I paced the dead and alive streets of North London without striking the faintest indication of a trail. After a week's futile wanderings I began to realize the immensity of the English metropolis—immense not only by its actual area, but by the multiplicity of its streets and windings, and by the indifference of each household to its neighbors, which makes every roof the cover of manifold mysterious existences and potentialities. To look for a needle in a bundle of hay were child's play to the task of finding a face in a London suburb, even assuming as I did my enigma lived in the northern district. I dared not return to the restaurant to inquire if perchance he had been seen. I was ashamed to confess myself baffled. I shifted my quarters from Leicester Square to Green Lanes and walked every day within a four mile radius of the restaurant, but fortune turned her face (and his) from me and I raged at my own folly in undertaking so futile a quest. At last, "Patience!" I cried. "Patience, and shuffle the cards!" It was my pet proverb when off the track of anything. To cut yourself adrift from the old plan and look at the problem with new eyes— that was my recipe. I tried it by going into the country for some stag hunting, which I had ascertained from a farmer whom I met in a coffee-house, could be obtained in some of the villages in the next county. But English field- sports I found little to my taste, for the deer had been unhorned and was let out of a cart, and it was only playing at sport. The Holy Mother save me from such bloodless make-believe! Though the hunting season was in full swing I returned in disgust to the town, and again confiding my fortunes to a common or garden omnibus, I surveyed the street panorama from my seat on the roof till the vehicle turned round for the backward journey. This time I found myself in Canonbury, a district within the radius I had previously explored. The coincidence gave me fresh hope—it seemed a happy augury of ultimate success. The saints would guide my footsteps after all; for he who wills aught intensely cajoles Providence. The dusk had fallen and the night lamps had been lit in the heavens and on the earth, though without imparting cheerfulness to the rigid rows of highly respectable houses. I walked through street after street of gray barracks, tall narrow structures holding themselves with the military stiffness and ranged in serried columns, the very greenery that relieved their fronts growing sympathetically symmetrical and sombre. I sighed for my native orange-groves, I longed for a whiff of the blue Mediterranean, I strove to recall the breezy expanses of the South American Pampas whence I had come, and had it not been for the interest of my search, I should have fled like St. Anthony from the lady, though for very opposite reasons. It seemed scarcely possible that romance should brood behind those dull façades; the grosser spirit of prose seemed to shroud them as in a fog.

Suddenly, as I paced with clogged footsteps in these heavy regions, I heard a voice calling somebody, and looking in the direction of the sound I could not but fancy it was myself whose attention was sought. A gentleman standing at the hall-door of one of the houses, at the top of the white steps, was beckoning in my direction. I halted, and gazing on all sides ascertained I was the sole pedestrian. Puzzled as to what he could want of me, I tried to scan his features by the rays of a street lamp which faced the house and under which I stood. They revealed a pleasant but not English-looking face, bearded and bronzed, but they revealed nothing as to the owner's designs. He stood there still beckoning, and the latent hypnotism of the appeal drew me towards the gate. I paused with my hand on the lock. What in the name of all the saints could he possibly want with me? I had sundry valuables about my person, but then they included a loaded revolver, so why refuse the adventure?

"Do come in," he said in English, seeing my hesitation. "*We are only waiting for you.*"

I accepted the strange invitation.

The mysterious language of the invitation sealed my fate. Evidently I had again been mistaken for somebody else. Was it that I resembled someone this man knew? If so, it would probably be the same someone the other man had dreaded. I seemed to feel the end of a clew at last, the other end which was tied to him I sought. Putting my hand to my breast pocket to make sure it held my pistol, I drew back the handle of the gate and ascended the steps. There was an expression of satisfaction on the face of my inviter, and, turning his back upon me he threw the door wide open and held it courteously as I entered. A whiff of warm stuffy air smote my nostrils as I stepped into the hall where an india-rubber plant stood upon a rack heavily laden with overcoats. My host preceded me a few paces and opened a door on the right. A confused babble of guttural speech broke upon my ear, and over his shoulder I caught a glimpse of a strange scene—a medley of swarthy men, wearing their hats, a venerable-looking old man who seemed their chief being prominent in a grim, black skull cap; there was a strange weird wick burning in a cup of oil on the mantelpiece, and on a sofa at the extreme end of the room sat a beautiful young lady weeping silently.

My heart gave a great leap. Instinct told me I had found the woman. I made the sign of the cross and entered.

A strange look of relief passed over the faces of the company as I entered. Instinctively I removed my hat, but he who had summoned me deprecated the courtesy with a gesture, remarking, "We are commencing at once."

I stared at him, more puzzled than ever, but kept silence lest speech should betray me and snatch the solution from me on the very eve of my arrival at it.

It was gathering in my mind that I must strikingly resemble one of the band, that the man of the restaurant had betrayed us, and that he went in fear of our vengeance. Only thus could I account for my reception both by him and by the rest of the gang.

The patriarchal-looking chieftain got up and turned his back to the company, as if surveying them through the mirror. He then addressed them at great length with averted face in a strange language, the others following him attentively and accompanying his remarks with an undercurrent of murmured sympathy, occasionally breaking out into loud exclamations of assent in the same tongue. I listened with all my ears, but could not form the least idea as to what the language was. There were gutturals in it as in German, but I can always detect German if I cannot understand it. There was never a word which had the faintest analogy with any of the European tongues. I came to the conclusion it was a patter of their own. The leader spoke hurriedly for the most part, but in his slower passages there was a rise and fall of the voice almost amounting to a musical inflection. Near the end, after an emphatic speech frequently interrupted by applause, he dropped his voice to a whisper and a hushed silence fell upon the room. The beautiful girl on the couch got up and, holding a richly-bound book in her hand, perused it quietly. Her lovely eyes were heavy with tears. I drifted upon a current of wonder into perusing her face, and it was with a start that, at the sudden resumption of the leader's speech, I woke from my dreams. The address came to a final close soon after, and then another member wound up the proceedings with a little speech, which was received with great enthusiasm.

While he was speaking, I studied the back of the patriarch's head. He moved it, and my eyes accidentally lighted on something on the mantelpiece which sent a thrill through my whole being. It was a photograph, and unless some hallucination tricked my vision, the photograph of the man I sought. I trembled with excitement. My instinct had been correct. I had found the woman. Saint Antony had guided my footsteps aright. The company was slowly dispersing, chatting as it went. Everybody took leave of the beautiful girl, who had by this time dried her eyes and resumed the queen. I should have to go with them, and without an inkling of comprehension of what had passed! What had they been plotting? What part had I been playing in these uncanny transactions? What had they been doing to bring suffering to this fair girl, before whom all bowed in mock homage? Was she the unwilling accomplice of their discreditable designs? I could not see an inch in the bewildering fog. And was I to depart like the rest, doomed to cudgel my brains till they ached like caned schoolboys? No, my duty was clear. A gentle creature was in trouble—it was my business to stay and succor her.

Then suddenly the thought flashed upon me that she loved the man who had betrayed us, that she had pleaded with fear for his life, and that her petition had been granted. The solution seemed almost complete, yet it found me no more willing to go. Had I not still to discover for what end we were leagued together?

As I stood motionless, thus musing, the minutes and the company slipped away. I was left with the man of the doorstep, the second speaker, and the beautiful girl.

While I was wondering by what pretext to remain, the second speaker came up to me and said cordially: "We are so much obliged to you for coming. It was very good of you."

His English was that of a native, as I enviously noted. He was a young, good-looking fellow, but, as I gazed at him, a vague resemblance to the stranger of the restaurant and to the photograph on the mantelpiece forced itself on my attention.

"Oh, it was no trouble; no trouble at all," I remarked cheerfully. "I will come again if you like."

"Thank you; but this is our last night, with the exception of Saturday, when one can get together twenty quite easily, so there is no need to trouble you, as you perhaps do not reside in the neighborhood."

"Oh, but I do," I hastened to correct him.

"In that case we shall be very pleased to see you," he replied readily. "I don't remember seeing you before in the district. I presume you are a newcomer."

"Yes, that's it," I exclaimed glibly, secretly more puzzled than ever. He did not remember seeing me before, nor did the man of the doorstep vouchsafe any information as to my identity. Then I could certainly not have been mistaken for somebody else. And yet—what was the meaning of that significant invitation: *"We are waiting only for you?"*

"I thought you were a stranger," he replied. "I haven't the pleasure of knowing your name."

This was the climax. But I concealed my astonishment, having always found the *nil admirari* principle the safest in enterprises of this nature. Should I tell him my real name? Yes, why not? I was utterly unknown in London, and my real name would be as effective a disguise as a pseudonym.

"Mendoza," I replied.

"Ah," said the man of the doorstep. "Any relation to the Mendozas of Highbury?"

"I think not," I replied, with an air of reflection.

"Ah well," said the second speaker, "we are all brothers."

"And sisters." I remarked gallantly, bowing to the beautiful maiden. On second thoughts it struck me the remark was rather meaningless, but second thoughts have an awkward way of succeeding first thoughts, which sometimes interferes with their usefulness. On third thoughts I went on in my best English, "May I in return be favored with the pleasure of knowing your name?"

The second speaker smiled in a melancholy way and said, "I beg you pardon, I forgot we were as strange to you as you to us. My name is Radowski, Philip Radowski; this is my friend Martin, and this my sister Fanny."

I distributed elaborate bows to the trinity.

"You will have a little refreshment before you go?" said Fanny, with a simple charm that would have made it impossible to refuse, even if I had been as anxious to go as I was to stay.

"Oh no, I could not think of troubling you," I replied warmly, and in due course I was sipping a glass of excellent old port and crumbling a macaroon.

This seemed to me the best time for putting out a feeler, and I remarked lightly, pointing to the photograph on the mantelpiece, "I did not see that gentleman here to-night." Instantly a portentous expression gathered upon all the faces. I saw I had said the wrong thing. The beautiful Fanny's mouth quivered, her eyes grew wistful and pathetic.

"My father is dead," she said in a low tone.

Dead? Her father? A great shock of horror and surprise traversed my frame. His secret had gone with him to the grave.

"Dead?" I repeated involuntarily. "Oh, forgive me, I did not know."

"Of course not, of course not. I understand perfectly," put in her brother soothingly. "You did not know whom it was we had lost. Yes, it was our father."

"Has he been dead long?"

He seemed a little surprised at the question, but answered: "It is he we are mourning now."

I nodded my head, as if comprehending.

"Ah, he was a good man," said Martin. "I wish we were all so sure of Heaven."

"There are very few Jews like him left," said Fanny quietly.

"Alas, he was one of the pious old school," assented Martin, shaking his head dolefully.

My heart was thumping violently as a great wave of light flooded my brain. These people then were Jews—that strange, scattered race of heretics I had often heard of, but never before come into contact with in my wild adventurous existence. The strange scene I had witnessed was not, then, a meeting of conspirators, but a religious funereal ceremonial; the sorrow of Fanny was filial grief; the address of the venerable old man a Hebrew prayer- reading; the short speech of Philip Radowski probably a psalm in the ancient language all spoke so fluently. But what had I come to do in that galley?

All these thoughts flashed upon me in the twinkling of an eye. There was scarce a pause between Martin's observation and Radowski's remark that followed it.

"He was, indeed, pious. It was wonderful how he withstood the influence of his English friends. You would never imagine he left Poland quite thirty years ago."

So I had found the Pole! But was it too late? Anyhow I resolved to know what *I* had been summoned for? The saints spared me the trouble of the search.

"Yes," returned Martin, "when you think how ready he was to go to the houses of mourners, I think it perfectly disgraceful that we had such difficulty in getting together ten brother-Jews for the services in his memory. But for the kindness of Mr. Mendoza I don't know what we should have done to-night. In your place, Philip, I confess I should have felt tempted to violate the law altogether. I can't see that it matters to the Almighty whether you have nine men or ten men or five men. And I don't see why Fanny couldn't count in quite as well as any man."

"Oh! Martin," said Fanny with a shocked look. "How can you talk so irreligiously? Once we begin to break the law where are we to stop? Jews and Christians may as well intermarry at once." Her righteous indignation was beautiful to see.

Two things were clear now. First, I had been mistaken for a Jew, probably on account of my foreign appearance. Secondly, Fanny would never wed a Christian. But for the first fact I would have regretted the second. For a third thing was clear—that I loved the glorious Jewess with all the love of a child of the South. We are not tame rabbits, we Andalusians: the flash from beauty's eye fires our blood and we love instantly and dare greatly. My heart glowed with gratitude to my patron saint for having brought about the mistake; a Jew I was and a Jew I would remain.

"You are quite right, Miss Radowski," I said, "Jew and Christian might as well intermarry at once."

"I am glad to hear you say so," said Fanny, turning her lovely orbs towards me. "Most young men nowadays are so irreligious."

Martin darted a savage glance at me. I saw at once how the land lay. He was either engaged to my darling or a *fiancé* in the making. I surveyed him impassively from his head to his shoes and decided to stand in them. It was impossible to permit a man of such dubious religious principles to link his life with a spiritually-minded woman like Fanny. Such a union could only bring unhappiness to both. What she needed was a good pious Jew, one of the old school. With the help of the saints I vowed to supply her needs.

"I think modern young women are quite as irreligious as modern young men," retorted Martin, as he left the room.

"Yes, it is so," sighed Fanny, the arrow glancing off unheeded. Then, uplifting her beautiful eyes heavenwards, she murmured: "Ah, if they had been blessed with fathers like mine."

Martin, who had only gone out for an instant, returned with Fanny's hat and a feather boa, and observing, "You must really take a walk at once—you have been confined indoors a whole week," helped her to put them on. I felt sure his zeal for her health was overbalanced by his enthusiasm for my departure. I could not very well attach myself to the walking party— especially as I only felt an attachment for one member of it. Disregarding the interruption I remarked in tones of fervent piety:

"It will be an eternal regret to me that I missed knowing your father."

She gave me a grateful look.

"Look!" she said, seating herself on the sofa for a moment and picking up the richly-bound book lying upon it. "Look at the motto of exhortation he wrote in my prayer-book before he died. Our minister says it is in the purest Hebrew."

I went to her side and leaned over the richly-bound book, which appeared to be printed backwards, and scanned the inscription with an air of appreciation.

"Read it," she said. "Read it aloud! It comforts me to hear it."

"Read it aloud," she said. "It comforts me."

I coughed violently and felt myself growing pale. The eyes of Martin were upon me with an expression that seemed waiting to become sardonic. I called inwardly upon the Holy Mother. There seemed to be only a few words and after a second's hesitation I murmured something in my most inarticulate manner, producing some sounds approximately like those I had heard during the service.

Fanny looked up at me, puzzled.

"I do not understand your pronunciation," she said.

I felt ready to sink into the sofa.

"Ah, I am not surprised," put in her brother. "From Mr. Mendoza's name and appearance I should take him to be a Sephardi like the Mendozas of Highbury. They pronounce quite differently from us, Fanny."

I commended him to the grace of the Virgin.

"That is so," I admitted. "And I found it not at all easy to follow your services."

"Are you an English Sephardi or a native Sephardi?" asked Martin.

"A native!" I replied readily. "I was born there." Where "there" was I had no idea.

"Do you know," said Fanny, looking so sweetly into my face, "I should like to see your country. Spain has always seemed to me so romantic, and I dote on Spanish olives."

I was delighted to find I had spoken the truth as to my nativity.

"I shall be charmed to escort you," I said, smiling.

She smiled in response.

"It is easy enough to go anywhere nowadays," said Martin surlily.

"I wish you would go to the devil," I thought. "That would certainly be easy enough."

But it would have been premature to force my own company upon Fanny any longer. I relied upon the presence of death and her brother to hinder Martin's suit from developing beyond the point it had already reached. It remained to be seen whether the damage was irreparable. I went again on the Saturday night, following with interest the service that had seemed a council-meeting. This time it began with singing, in which everybody joined and in which I took part with hearty inarticulateness. But a little experience convinced me that my course was beset with pitfalls, that not Mary Jane aspiring to personify a duchess could glide on thinner ice than I attempting to behave as one of these strange people, with their endless and all-embracing network of religious etiquette. To my joy I discovered that I could pursue my suit without going to synagogue, a place of dire peril, for it seems that the Spaniards are a distinct sect, mightily proud of their blood and their peculiar pronunciation, and the Radowskis, being Poles, did not expect to see me worshipping with themselves, which enabled me to continue my devotions in the Holy Chapel of St. Vincent. It also enabled me to skate over many awkward moments, the Poles being indifferently informed as to the etiquette of their Peninsular cousins. That I should have been twice taken for one of their own race rather surprised me, for my physiognomical relationship to it seemed of the slightest. The dark complexion, the foreign air, doubtless gave me a superficial resemblance, and in the face it is the surface that tells. I read up Spanish history and learnt that many Jews had become Christians during the persecutions of the Holy Inquisition, and that many had escaped the fires of the *auto-da-fé* by feigning conversion, the while secretly performing their strange rites, and handing down to their descendants the traditions of secrecy and of Judaism, these unhappy people being styled Marranos. Perchance I was sprung from some such source, but there was no hint of it in my genealogy so far as known to me; my name Mendoza was a good old Andalusian name, and my ancestors had for generations been good sons of the only true Church. The question has no interest for me now.

For, although like Cæsar I am entitled to say that I came, saw, and conquered, conquering not only Fanny but my rival, yet am I still a bachelor. I had driven Martin on one side as easily as a steamer bearing down upon a skiff, yet my own lips betrayed me. It was the desire to penetrate the mystery of the restaurant that undid me, for if a woman cannot keep a secret, a man cannot refrain from fathoming one. The rose-gardens of Love were open for my walking when the demon in possession prompted me to speech that silvered the red roses with hoar-frost and ice.

One day I sat holding her dear hand in mine. She permitted me no more complex caresses, being still in black. Such was the sense of duty of this beautiful, warm-blooded Oriental creature, that she was as cold as her father's tombstone, and equally eulogistic of his virtues. She spoke of them now, though I would fain have diverted the talk to hers. Failing that, I seized the opportunity to solve the haunting puzzle.

"Do you know, I fancy I once saw your father," I said, earnestly.

"Indeed!" she observed, with much interest. "Where?"

"In a restaurant not many miles from here. It was before noon."

"In a restaurant?" she repeated. "Hardly very likely. There isn't any restaurant near here he would be likely to go to, and certainly not at the time you mention, when he would be in the city. You must be mistaken."

I shook my head. "I don't think so. I remember his face so well. When I saw his photograph I recognized him at once."

"How long ago was it?"

"I can tell you exactly," I said. "The date is graven on my heart. It was the twenty-fourth of October."

"This year?"

"This year."

"The twenty-fourth of October!" she repeated musingly. "Only a few weeks before he died. Poor father, peace be upon him! The twenty-fourth of October, did you say?" she added, suddenly.

"What is the matter?" I asked. "You are agitated."

"No, it is nothing. It cannot be," she added, more calmly. "Of course not." She smiled faintly. "I thought——" she paused.

"You thought what?"

"Oh, well, I'll show you I was mistaken." She rose, went to the book-case, drew out a little brown-paper covered volume, and turned over the pages scrutinizingly. Suddenly a change came over the beautiful face; she stood motionless, pale as a statue.

A chill shadow fell across my heart, distracted between tense curiosity and dread of a tragic solution.

"My dear Fanny, what in Heaven's name is it?" I breathed.

"Don't speak of Heaven," said Fanny, in strange, harsh tones, "when you libel the dead thus."

"Libel the dead? How?"

"Why, the twenty-fourth of October was *Yom Kippur*."

"Well," I said, unimpressed and uncomprehending, "and what of it?"

She stared at me, staggered and clutched at the book-case for support.

"What of it?" she cried, in passionate emotion. "Do you dare to say that you saw my poor father, who was righteousness itself, breaking his fast in a restaurant on the Day of Atonement? Perhaps you will insinuate next that his speedy death was Heaven's punishment on him for his blasphemy!"

In the same instant I saw the truth and my terrible blunder. This fast-day must be of awful solemnity, and Fanny's father must have gone systematically to a surreptitious breakfast in that queer, out-of-the-way restaurant. His nervousness, his want of ease, his terror at the sight of me, whom he mistook for a brother-Jew, were all accounted for. Once a year—the discrepancy in the date being explained by the discord between Jewish and Christian chronology —he hied his way furtively to this unholy meal, enjoying it and a reputation for sanctity at the same time. But to expose her father's hypocrisy to the trusting, innocent girl would be hardly the way to advance love-matters. It might be difficult even to repair the mischief I had already done.

"I beg your pardon," I said humbly. "You were right. I was misled by some chance resemblance. If your father was the pious Jew you paint him, it is impossible he could have been the man I saw. Yes, and now I think of it, the eyebrows were bushier and the chin plumper than those of the photograph."

A sigh of satisfaction escaped her lips. Then her face grew rigid again as she turned it upon me, and asked in low tones that cut through me like an icy blast: "Yes, but what were *you* doing in the restaurant on the Day of Atonement?"

"I—I——?" I stammered.

Her look was terrible.

"I—I—was only having a cup of chocolate," I replied, with a burst of inspiration.

As everybody knows, since the pronunciamento of Pope Paul V., chocolate may be imbibed by good Catholics without breaking the fasts of the Church. But, alas! it seems these fanatical Eastern flagellants allow not even a drop of cold water to pass their lips for over twenty-four hours.

"I am glad you confess it," said Fanny, witheringly. "It shows you have still one redeeming trait. And I am glad you spoke ill of my poor father, for it has led to the revelation of your true character before it was too late. You will, of course, understand, Mr. Mendoza, that our acquaintance is at an end."

"Fanny!" I cried, frantically.

"Spare me a scene, I beg of you," she said, coldly. "You, you the man who pretended to such ardent piety, to such enthusiasm for our holy religion, are an apostate from the faith into which you were born, a blasphemer, an atheist."

I stared at her in dumb horror. I had entangled myself inextricably. How could I now explain that it was her father who was the renegade, not I?

"Good-bye," said Fanny. "Heaven make you a better Jew."

I moved desperately towards her, but she waved me back. "Don't touch me," she cried. "Go, go!"

"But is there no hope for me?" I exclaimed, looking wildly into the cold, statue-like face, that seemed more beautiful than ever, now it was fading from my vision.

"None," she said. Then, in a breaking voice, she murmured, "Neither for you nor for me."

"Ah, you love me still," I cried, striving to embrace her. "You will be my wife."

She struggled away from me. "No, no," she said, with a gesture of horror. "It would be sacrilege to my dead father's memory. Rather would I marry a Christian, yes, even a Catholic, than an apostate Jew like you. Leave me, I pray you; or, must I ring the bell?"

I went—a sadder and a wiser man. But even my wisdom availed me not, for when I repaired to the restaurant to impart it to the proprietor, the last consolation was denied me. He had sold his business and returned to Italy.

To-morrow I start for Turkestan.

CHAPTER XII.

THE ARITHMETIC AND PHYSIOLOGY OF LOVE.

"Well, have you seen this Fanny Radowski?" said Lord Silverdale, when he returned the manuscript to the President of the Old Maids' Club.

"Of course. Didn't I tell you I had the story from her own mouth, though I have put it into Mendoza's?"

"Ah, yes, I remember now. It certainly is funny, her refusing a good Catholic on the ground that he was a bad Jew. But then according to the story she doesn't know he's a Catholic?"

"No, it was I who divined the joke of the situation. Lookers-on always see more of the game. I saw at once that if Mendoza were really a Jew, he would never have been such an ass as to make the slip he did; and so from this and several other things she told me about her lover, I constructed deductively the history you have read. She says she first met him at a mourning service in memory of her father, and that it is a custom among her people when they have not enough men to form a religious quorum (the number is the mystical ten) to invite any brother Jew who may be passing to step in, whether he is an acquaintance or not."

"I gathered that from the narrative," said Lord Silverdale. "And so she wishes to be an object lesson in female celibacy, does she?"

"She is most anxious to enlist in the Cause."

"Is she really beautiful, et cetera?"

"She is magnificent."

"Then I should say the very member we are looking for. A Jewess will be an extremely valuable element of the Club, for her race exalts marriage even above happiness, and an old maid is even more despised than among us. The lovely Miss Radowski will be an eloquent protest against the prejudices of her people."

Lillie Dulcimer shook her head quietly. "The racial accident which makes her seem a desirable member to you, makes me regard her as impossible."

"How so?" cried Silverdale in amazement. "You surely are not going to degrade your Club by anti-Semitism."

"Heaven forefend! But a Jewess can never be a whole Old Maid."

"I don't understand."

"Look at it mathematically a moment."

Silverdale made a grimace.

"Consider! A Jewess, orthodox like Miss Radowski, can only be an Old Maid fractionally. An Old Maid must make 'the grand refusal!'—she must refuse mankind at large. Now Miss Radowski, being cut off by her creed from marrying into any but an insignificant percentage of mankind, is proportionately less valuable as an object-lesson; she is unfitted for the functions of Old Maidenhood in their full potentiality. Already by her religion she is condemned to almost total celibacy. She cannot renounce what she never possessed. There are in the world, roughly speaking, eight million Jews among a population of a thousand millions. The force of the example, in other words, her value as an Old Maid, may therefore be represented by .008."

"I am glad you express her as a decimal rather than a vulgar fraction," said Lord Silverdale laughing. "But I must own your reckoning seems correct. As a mathematical wrangler you are terrible. So I shall not need to try Miss Radowski?"

"No; we cannot entertain her application," said Lillie peremptorily, the thunder-cloud no bigger than a man's hand gathering on her brow at the suspicion that Silverdale did not take her mathematics seriously. Considering that in keeping him at arm's length her motive were merely mathematical (though Lord Silverdale was not aware of this) she was peculiarly sensitive on the point. She changed the subject quickly by asking what poem he had brought her.

"Do not call them poems," he answered.

"It is only between ourselves. There are no critics about."

"Thank you so much. I have brought one suggested by the strange farrago of religions that figured in your last human document. It is a pæan on the growing hospitality of the people towards the gods of other nations. There was a time when free trade in divinities was tabu, each nation protecting, and protected by, its own. Now foreign gods are all the rage."

"THE END OF THE CENTURY" CATHOLIC CREDO.

I'm a Christo-Jewish Quaker,
Moslem, Atheist and Shaker,
Auld Licht Church of England Fakir,
Antinomian Baptist, Deist,
Gnostic, Neo-Pagan Theist,

Presbyterianish Papist,
Comtist, Mormon, Darwin-apist,
Trappist, High Church Unitarian,
Sandemanian Sabbatarian,
Plymouth Brother, Walworth Jumper,
Southcote South-Place Bible-Thumper,
Christadelphian, Platonic,
Old Moravian, Masonic,
Corybantic Christi-antic,
Ethic-Culture-Transatlantic,
Anabaptist, Neo-Buddhist,
Zoroastrian Talmudist,
Laotsean, Theosophic,
Table-rapping, Philosophic,
Mediæval, Monkish, Mystic,
Modern, Mephistophelistic,
Hellenistic, Calvinistic,
Brahministic, Cabbalistic,
Humanistic, Tolstoistic,
Rather Robert Elsmeristic,
Altruistic, Hedonistic
And Agnostic Manichæan,
Worshipping the Galilean.

For with equal zeal I follow
Sivah, Allah, Zeus, Apollo,
Mumbo Jumbo, Dagon, Brahma,
Buddha *alias* Gautama,
Jahvé, Juggernaut and Juno—
Plus some gods that but the few know.

Though I reverence the Mishna,
I can bend the knee to Vishna;
I obey the latest mode in
Recognizing Thor and Odin,
Just as freely as the Virgin;
For the Pope and Mr. Spurgeon,
Moses, Paul and Zoroaster,
Each to me is seer and master.
I consider Heine, Hegel,
Schopenhauer, Shelley, Schlegel,
Diderot, Savonarola,
Dante, Rousseau, Goethe, Zola,

Whitman, Renan (priest of Paris),
Transcendental Prophet Harris,
Ibsen, Carlyle, Huxley, Pater
Each than all the others greater.
And I read the Zend-Avesta,
Koran, Bible, Roman Gesta,
Ind's Upanischads and Spencer
With affection e'er intenser.
For these many appellations
Of the gods of different nations,
I believe—from Baal to Sun-god—
All at bottom cover *one* god.
Him I worship—dropping gammon—
And his mighty name is MAMMON.

"You are very hard upon the century—or rather upon the end of it," said Lillie.

"The century is dying unshriven," said the satirist solemnly. "Its conscience must be stirred. Truly, was there ever an age which had so much light and so little sweetness? In the reckless fight for gold Society has become a mutual swindling association. Cupidity has ousted Cupid, and everything is bought and sold."

"Except your poems, Lord Silverdale," laughed Lillie.

It was tit for the tat of his raillery of her mathematics.

Before his lordship had time to make the clever retort the thought of next day, Turple the magnificent brought in a card.

"Miss Winifred Woodpecker?" said Lillie queryingly. "I suppose it's another candidate. Show her in."

Miss Woodpecker was a tall stately girl, of the kind that pass for lilies in the flowery language of the novelists.

"Have I the pleasure of speaking to Miss Dulcimer?"

"Yes, I am Miss Dulcimer," said Lillie.

"And where is the Old Maids' Club?" further inquired Miss Woodpecker, looking around curiously.

"Here," replied Lillie, indicating the epigrammatic antimacassars with a sweeping gesture. "No, don't go, Lord Silverdale. Miss Woodpecker, this is my friend Lord Silverdale. He knows all about the Club, so you needn't mind speaking before him."

"Well, you know, I read the leader in the *Hurrygraph* about your Club this morning."

"Oh, is there a leader?" said Lillie feverishly. "Have you seen it, Lord Silverdale?"

"I am not sure. At first I fancied it referred to the Club, but there was such a lot about Ptolemy, Rosa Bonheur's animals and the Suez Canal that I can hardly venture to say what the leader itself was about. And so, Miss Woodpecker, you have thought about joining our institution for elevating female celibacy into a fine art?"

"I wish to join at once. Is there any entrance fee?"

"There *is*—experience. Have you had a desirable proposal of marriage?"

"Eminently desirable."

"And still you do not intend to marry?"

"Not while I live."

"Ah, that is all the guarantee we want," said Lord Silverdale smiling. "Afterwards—in heaven—there is no marrying, nor giving in marriage."

"That is what makes it heaven," added Lillie. "But tell us your story."

"It was in this way. I was staying at a boarding-house in Brighton with a female cousin, and a handsome young man in the house fell in love with me and we were engaged. Then my mother came down. Immediately afterwards my lover disappeared. He left a note for me containing nothing but the following verses."

She handed a double tear-stained sheet of letter-paper to the President, who read aloud as follows:

A VISION OF THE FUTURE.

"Well is it for man that he knoweth not what the future will bring forth."

She had a sweetly spiritual face,
Touched with a noble, stately grace,
Poetic heritage of race.

Her form was graceful, slim and sweet,
Her frock was exquisitely neat,
With airy tread she paced the street.

She seemed some fantasy of dream,
A flash of loveliness supreme,
A poet's visionary gleam.

And yet she was of mortal birth,
A lovely child of lovely earth,
For kisses made and joy and mirth.

Sweet whirling thoughts my bosom throng,
To link her life with mine I long,
And shrine her in immortal song.

I steal another glance—and lo!
Dread shudders through my being flow,
My veins are filled with liquid snow.

Another form beside her walks,
Of servants and expenses talks,
Her nose is not unlike a hawk's.

Her face is plump, her figure fat,
She's prose embodied, stout gone flat,—
A comfortable Persian cat.

Her life is full of petty fuss,
She wobbles like an omnibus,
And yet it was not always thus.

Alas for perishable grace!
How unmistakably I trace
The daughter's in the mother's face.

Beneath the beak I see the nose,
The poetry beneath the prose,
The figure 'neath the adipose.

And so I sadly turn away:
How *can* I love a clod of clay,
Doomed to grow earthlier day by day?

Vain, vain the hope from Fate to flee,
What special Providence for me?
I know that what hath been will be.

The Present and the Future.

Lillie and Silverdale looked at each other.

"Well, but," said Lillie at last, "according to this he refused you, not you him. Our rules——"

"You mistake me," interrupted Winifred Woodpecker. "When the first fit of anguish was over, I saw my Frank was right, and I have refused all the offers I have had since—five in all. It would not be fair to a lover to chain him to a beauty so transient. In ten or twenty years from now I shall go the way of all flesh. Under such circumstances is not marriage a contract entered into under false pretences? There is no chance of the law of this country allowing a time-limit to be placed in the contract; celibacy is the only honest policy for a woman."

Involuntarily Lillie's hand seized the candidate's and gripped it sympathetically. She divined a sister soul.

"You teach me a new point of view," she said, "a finer shade of ethical feeling."

Silverdale groaned inwardly; he saw a new weapon going into the anti-hymeneal armory, and the Old Maids' Club on the point of being strengthened by the accession of its first member.

"The law will have to accommodate itself to these finer shades," pursued Lillie energetically. "It is a rusty machine out of harmony with the age. Science has discovered that the entire physical organism is renewed every seven years, and yet the law calmly goes on assuming that the new man and the new woman are still bound by the contract of their predecessors and still possess the good-will of the original partnership. It seems to me if the short lease principle demanded by physiology is not to be conceded, there should at any rate be provincial and American rights in marriage as well as London rights. In the metropolis the matrimonial contract should hold good with A, in the country with B, neither party infringing the other's privileges, in accordance with theatrical analogy."

"That is a literal latitudinarianism in morals you will never get the world to agree to," laughed Lord Silverdale. "At least not in theory; we cannot formally sanction theatrical practice."

"Do not laugh," said Lillie. "Law must be brought more in touch with life."

"Isn't it rather *vice versâ*? Life must be brought more in touch with law. However, if Miss Woodpecker feels these fine ethical shades, won't she be ineligible?"

"How so?" said the President in indignant surprise.

"By our second rule every candidate must be beautiful and undertake to continue so."

Poor little Lillie drooped her head.

And now it befalls to reveal to the world the jealously-guarded secret of the English Shakespeare, for how else can the tale be told of how the Old Maids' Club was within an ace of robbing him of his bride?

CHAPTER XIII.

"THE ENGLISH SHAKESPEARE."

By a thorough knowledge of the natural laws which govern the operations of human nature and by a careful application of the fine properties of well-selected men, and a judicious use of every available instrument of log-rolling, the Mutual Depreciation Society gradually built up a constitution strong enough to defy every tendency to disintegration. Hundreds of subtle malcontents floated round, ready to attack wherever there was a weak point, but foiled by ignorance of the Society's existence, and the members escaped many a fatal shaft by keeping themselves entirely to themselves. The idea of the Mutual Depreciation Society was that every member should say what he thought of the others. The founders, who all took equal shares in it, were

Tom Brown,
Dick Jones,
Harry Robinson.

Their object in founding the Mutual Depreciation Society was of course to achieve literary success, but they soon perceived that their phalanx was too small for this, and as they had no power to add to their number except by inviting strangers from without, they took steps to induce three other gentlemen to solicit the privileges of membership. The second batch comprised,

Taffy Owen,
Andrew Mackay,
Patrick Boyle.

Tom Brown, the Supreme Thinker.

These six gentlemen being all blessed with youth, health and incompetence, resolved to capture the town. Their tactics were very simple, though their first operations were hampered by their ignorance of one another's. Thus, it was some time before it was discovered that Andrew Mackay, who had been deployed to seize the *Saturday Slasher*, had no real acquaintance with the editor's fencing-master, while Dick Jones, who had undertaken to bombard the *Acadæum*, had started under the impression that the eminent critic to whom he had dedicated his poems (by permission) was still connected with the staff. But these difficulties were eliminated as soon as the Society got into working order. Everything comes to him who will not wait, and almost before they had time to wink our six gentlemen had secured the makings of an Influence. Each had loyally done his best for himself and the rest, and the first spoils of the campaign, as announced amid applause by the Secretary at the monthly dinner, were

Two Morning Papers,
Two Evening Papers,
Two Weekly Papers.

They were not the most influential, nor even the best circulated, still it was not a bad beginning, though of course only a nucleus. By putting out tentacles in every direction, by undertaking to write even on subjects with which they were acquainted, they gradually secured a more or less tenacious connection with the majority of the better journals and magazines. On taking stock they found that the account stood thus:

Three Morning Papers,
Four Evening Papers,
Eleven Weekly Papers,
Thirteen London Letters,
Seven Dramatic Columns,
Six Monthly Magazines,
Thirteen Influences on Advertisements,
Nine Friendships with Eminent Editors,
Seventeen ditto with Eminent Sub-editors,
Six ditto with Lady Journalists,
Fifty-three Loans (at two-and-six each) to Pressmen,
One hundred and nine Mentions of Editor's Womenkind at Fashionable
      Receptions.

It showed what could be achieved by six men, working together shoulder to shoulder for the highest aims in a spirit of mutual good-will and brotherhood. They were undoubtedly greatly helped by having all been to Oxford or Cambridge, but still much was the legitimate result of their own manœuvres.

By the time the secret campaign had reached this stage, many well-meaning, unsuspecting men, not included in the above inventory, had been pressed into the service of the Society, with the members of which they were connected by the thousand and one ties which spring up naturally in the intercourse of the world, so that there was hardly any journal in the three kingdoms on which the Society could not, by some hook or the other, fasten a paragraph, if we except such publications as the *Newgate Calendar* and *Lloyds' Shipping List*, which record history rather than make it.

Indeed, the success of the Society in this department was such as to suggest the advisability of having themselves formally incorporated under the Companies' Acts for the manufacture and distribution of paragraphs, for which they had unequalled facilities, and had obtained valuable concessions, and it was only the publicity required by law which debarred them from enlarging their home trade to a profitable industry for the benefit of non- members. For, by the peculiar nature of the machinery, it could only be worked if people were unaware of its existence. They resolved, however, that when they had made their pile, they would start the newspaper of the future, which any philosopher with an eye to the trend of things can see will be a journal written by advertisers for gentlemen, and will contain nothing calculated to bring a blush to the cheek of the young person except cosmetics.

Contemporaneously with the execution of one side of the Plan of Campaign, the Society was working the supplementary side. Day and night, week-days and Sundays, in season and out, these six gentlemen praised themselves and one another, or got themselves and one another praised by non-members. There are many ways in which you can praise an author, from blame downwards. There is the puff categorical and the puff allusive, the lie direct and the eulogy insinuative, the downright abuse and the subtle innuendo, the exaltation of your man or the depression of his rival. The attacking method of log-rolling must not be confounded with depreciation. In their outside campaign, the members used every variety of puff, but depreciation was strictly reserved for their private gatherings. For this was the wisdom of the Club, and herein lay its immense superiority over every other log-rolling club, that whereas in those childish cliques every man is expected to admire every other, or to say so, in the Mutual Depreciation Society the obligation was all the other way. Every man was bound by the rules to sneer at the work of his fellow-members and, if he should happen to admire any of it, at least to have the grace to keep his feelings to himself. In practice, however, the latter contingency never arose, and each was able honestly to express all he thought, for it is impossible for men to work together for a common object without discovering that they do not deserve to get it. Needless to point out how this sagacious provision strengthened them in their campaign, for not having to keep up the tension of mutual admiration, and being able to relax and breathe (and express themselves) freely at their monthly symposia, as well as to slang one another in the street, they were able to write one another up with a clear conscience. It is well to found on human nature. Every other basis proves shifting sand. The success of the Mutual Depreciation Society justified their belief in human nature.

Not only did they depreciate one another, but they made reparation to the non-members they were always trying to write down during business hours, by eulogizing them in the most generous manner in those blessed hours of leisure when knife answers fork and soul speaks to soul. At such times even popular authors were allowed to have a little merit.

It was at one of these periods of soul-expansion, when the most petty-souled feels inclined to loosen the last two buttons of his waistcoat, that the idea of the English Shakespeare was first mooted. But we are anticipating, which is imprudent, as anticipations are seldom realized.

One of the worst features of prosperity is that it is cloying, and when the first gloss of novelty and adventure had worn off, the free lances of the Mutual Depreciation Society began to bore one another. You can get tired even of hearing your own dispraises; and the members were compelled to spice their mutual adverse criticism in the highest manner, so as to compensate for its staleness. The jaded appetite must needs be pampered if it is to experience anything of that relish which a natural healthy hunger for adverse criticism can command so easily.

This was the sort of thing that went on at the dinners:

"I say, Tom," said Andrew Mackay, "what in Heaven's name made you publish your waste-paper basket under the name of 'Stray Thoughts?' For utter and incomprehensible idiocy they are only surpassed by Dick's last volume of poems. I shouldn't have thought such things could come even out of a lunatic asylum, certainly not without a keeper. Really you fellows ought to consider me a little——"

"We do. We consider you as little as they make them," they interrupted simultaneously.

"It isn't fair to throw all the work on me," he went on. "How can I go on saying that Tom Brown is the supreme thinker of the time, the deepest intellect since Hegel, with a gift of style that rivals Berkeley's, if you go on turning out twaddle that a copy-book would boggle at? How can I keep repeating that for sure and consummate art, for unfailing certainty of insight, for unerring visualization, for objective subjectivity and for subjective objectivity, for Swinburnian sweep of music and Shakespearean depth of suggestiveness, Dick Jones can give forty in a hundred (spot stroke barred) to all other contemporary poets, if you continue to spue out rhymes as false as your teeth, rhythms as musical as your voice when you read them, and words that would drive a drawing-room composer mad with envy to set them? I maintain, it is not sticking to the bargain to expose me to the danger of being found out. You ought at least to have the decency to wrap up your fatuousness in longer words or more abstruse themes. You're both so beastly intelligible that a child can understand you're asses."

"Tut, tut, Andrew," said Taffy Owen, "it's all very well of you to talk who've only got to do the criticism. And I think it's deuced ungrateful of you after we've written you up into the position of leading English critic to want us to give you straw for your bricks! Do we ever complain when you call us cataclysmic, creative, esemplastic, or even epicene? We know it's rot, but we put up with it. When you said that Robinson's last novel had all the glow and genius of Dickens without his humor, all the ripe wisdom of Thackeray without his social knowingness, all the imaginativeness of Shakespeare without his definiteness of characterization, we all saw at once that you were incautiously allowing the donkey's ears to protrude too obviously from beneath the lion's skin. But did anyone grumble? Did Robinson, though the edition was sold out the day after? Did I, though you had just called me a modern Buddhist with the soul of an ancient Greek and the radiant fragrance of a Cingalese tea-planter? I know these phrases take the public and I try to be patient."

"Owen is right," Harry Robinson put in emphatically. "When you said I was a cross between a Scandinavian skald and a Dutch painter, I bore my cross in silence."

"Yes, but what else can a fellow say, when you give the public such heterogeneous and formless balderdash that there is nothing for it but to pretend it's a new style, an epoch-making work, the foundation of a new era in literary art? Really I think you others have out and away the best of it. It's much easier to write bad books than to eulogize their merits in an adequately plausible manner. I think it's playing it too low upon a chap, the way you fellows are going on. It's taking a mean advantage of my position."

"And who put you into that position, I should like to know?" yelled Dick Jones, becoming poetically excited. "Didn't we lift you up into it on the point of our pens?"

"Fortunately they were not very pointed," ejaculated the great critic, wriggling uncomfortably at the suggestion. "I don't deny that, of course. All I say is, you're giving me away now."

"You give yourself away," shrieked Owen vehemently, "with a pound of that Cingalese tea. How is it Boyle managed to crack up our plays without being driven to any of this new-fangled nonsense?"

"Plays!" said Patrick, looking up moodily. "Anything is good enough for plays. You see I can always fall back on the acting and crack up that. I had to do that with Owen's thing at the *Lymarket*. My notice read like a gushing account of the play, in reality it was all devoted to the players. The trick of it is not easy. Those who can read between the lines could see that there were only three of them about the piece itself, and yet the outside public would never dream I was shirking the expression of an opinion about the merits of the play or the pinning myself to any definite statement. The only time, Owen, I dare say, that your plays are literature is when they are a frost, for that both explains the failure and justifies you. But, an you love me, Taffy, or if you have any care for my reputation, do not, I beg of you, be enticed into the new folly of printing your plays."

"But things have come to that stage I *must* do it," said Owen, "or incur the suspicion of illiterateness."

"No, no!" pleaded Patrick in horror. "Sooner than that I will damn all the other printed plays *en bloc*, and say that the real literary playwrights, conscious of their position, are too dignified to resort to this cheap method of self-assertion."

"But you will not carry out your threat? Remember how dangerously near you came to exposing me over your *Naquette*."

The Club laughed. Everyone knew the incident, for it was Patrick's stock grievance against the dramatist. Patrick being out of town, had written his eulogy of this play of Owen's from his inner consciousness. On the fourth night in deference to Owen's persuasions he had gone to see *Naquette*.

After the tragedy, Owen found him seated moodily in the stalls, long after the audience had filed out.

"Knocked you, old man, this time, eh?" queried Owen laughing complacently.

"Knocked you, old man, this time, eh?"

"Yes, all to pieces!" snarled Patrick savagely. "I shall never believe in my critical judgment again. I dare not look my notice in the face. When I wrote *Naquette* was a masterpiece, I thought at least there would be some merit in it —I didn't bargain for such rot as this."

In this wise things would have gone on—from bad to worse—had Heaven not created Cecilia nineteen years before.

Cecilia was a tall, fair girl, with dreamy eyes and unpronounced opinions, who longed for the ineffable with an unspeakable yearning.

Frank Grey loved her. He always knew he was going to and one day he did it. After that it was impossible to drop the habit. And at last he went so far as to propose. He was a young lawyer, with a fondness for manly sports and a wealth of blonde moustache.

"Cecilia," he said, "I love you. Will you be mine?"

He had a habit of using unconventional phrases.

"No, Frank," she said gently, and there was a world and several satellites of tenderness in her tremulous tones. "It cannot be."

"Ah, do not decide so quickly," he pleaded. "I will not press you for an answer."

"I would press you for an answer, if I could," replied Cecilia, "but I do not love you."

"Why not?" he demanded desperately.

"Because you are not what I should like you to be?"

"And what would you like me to be?" he demanded eagerly.

"If I told you, you would try to become it?"

"I would," he said, enthusiastically. "Be it what it may, I would leave no stone unturned. I would work, strive, study, reform—anything, everything."

"I feared so," she said despondently. "That is why I will not tell you. Don't you understand that your charm to me is your being just yourself—your simple, honest, manly self? I will not have my enjoyment of your individuality spoilt by your transmogrification into some unnatural product of the forcing house. No, Frank, let us be true to ourselves, not to each other. I shall always remain your friend, looking up to you as to something stanch, sturdy, stalwart, coming to consult you (unprofessionally) in all my difficulties. I will tell you all my secrets, Frank, so that you will know more of me than if I married you. Dear friend, let it remain as I say. It is for the best."

So Frank went away broken-hearted, and joined the Mutual Depreciation Society. He did not care what became of him. How they came to let him in was this. He was the one man in the world outside who knew all about them, having been engaged as the Society's legal adviser. It was he who made their publishers and managers sit in an erect position. In applying for a more intimate connection, he stated that he had met with a misfortune, and a little monthly abuse would enliven him. The Society decided that, as he was already half one of themselves, and as he had never written a line in his life, and so could not diminish their takings, nothing but good could ensue from the infusion of new blood. In fact, they wanted it badly. Their mutual recriminations had degenerated into mere platitudes. With a new man to insult and be insulted by, something of the old animation would be restored to their proceedings. The wisdom of the policy was early seen, for the first fruit of it was the English Shakespeare, who for a whole year daily opened out new and exciting perspectives of sensation and amusement to a *blasé* Society. Andrew Mackay had written an enthusiastic article in the so-called *Nineteenth Century* on "The Cochin-China Shakespeare," and set all tongues wagging about the new literary phenomenon with whose verses the boatmen of the Irrawady rocked their children to sleep on the cradle of the river, and whose dramas were played in eight hours slices in the strolling-booths of Shanghai. Andrew had already arranged with Anyman to bring out a translation from the original Cochin-Chinese, for there was no language he could not translate from, provided it were sufficiently unknown.

"Cochin-Chinese Shakespeare, indeed!" said Dick Jones, at the next symposium. "Why, judging from the copious extracts you gave from his greatest drama, Baby Bantam, it is *the* most tedious drivel. You might have written it yourself. Where is the Shakespearean quality of this, which is, you say, the whole of Act Thirteen?

"'Hang-ho: Out, Fu-sia, does your mother know you are?

"'Fu-sia: I have no mother, but I have a child.'"

"Where is the Shakespearean quality?" repeated Andrew. "Do you not feel the perfect pathos of those two lines, the infiniteness of incisive significance? To me they paint the whole scene in two strokes of matchless simplicity, strophe and anti-strophe. Fu-sia the repentant outcast and Hang-ho whose honest love she rejected, stand out as in a flash of lightning. Nay, Shakespeare himself never wrote an act of such tragic brevity, packed so full of the sense of anagke. Why, so far from it being tedious drivel, a lady in whose opinion I have great confidence and to whom I sent my article, told me afterwards that she couldn't sleep till she had read it."

"She told me she couldn't sleep till she had read it."

The Mutual Depreciation Society burst into a roar of laughter and Andrew realized that he had put his foot into it.

"Don't you think it a shame," broke in Frank Grey, "that we English are debarred from having a Shakespeare. There's been one discovered lately in Belgium, and we have already a Dutch Shakespeare, a French Shakespeare, a German Shakespeare, and an American Shakespeare. English is the only language in which we can't get one. It seems cruel that we should be just the one nation in the world to be cut off from having a nineteenth century Shakespeare. Every patriotic Briton must surely desire that we could discover an English Shakespeare to put beside these vaunted foreign phenomena."

"But an English Shakespeare is a bull," said Patrick Boyle, who had a keen eye for such.

"Precisely. A John Bull," replied Frank.

"Peace. I would willingly look out for one," said Andrew Mackay, thoughtfully. "But I cannot venture to insinuate yet that Shakespeare did not write English. The time is scarcely ripe, though it is maturing fast. Otherwise the idea is tempting."

"But why take the words in their natural meaning?" demanded Tom Brown, the philosopher, in astonishment. "Is it not unapparent that an English Shakespeare would be a great writer more saturated with Anglo-Saxon spirit than Shakespeare, who was cosmic and for all time and for every place? Hamlet, Othello, Lady Macbeth—these are world-types, not English characters. Our English Shakespeare must be more autochthonic, more chauviniste; or more provincial and more *borné*, if you like to put it that way. His scenes must be rooted in English life, and his personages must smack of British soil." There was much table-thumping when the philosopher ceased.

"Excellent!" said Andrew. "He must be found. It will be the greatest boom of the century. But whom can we discover?"

"There is John P. Smith," said Tom Brown.

"No, why John P. Smith? He has merit," objected Taffy Owen. "And then he has never been in our set."

"And besides he would not be satisfied," said Patrick Boyle.

"That is true," said Andrew Mackay reflectively. "I know, Owen, *you* would like to be the subject of the discovery. But I am afraid it is too late. I have taken your measurements and laid down the chart of your genius too definitely to alter now. You are permanently established in business as the dainty neo-Hellenic Buddhist who has chosen to express himself through farcical comedy. If you were just starting life, I could work you into this English Shakespeardom—I am always happy to put a good thing in the way of a friend—but at your age it is not easy to go into a new line."

"Well, but," put in Harry Robinson, "if none of us is to be the English Shakespeare, why should we give over the appointment to an outsider? Charity begins at home."

"That *is* a difficulty," admitted Andrew, puckering his brow. "It brings us to a standstill. Seductive, therefore, as the idea is, I am afraid it has occurred to us too late."

They sat in thoughtful silence. Then suddenly Frank Grey flashed in with a suggestion that took their breath away for a moment and restored it to them, charged with "Bravos" the moment after.

"But why should he exist at all?"

Why indeed? The more they pondered the matter, the less necessity they saw for it.

"'Pon my word, Grey, you are right," said Andrew. "Right as Talleyrand when he told the thief who insisted that he must live: *Mais, monsieur, je n'en vois pas la nécessité.*"

"It's an inspiration!" said Tom Brown, moved out of his usual apathy. "We all remember how Whateley proved that the Emperor Napoleon never existed —and the plausible way he did it. How few persons actually saw the Emperor? How did even these know that what they saw *was* the Emperor? Conversely, it should be as easy as possible for us six to put a non-existent English Shakespeare on the market. You remember what Voltaire said of God —that if there were none it would be necessary to invent Him. In like manner patriotism calls upon us to invent the English Shakespeare."

"Yes, won't it be awful fun?" said Patrick Boyle.

The idea was taken up eagerly—the *modus operandi* was discussed, and the members parted, effervescing with enthusiasm and anxious to start the campaign immediately. The English Shakespeare was to be named Fladpick, a cognomen which once seen would hook itself on to the memory.

The very next day a leading article in the *Daily Herald* casually quoted Fladpick's famous line:

"Coffined in English yew, he sleeps in peace."

And throughout the next month, in the most out-of-the-way and unlikely quarters, the word Fladpick lurked and sprang upon the reader. Lines and phrases from Fladpick were quoted. Gradually the thing worked up, gathering momentum on its way, and going more and more of itself, like an ever-swelling snowball which needs but the first push down the mountain-side. Soon a leprosy of Fladpick broke out over the journalism of the day. The very office-boys caught the infection, and in their book reviews they dragged in Fladpick with an air of antediluvian acquaintance. Writers were said not to possess Fladpick's imagination, though they might have more sense of style, or they were said not to possess Fladpick's sense of style, though they might have more imagination. Certain epithets and tricks of manner were described as quite Fladpickian, while others were mentioned as extravagant and as disdained by writers like, say, Fladpick. Young authors were paternally invited to mould themselves on Fladpick, while others were contemptuously dismissed as mere imitators of Fladpick. By this time Fladpick's poetic dramas began to be asked for at the libraries, and the libraries said that they were all out. This increased the demand so much that the libraries told their subscribers they must wait till the new edition, which was being hurried through the press, was published. When things had reached this stage, queries about Fladpick appeared in the literary and professionally inquisitive papers, and answers were given, with reference to the editions of Fladpick's book. It began to leak out that he was a young Englishman who had lived all his life in Tartary, and that his book had been published by a local firm and enjoyed no inconsiderable reputation among the English Tartars there, but that the copies which had found their way to England were extremely scarce and had come into the hands of only a few *cognoscenti*, who being such were enabled to create for him the reputation he so thoroughly deserved. The next step was to contradict this, and the press teemed with biographies and counter- biographies. *Dazzler* also wired numerous interviews, but an authoritative statement was inserted in the *Acadæum*, signed by Andrew Mackay, stating that they were unfounded, and paragraphs began to appear detailing how Fladpick spent his life in dodging the interviewers. Anecdotes of Fladpick were highly valued by editors of newspapers, and very plenteous they were, for Fladpick was known to be a cosmopolitan, always sailing from pole to pole and caring little for residence in the country of which he yet bade fair to be the laureate. These anecdotes girdled the globe even more quickly than their hero, and they returned from foreign parts bronzed and almost unrecognizable, to set out immediately on fresh journeys in their new guise.

A parody of one of his plays was inserted in a comic paper, and it was bruited abroad that Andrew Mackay was collaborating with him in preparing one of his dramas for representation at the Independent Theatre. This set the older critics by the ears, and they protested vehemently in their theatrical columns against the infamous ethics propagated by the new writer, quoting largely from the specimens of his work given in Mackay's article in the *Fortnightly Review*. Patrick, who wrote the dramatic criticism for seven papers, led the attack upon the audacious iconoclast. Journalesia was convulsed by the quarrel, and even young ladies asked their partners in the giddy waltz whether they were Fladpickiets or Anti-Fladpickiets. You could never be certain of escaping Fladpick at dinner, for the lady you took down was apt to take you down by her contempt of your ignorance of Fladpick's awfully sweet writings. Any amount of people promised one another introductions to Fladpick, and those who had met him enjoyed quite a reflected reputation in Belgravian circles. As to the Fladpickian parties, which brother geniuses like Dick Jones and Harry Robinson gave to the great writer, it was next to impossible to secure an invitation to them, and comparatively few boasted of the privilege. Fladpick reaped a good deal of *kudos* from refusing to be lionized and preferring the society of men of letters like himself, during his rare halting moments in England.

Long before this stage Mackay had seen his way to introducing the catchword of the conspiracy, "The English Shakespeare." He defended vehemently the ethics of the great writer, claiming they were at core essentially at one with those of the great nation from whence he sprang and whose very life- blood had passed into his work. This brought about a reaction, and all over the country the scribblers hastened to do justice to the maligned writer, and an elaborate analysis of his most subtle characters was announced as having been undertaken by Mr. Patrick Boyle. And when it was stated that he was to be included in the Contemporary Men of Letters Series, the advance orders for the work were far in advance of the demand for Fladpick's actual writings. "Shakespearean," "The English Shakespeare," was now constantly used in connection with his work, and even the most hard-worked reviewers promised themselves to skim his book in their next summer holidays. About this time, too, *Dazzler* unconsciously helped the Society by announcing that Fladpick was dying of consumption in a snow-hut in Greenland, and it was felt that he must either die or go to a warmer climate, if not both. The news of his phthisic weakness put the seal upon his genius, and the great heart of the nation went out to him in his lonely snow-hut, but returned on learning that the report was a *canard*. Still, the danger he had passed through endeared him to his country, and within a few months Fladpick, the English Shakespeare, was definitely added to the glories of the national literature, founding a whole school of writers in his own country, attracting considerable attention on the Continent, and being universally regarded as the centre of the Victorian Renaissance.

But this was the final stage. A little before it was reached Cecilia came to Frank Grey to pour her latest trouble into his ear, for she had carefully kept her promise of bothering him with her most intimate details, and the love-sick young lawyer had listened to her petty psychology with a patience which would have brought him in considerable fees if invested in the usual way. But this time the worry was genuine.

"Frank," she said, "I am in love."

The young man turned as white as a sheet. The sword of Damocles had fallen at last, sundering them forever.

"With whom?" he gasped.

"With Mr. Fladpick!"

"The English Shakespeare?"

"The same!"

"But you have never seen him!"

"I have seen his soul. I have divined him from his writings. I have studied Andrew Mackay's essays on him. I feel that he and I are *en rapport*."

"But this is madness!"

"I know it is. I have tried to fight against it. I have applied for admission to the Old Maids' Club, so as to stifle my hopeless passion. Once I have joined Miss Dulcimer's Society, I shall perhaps find peace again."

"Great Heavens! Think; think before you take this terrible step. Are you sure it is love you feel, not admiration?"

"No, it is love. At first I thought it was admiration, and probably it was, for I was not likely to be mistaken in the analysis of my feelings, in which I have had much practice. But gradually I felt it efflorescing and sending forth tender shoots clad in delicate green buds, and a sweet wonder came upon me, and I knew that love was struggling to get itself born in my soul. Then suddenly the news came that he I loved was ill, dying in that lonely snow-hut in grim Greenland, and then in the tempest of grief that shook me I knew that my life was bound up with his. Watered by my hot tears, the love in my heart bourgeoned and blossomed like some strange tropical passion-flower, and when the reassuring message that he was strong and well flashed through the world, I felt that if he lived not for me, the universe were a blank and next year's daisies would grow over my early grave."

"He I loved was dying in Greenland."

She burst into tears. "A great writer has always been the ideal which I would not tell you of. It is the one thing I have kept from you. But oh, Frank, Frank, he can never be mine. He will probably never know of my existence and the most I can ever hope for is his autograph. To-morrow I shall join the Old Maids' Club, and then all will be over." A paroxysm of hopeless sobs punctuated her remarks.

It was a terrible position. Frank groaned inwardly.

How was he to explain to this fair young thing that she loved nobody and could never hope to marry him? There was no doubt that with her intense nature and her dreamy blue eyes she would pine away and die. Or worse, she would live to be an old maid.

He made an effort to laugh it off.

"Tush!" he said, "all this is mere imagination. I don't believe you really love anybody!"

"Frank!" She drew herself up, stony and rigid, the warm tears on her poor white face frozen to ice. "Have you nothing better than this to say to me, after I have shown you my inmost soul?"

The wretched young lawyer's face returned from white to red. He could have faced a football team in open combat, but these complex psychical positions were beyond the healthy young Philistine.

"For—or—give me," he stammered. "I—I am—I—that is to say, Fladpick —oh how can I explain what I mean?"

Cecilia sobbed on. Every sob seemed to stick in Frank's own throat. His impotence maddened him. Was he to let the woman he loved fret herself to death for a shadow? And yet to undeceive her were scarcely less fatal. He could have cut out the tongue that first invented Fladpick. Verily, his sin was finding him out.

"Why can you not explain what you mean?" wept Cecilia.

"Because I—oh, hang it all—because I am the cause of your grief."

"You?" she said. A strange, wonderful look came into her eyes. The thought shot from her eyes to his and dazzled them.

Yes! why not? why should he not sacrifice himself to save this delicate creature from a premature tomb? Why should he not become "the English Shakespeare?" True, it was a heavy burden to sustain, but what will a man not dare or suffer for the woman he loves? Moreover, was he not responsible for Fladpick's being, and thus for all the evil done by his Frankenstein? He had employed Fladpick for his own amusement and the Employers' Liability Act was heavy upon him. The path of abnegation, of duty, was clear. He saw it and he went for it then and there—went, like a brave young Englishman, to meet his marriage.

"Yes," he said, "I am glad you love Mr. Fladpick."

"Why?" she murmured breathlessly.

"Because I love you." "But—I—do—not—

love—you," she said slowly.

"You will, when I tell you it is I who have provoked your love."

"Frank, is this true?"

"On my word of honor as an Englishman."

"You are Fladpick?"

"If I am not, he does not exist. There is no such person."

"Oh, Frank, this is no cruel jest?"

"Cecilia, it is the sacred truth. Fladpick is nobody, if he is not Frank Grey."

"But you never lived in Tartary?"

"Of course not. All that about Fladpick is the veriest poetry. But I did not mind it, for nobody suspected me. I'll introduce you to Andrew Mackay himself, and you shall hear from his own lips how the newspapers have lied about Fladpick."

"My noble, modest boy! So this was why you were so embarrassed before! But why not have told *me* that you were Fladpick?"

"Because I wanted you to love me for myself alone."

She fell into his arms.

"Frank—Frank—Fladpick, my own, my English Shakespeare," she sobbed ecstatically.

At the next meeting of the Mutual Depreciation Society, a bombshell in a stamped envelope was handed to Mr. Andrew Mackay. He tore open the envelope and the explosion followed—as follows:

"Gentlemen,

"I hereby beg to tender the resignation of my membership in your valued Society, as well as to anticipate your objections to my retaining the post of legal adviser I have the honor to hold. I am about to marry— the cynic will say I am laying the foundation of a Mutual Depreciation Society of my own. But this is not the reason of my retirement. That is to be sought in my having accepted the position of the English Shakespeare which you were good enough to open up for me. It would be a pity to let the pedestal stand empty. From the various excerpts you were kind enough to invent, especially from the copious extracts in Mr. Mackay's articles, I have been able to piece together a considerable body of poetic work, and by carefully collecting every existing fragment, and studying the most authoritative expositions of my aims and methods, I have constructed several dramas, much as Professor Owen re-constructed the

185

mastodon from the bones that were extant. As you know I had never written a line in my life before, but by the copious aid of your excellent and genuinely helpful criticism I was enabled to get along without much difficulty. I find that to write blank verse you have only to invert the order of the words and keep on your guard against rhyme. You may be interested to know that the last line in the last tragedy is:

'Coffined in English yew he sleeps in peace.'

When written, I got my dramas privately printed with a Tartary trademark, after which I smudged the book and sold the copyright to Makemillion & Co. for ten thousand pounds. Needless to say I shall never write another book. In taking leave of you I cannot help feeling that, if I owe you some gratitude for the lofty pinnacle to which you have raised me, you are also not unindebted to me for finally removing the shadow of apprehension that must have dogged you in your sober moments—I mean the fear of being found out. Mr. Andrew Mackay, in particular, as the most deeply committed, I feel owes me what he can never hope to repay for my gallantry in filling the mantle designed by him, whose emptiness might one day have been exposed, to his immediate downfall.

"I am, gentlemen,
"Your most sincere and humble Depreciator,
"THE ENGLISH SHAKESPEARE."

CHAPTER XIV.

THE OLD YOUNG WOMAN AND THE NEW.

"Providence has granted what I dared not hope for," wrote Cecilia to the President.

"If she had hoped for it, Providence would not have granted it," interpolated the Honorary Trier.

"This is hardly the moment for jesting," said Lillie, with marked pique.

"Pardon me. The moment for jesting is surely when you have received a blow. In a happy crisis jesting is a waste of good jokes. The retiring candidate does not state *what* Providence has granted, does she?"

"No," said Lillie savagely. "She was extremely reticent about her history—reticent almost to the point of indiscretion. But I daresay it's a husband."

"Ah, then it can hardly be Providence that has granted it," said Silverdale.

"Providence is not always kindly," said Lillie laughing. The gibe at Benedicts restored her good-humor and when the millionaire strolled into the Club she did not immediately expel him.

"Well, Lillie," he said, "when are you going to give the *soirée* to celebrate the foundation of the Club? I am staying in town expressly for it."

"As soon as possible, father. I am only waiting for some more members."

"Why, have you any difficulty about getting enough? I seem always to be meeting young ladies on the staircases."

"We are so exclusive."

"So it seems. You exclude even me," grumbled the millionaire. "I can't make out why you are so hard to please. A more desirable lot of young ladies I never wish to see. I should never have believed it possible that such a number of pretty girls would be anxious to remain single merely for the sake of a principle."

"You see!" said Lillie eagerly, "we shall be a standing proof to men of how little they have understood our sex."

"Men do not need any proof of that," remarked Lord Silverdale dryly.

This time it was Lillie whom Turple the magnificent prevented from making the retort which was not on the tip of her tongue.

"A gentleman who gives his name as a lady is waiting in the ante-room," he announced.

They all stared hard at Turple the magnificent, almost tempted to believe he was joking and that the end of the world was at hand.

But the countenance of Turple the magnificent was as stolid and expressionless as a Bath bun. He might have been beaming behind his face, possibly even the Old Maids' Club tickled him vastly, so that his mental midriff was agitated convulsively; but this could not be known by outsiders.

Lillie took the card he tendered her and read aloud: "Nelly Nimrod."

"Nelly Nimrod!" cried the Honorary Trier. "Why, that's the famous girl who travelled from Charing Cross to China-Tartary on an elephant and wrote a book about it under the pen-name of Wee Winnie."

"Shall I show him in?" interposed Turple the magnificent.

"Certainly," said Lillie eagerly. "Father, you must go."

"Oh, no! Not if it's only a gentleman."

"It may be only no lady," murmured Silverdale. Lillie caught the words and turned upon him the dusky splendors of her fulminant eyes.

"*Et tu, Brute!*" she said. "Do you too hold that false theory that womanliness consists in childishness?"

"No, nor that other false theory that it consists in manliness," retorted the Honorary Trier.

The entry of Nelly Nimrod put an end to the dispute. In the excitement of the moment no one noticed that the millionaire was still leaning against an epigram.

"Good-morning, Miss Dulcimer. I am charmed to make your acquaintance," said Wee Winnie, gripping the President's soft hand with painful cordiality. She was elegantly attired in a white double-breasted waistcoat, a zouave jacket, a check-tweed skirt, gaiters, a three inch collar, a tricorner hat, a pair of tanned gloves and an eyeglass. In her hand she carried an ebony stick. Her hair was parted at the side. Nelly was nothing if not original, so that when the spectator looked down for the divided skirt he was astonished not to find it. Wee Winnie in fact considered it ungraceful and *Divide et Impera* a contradiction in terms. She was a tall girl, and looked handsome even under the most masculine conditions.

"I am happy to make yours," returned the President. "Is it to join the Old Maids' Club that you have called?"

"It is. Wherever there is a crusade you will always find me in the van. I don't precisely know your objects yet, but any woman who strikes out anything new commands my warmest sympathies."

"Be seated, Miss Nimrod. Allow me to introduce Lord Silverdale—an old friend of mine."

"And of mine," replied Nelly, bowing with a sweet smile.

"Indeed!" cried Lillie flushing.

"In the spirit, only in the spirit," said Nelly. "His lordship's 'Poems of Passion' formed my sole reading in the deserts of China-Tartary."

"In the letter, you should say then," said the peer. "By the way, you are confusing me with a minor poet, Silverplume, and his book is not called Poems of Passion but Poems of Compassion."

"Ah well, there isn't much difference," said Nelly.

"No, according to the proverb Compassion *is* akin to Passion," admitted Silverdale.

"Well, Miss Nimrod," put in Lillie, "our object is easily defined. We are an association of young and beautiful girls devoted to celibacy in order to modify the meaning of the term 'Old Maid.'"

Nelly Nimrod started up enthusiastically.

"Bravo, old girl!" she cried, slapping the President on the back. "Put me down for a flag. I catch the conception of the campaign. It is magnificent."

"But it is not war," said Lillie. "Our methods are peaceful, unaggressive. Our platform is merely metaphorical. Our lesson is the self-sufficiency of spinsterhood. We preach it by existing."

"Not exist by preaching it," added Silverdale. "This is not one of the cliques of the shrieking sisterhood?"

"What do you mean by the term shrieking sisterhood," said Nelly. "I use it to denote the mice-fearing classes."

"Hear, hear," said Lillie. "It is true, Miss Nimrod, that our members are required not to exhibit in public, but only because that is a part of the old unhappy signification of 'Old Maid.'"

"I quite understand. You would not call a book a public exhibition of oneself, I suppose."

"Certainly not—if it is an autobiography," said Silverdale.

"That's all right then. My book *is* autobiographical."

"I knew a celebrity once," said Silverdale, "a dreadfully shy person. All his life he lived retired from the world, and even after his death he concealed himself behind an autobiography."

Lillie frowned at these ironical insinuations, though Miss Nimrod appeared impervious to them.

"I have not concealed myself," she said simply. "All I thought and did is written in my book."

"I liked that part about the fleas," murmured the millionaire.

"What's that? Didn't catch that," said Nelly, looking round in the direction of the voice.

"Good gracious, father, haven't you gone?" cried Lillie, no less startled. "It's too bad. You are spoiling one of my best epigrams. Couldn't you lean against something else?"

Before the millionaire could be got rid of, Turple the magnificent reappeared.

"A lady who gives the name of a gentleman," he said.

The assemblage pricked up its ears.

"What name?" asked Lillie.

"Miss Jack, she said."

"That's her surname," said Lillie, in a disappointed tone.

Turple the magnificent stood reproved a moment, then he went out to fetch the lady. The gathering was already so large that Lillie thought there was nothing to be gained by keeping her waiting.

Miss Jack proved to be an extremely eligible candidate so far as appearances went. She bowed stiffly on being introduced to Miss Nimrod.

"May I ask if that is to be the uniform of the Old Maids' Club?" she inquired of the President. "Because if so I am afraid I have made a mistaken journey. It is as a protest against unconventional females that I designed to join you."

"Is that the uniform of the Old Maids' Club?"

"Is it to me you are referring as an unconventional female?" asked Miss Nimrod, bridling up.

"Certainly," replied Miss Jack, with exquisite politeness. "I lay stress upon your sex, merely because it is not obvious."

"Well, I *am* an unconventional female, and I glory in it," said Nelly Nimrod, seating herself astride the sofa. "I did not expect to hear the provincial suburban note struck within these walls. I claim the right of every woman to lead her own life in her own toilettes."

"And a pretty life you have led!"

"I have, indeed!" cried Miss Nimrod, goaded almost to oratory by Miss

Jack's taunts. "Not the ugly, unlovely life of the average woman. I have exhausted all the sensations which are the common guerdon of youth and health and high spirits, and which have for the most part been selfishly monopolized by man. The splendid audacity of youth has burnt in my veins and fired me to burst my swaddling clothes and strike for the emancipation of my sex. I have not merely played cricket in a white shirt and lawn tennis in a blue serge skirt, I have not only skated in low-heeled boots and fenced in corduroy knickerbockers, but I have sailed the seas in an oil-skin jacket and a sou'-wester and swum them in nothing and walked beneath them in the diver's mail. I have waded after salmon in long boots and caught trout in tweed knickerbockers and spats. Nay, more! I have proclaimed the dignity of womanhood upon the moors, and have shot grouse in brown leather gaiters and a sweet Norfolk jacket with half-inch tucks. But this is not the climax, I have——"

Wee Winnie on her Travels.

"Yes, I know. You are Wee Winnie. You travelled alone from Charing Cross to China-Tartary. I have not read your book, but I have heard of it."

"And what have you heard of it?"

"That it is in bad taste."

"Your remark is in worse," interposed Lillie severely.

"Ladies, ladies!" murmured Silverdale. "This is the first time we have had two of them in the room together," he thought. "I suppose when the thing is once started we shall change the name to the Kilkenny Cats' Club."

"In bad taste, is it?" said Miss Nimrod, promptly whipping a book out of her skirt pocket. "Well, here is the book. If you can find one passage in bad taste I'll—I'll delete it in the next edition. There!"

She pushed the book into the hands of Miss Jack, who took it rather reluctantly.

"What's this?" asked Miss Jack, pointing to a weird illustration.

"That's a picture of me on my elephant, sketched by myself. Do you mean to say there's any bad taste about that?"

"Oh, no; I merely asked for information. I didn't know what animal it was."

"You astonish me," said the artist. "Have you never been to a circus? Yes, this is Mumbo Jumbo himself."

"Surely, Miss Jack," said Lord Silverdale gravely. "You must have heard, if you have not read, how Miss Nimrod chartered an elephant, packed up her Kodak and a few bonnet-boxes and rode him on the curb through Central Asia. But may I ask, Miss Nimrod, why you did not enrich the book with more sketches? There is only this one. All the rest are Kodaks."

"Well, you see, Lord Silverdale, it's simpler to photograph."

"Perhaps, but your readers miss the artistic quality that pervades this sketch. I am glad you made an exception in its favor."

"Oh, only because one can't Kodak oneself. Everything else I caught as I flew past."

"Did you catch any Tartars?"

"Hundreds. I destroyed most of them."

"By the way, you did not come across Mr. Fladpick in Tartary?"

"The English Shakespeare? Oh, yes! I lunched with him. He is charm ____"

"Ah, here are the fleas!" interrupted Miss Jack.

The millionaire started as if he had been stung.

"I won't have them taken apart from the context, I warn you. That wouldn't be fair," said Miss Nimrod.

"Very well, I will read the whole passage," said Miss Jack.

"'Mumbo Jumbo bucked violently (*see illustration*) but I settled myself tightly on the saddle and gave myself up to meditations on the vanity of Lifeguardsmen. Mumbo Jumbo seemed, however, determined to have his fling, and bounded about with the agility of an india-rubber ball. At last his convulsions became so terrific that I grew quite nervous about my fragile bonnet-boxes. They might easily dash one another to bits. I determined to have leather hat-boxes the next time I travelled in untrodden paths. "Steady, my beauty, steady!" I cried. Recognizing my familiar accents, my pet easied a little. To pacify him entirely I whistled 'Ba, ba, ba, boodle-dee,' to him, but his contortions recommenced and became quite grotesque. First he lifted one paw high in the air, then he twirled his trunk round the corner, then the first paw came down with a thud that shook the desert, while the other three paws flew up towards the sky. It suddenly occurred to me that he was dancing to the air of 'Ba, ba, ba, boodle-dee,' and I laughed so loud and long, that any stray Mahatma who happened to be smoking at the door of his cave in the cool of the evening must have thought me mad. But while I was laughing, Mumbo Jumbo continued to stand upon his tail, so that I saw it could not be 'Ba, ba, ba, boodle-dee' he was suffering from. I wondered whether perhaps he could be teething—or should I say, tusking? I do not know whether elephants get a second set, or whether they cut their wisdom tusks, but, as they are so sagacious, I suppose they do. Suddenly the consciousness of what was really the matter with him flashed sharply upon my brain. I looked down upon my hand, and there, poised lightly yet firmly, like a butterfly on a lily, was a giant flea. Instantly, without uttering a single cry or reeling in my saddle, I grasped the situation; and coolly seizing the noxious insect with my other hand, I choked the life out of him, while Mumbo Jumbo cantered along in restored calm. The sensitive beast had evidently been suffering untold agonies.'"

"Now, Lord Silverdale," said Miss Nimrod, "I appeal to you. Is there anything in that passage in the least calculated to bring a blush to the cheek of the young person?"

"No, there is not," said his lordship emphatically. "Only I wish you had caught that flea with your Kodak."

"Why?" said Miss Nimrod.

"Because I have always longed to see him. A flea that could penetrate the pachydermatous hide of an elephant must have been, indeed, a monster. In England we only see that sort under microscopes. They seem to thrive nowhere else. Yours must have been one that had escaped from under the lens. He was magnified three thousand diameters and he never recovered from it. You probably took him over in your trunk."

"Oh, no, I'm sure I didn't," protested Miss Nimrod.

"Well, then, Mumbo Jumbo did in his."

"Excuse me," interposed Miss Jack. "We are getting off the point. I didnot say the passage was calculated to raise a blush, I said it was a grave error of taste."

"It is a mere flea-bite," broke in the millionaire, impatiently. "I liked it when I first read it, and I like it now I hear it again. It is a touch of nature that brings the Tartary traveller home to every fireside."

"Besides," added Lord Silverdale. "The introduction of the butterfly and the lily makes it quite poetical."

"Ladies and gentlemen," interposed the President, at last, "we are not here to discuss entomology or æsthetics. You stated, Miss Jack, that you thought of joining us as a protest against female unconventionally."

"I said unconventional females," persisted Miss Jack.

"Even so, I do not follow you," said Lillie.

"It is extremely simple. I am unable to marry because I have a frank nature, not given to feigning or fawning. I cannot bring a husband what he expects nowadays in a wife."

"What is that?" inquired Lillie curiously.

"A chum," answered Miss Jack. "Formerly a man wanted a wife, now he wants a woman to sympathize with his intellectual interests, to talk with him intelligently about his business, discuss politics with him—nay, almost to smoke with him. Tobacco for two is destined to be the ideal of the immediate future. The girls he favors are those who flatter him by imitating him. It is women like Wee Winnie who have depraved his taste. There is nothing the natural man craves less for than a clever, learned wife. Only he has been talked over into believing that he needs intellectual companionship, and now he won't be happy till he gets it. I have escaped politics and affairs all my life, and I am determined not to marry into them."

"What a humiliating confession!" sneered Miss Nimrod. "It is a pity you don't wear doll's-clothes."

"I claim for every woman the right to live her own life in her own toilettes," retorted Miss Jack. "The sneers about dolls are threadbare. I have watched these intellectual camaraderies, and I say they are a worse injustice to woman than any you decry."

"That sounds a promising paradox," muttered Lord Silverdale.

"The man expects the woman to talk politics—but he refuses to take a reciprocal interest in the woman's sphere of work. He will not talk nursery or servants. He will preach economy, but he will not talk it."

"That is true," said Lillie impressed. "What reply would you make to that, Miss Nimrod?"

"There is no possible reply," said Miss Jack hurriedly. "So much for the mock equality which is the cant of the new husbandry. How stands the account with the new young womanhood? The young ladies who are clamoring for equality with men want to eat their cake and to have it too. They want to wear masculine hats, yet to keep them on in the presence of gentlemen; to compete with men in the market-place, yet to take their seats inside omnibuses on wet days and outside them on sunny; to be 'pals' with men in theatres and restaurants and shirk their share of the expenses. I once knew a girl named Miss Friscoe who cultivated Platonic relations with young men, but never once did she pay her half of the hansom."

"Pardon me," interrupted Wee Winnie. "My whole life gives the lie to your superficial sarcasm. In my anxiety to escape these obvious objurgations I have even, I admit it, gone to the opposite extreme. I have made it a point to do unto men as they would have done unto me, if I had not anticipated them. I always defray the bill at the restaurants, buy the stalls at the box-office and receive the curses of the cabman. If I see a young gentleman to the train, I always get his ticket for him and help him into the carriage. If I convey him to a ball, I bring him a button-hole, compliment him upon his costume and say soft nothings about his moustache, while if I go to a dance alone I stroll in about one in the morning, survey mankind through my eyeglass, loll a few minutes in the doorway, then go downstairs to interview the supper, and having sated myself with chicken, champagne and trifle return to my club."

"To your club!" exclaimed the millionaire.

"Yes—do you think the Old Maids' is the only one in London? Mine is the Lady Travellers'—do you know it, Miss Dulcimer?"

"No—o," said Lillie shamefacedly. "I only know the Writers'."

"Why, are you a member of that? I'm a member, too. It's getting a great club now, what with Ellaline Rand (Andrew Dibdin, you know) and Frank Maddox and Lillie Dulcimer. I wonder we haven't met there."

"I'm so taken up with my own club," explained Lillie.

"Naturally. But you must come and dine with me some evening at the Lady Travellers'—snug little club—much cosier than the Junior Widows', and they give you a better bottle of wine, and then the decorations are so sweetly pretty. The only advantage the Junior Widows' has over the Lady

Travellers' is the lovely smoking-room lined with mirrors, which makes it much nicer when you have men to dinner. I always ask them there."

"Why, are you allowed to have men?" asked Miss Jack.

"Certainly—in the dining and smoking rooms. Then of course there are special gentlemen's nights. We get down a lot of music-hall talent just to let them have a peep into Bohemia."

"But how can you be a member of the Junior Widows'?" asked the millionaire.

"Oh, I'm not an original member. But when they were in want of funds they let a lot of married women and girls in, without asking questions."

"I suppose, though, they all look forward to becoming widows in time," observed Silverdale cheerfully.

"Oh no," replied Miss Nimrod emphatically. "I don't say that if they hadn't let me in, the lovely smoking-room lined with mirrors mightn't have tempted me to marry so as to qualify myself. But as it is, thank Heaven, I'm an Old Maid for life. Why should I give up my freedom and the comforts of my club and saddle myself with a husband who would want to monopolize my society and who would be jealous of my bachelor friends and want me to cut them, who would hanker to read my letters, who would watch my comings and goings, and open my parcels of cosmetics marked confectionery? Doubtless in the bad old times which Miss Jack has the inaptitude to regret, marriage was the key to comparative freedom, but in these days when woman has at last emancipated herself from the thraldom of mothers, it would be the height of folly to replace them by husbands. Will you tell me, Miss Jack, what marriage has to offer to a woman like me?"

"Nothing," replied Miss Jack.

"Aha! You admit it!" cried Miss Nimrod triumphantly. "Why should I embrace a profession to which I feel no call? Marriage has practically nothing to offer any independent woman except a trousseau, wedding presents, and the jealousy of her female friends. But what are these weighed against the cramping of her individuality? Perhaps even children come to fetter her life still more and she has daughters who grow up to be younger than herself. No, the future lies with the Old Maid; the woman who will retain her youth and her individuality till death; who dies, but does not surrender. The ebbing tide is with you, Miss Jack; the flowing tide is with us. The Old Maids' Club will be the keystone of the arch of the civilization of to-morrow, and Miss Dulcimer's name will go down to posterity linked with——"

"Lord Silverdale's," said the millionaire.

"Father! What are you saying?" murmured Lillie, abashed before her visitors.

"I was reminding Miss Nimrod of the part his lordship has played in the movement. It is not fair posterity should give you all the credit."

"I have done nothing for the club—nothing," said the peer modestly.

"And I will do the same," said Miss Jack. "I came here under the delusion that I was going to associate myself with a protest against the defeminization of my sex, with a band of noble women who were resolved never to marry till the good old times were restored and marriages became true marriages once more. But instead of that I find—Wee Winnie."

"You are, indeed, fortunate beyond your deserts," replied that lady. "You may even hope to encounter a suitable husband some day."

"I do hope," said Miss Jack frankly. "But I will never marry till I meet a thoroughly conventional man."

"There I have the advantage of you," said Miss Nimrod. "I shall never marry till I meet a thoroughly *un*conventional man."

"A thoroughly unconventional man would never want to marry at all," said Lillie.

"Of course not. That is the beauty of the situation. That is the paradox which guarantees my spinsterhood. Well, I've had a charming afternoon, Miss Dulcimer, but I must really run away now. I hate keeping men waiting, and I have an appointment with a couple of friends at the Junior Widows'. Such fun! While riding in the park before lunch, I met Guy Fledgely out for a constitutional with his father, the baronet. I asked Guy if he would have a chop with me at the club this evening, and what do you think? The baronet coughed and looked at Guy meaningly, and Guy blushed and hemmed and hawed and looked sheepish and at last gave me to understand he never went out to dine with a lady unless accompanied by his father. So I had to ask the old man, too. Isn't it awful? By the way, Miss Jack, I should be awfully delighted if you would join our party!"

"I asked them to have a chop at the club with me."

"Thank you, Wee Winnie," said Miss Jack, disdainfully.

"But think how thoroughly conventional the baronet is! He won't even let his son go out without a chaperon."

"That is true," admitted Miss Jack, visibly impressed. "He is about the most conventional man I ever heard of."

"A widower, too," pursued Miss Nimrod, pressing her advantage.

Miss Jack hesitated.

"And he dines seven sharp at the Junior Widows'."

"Ah then, there is no time to lose," said Miss Jack. They went out arm in arm.

———

"Have you seen Patrick Boyle's poem in the *Playgoers' Review*?" asked

Lillie, when the club was clear.

"You mean the great dramatic critic's? No, I haven't seen it, but I have seen extracts and eulogies in every paper."

"I have it here complete," said Lillie. "It is quite interesting to find there is a heart beneath the critic's waistcoat. Read it aloud. No, you don't want the banjo!"

Lord Silverdale obeyed. The poem was entitled.

CRITICUS IN STABULIS (?).

Rallying-point of all playgoers earnest,
    Packed with incongruous types of humanity,
Easily pleased, yet of critics the sternest,
    Crudely ignoring that all things are vanity.
Pit, in thee laughter and tears blend in medley—
    Would I could sit in thy cozy concavity!
No! to the stalls I am drawn, to the deadly
        Centre of gravity.

Florin, or shilling, or sixpence admission,
    Often I've paid in my raw juvenility,
Purchasing Banbury cakes in addition,
    Ginger-beer, too, to my highest ability.
Villains I hissed like a venomous gander,
    Virtue I loved next to cheesecakes or chocolate;
Now no atrocity raises my dander,
        No crime can shock o' late.

Then I could dote on a red melodrama,
    Now I demand but limelight on Philosophy,
Learned allusions to Buddha and Brahma,
    Science and Faith and a touch of Theosophy.
Farces I slate, on Burlesque I am scathing,
    Pantomime shakes for a week my serenity;
Nothing restores my composure but bathing
        Deep in Ibsenity.

Actors were Gods to my boyish devotion,
    Actresses angels—in tights and low bodices;
Drowned is that pretty and puerile notion,
    Thrown overboard in the first of my Odysseys.
Syrens may sing submarine fascinations,
    Adult Ulysses remain analytical,

Flat notes recording, or reedy vibrations,
 Tranquilly critical.

Here in the stalls we are stiff as if starch, meant
 Only for shirt-fronts, to faces had mounted up;
Dowagers' wills may be read on their parchment,
 Beautiful busts on your thumbs may be counted up.
Girls in the pit are remarkably rosy,
 Each claspt by lover who passes the paper-bag;
Here I can't even, the girls are so prosy,
 One digit taper bag.

Yet could I sit in the pit of the Surrey,
 Munching an orange or spooning with 'Arriet;
Sadly I fear I should be in no hurry
 Backward to drive my existence's chariot.
"Squeezes" are ill compensated by crushes—
 Stalls may be dull, but they're jolly luxurious;
Really the way o'er past joys we can gush is
 Awfully curious!

Life is a chaos of comic confusion,
 Past things alone take a haloharmonious;
So from illusion we wake to illusion,
 Each as the rest just as true and erroneous.
Fin de siècle I am, and so be it!
 Here's to the problems of sad sociology!
This is my weird,—like a man I must dree it,
 Great is chronology!

Even so, once the great drama allured me,
 Which we all play on the stage universal;
"Going behind" the "green" curtain has cured me.
 All my hope now is 'tis not a *rehearsal*.
Still I've played on; to old men's parts I grew from
 Juvenile lead, as I'd risen from small-boy,
So I'll play on till I get my last cue from
 Death, the old call-boy.

 "Hum! Not at all bad," concluded Lord Silverdale. "I wonder who wrote it."

CHAPTER XV.

THE MYSTERIOUS ADVERTISER.

> "Junior Widows' Club.
> "*Midnight.*

"Dear Miss Dulcimer,

"Just a line to tell you what a lovely evening we have had. The baronet seemed greatly taken with Miss Jack and she with him, and they behaved in a conventional manner. Guy and I were able to have a real long chat and he told me all his troubles. It appears that he has just been thrown over by his promised bride under circumstances of a most peculiar character. I gave him the sympathy he needed, but at the same time thought to myself, aha! here is another member for the Old Maids' Club. You rely on me, I will build you up a phalanx of Old Maids that shall just swamp the memory of Hippolyte and her Amazons. I got out of Guy the name and address of the girl who jilted him. I shall call upon Miss Sybil Hotspur the first thing in the morning, and if I do not land her my name is not

"Yours cheerily,

"Wee Winnie."

"This may be awkward," said the Honorary Trier, returning the letter to the President. "Miss Nimrod seems to take her own election for granted."

"And to think that we are anxious for members," added Lillie.

"Well, we ought to have somebody to replace Miss Jack," said Silverdale, with a suspicion of a smile. "But do you propose to accept Wee Winnie?"

"I don't know—she is certainly a remarkable girl. Such originality and individuality! Suppose we let things slide a little."

"Very well; we will not commit ourselves yet by saying anything to Miss Nim——"

"Miss Nimrod," announced Turple the magnificent.

"Aha! Here we are again!" cried Wee Winnie. "How are you, everybody? How is the old gentleman? Isn't he here?"

"He is very well, thank you, but he is not one of us," said Lillie.

"Oh! Well, anyhow, I've got another of us."

"Miss Sybil Hotspur?"

"The same. I found her raging like a volcano."

"What—smoking?" queried Silverdale.

"No, no, she is one of the old sort. She merely fumes," said Wee Winnie, laughing as if she had made a joke. "She was raving against the infidelity of men. Poor Guy! How his ears must have tingled. He has sent her a long explanation, but she laughs it to scorn. I persuaded her to let you see it—it is so quaint."

"Have you it with you?" asked Lillie eagerly. Her appetite for tales of real life was growing by what it fed upon.

"Yes—here is his letter, several quires long. But before you can understand it, you must know how the breach came about."

"Lord Silverdale, pass Miss Nimrod the chocolate creams. Or would you like some lemonade?"

"Lemonade by all means," replied Wee Winnie, taking up her favorite attitude astride the sofa. "With just a wee drappie of whiskey in it, if you please. I daresay I shall be as dry as a lime-kiln before I've finished the story and read you this letter."

Turple the magnificent duly attended to Miss Nimrod's wants. Whatever he felt, he made no sign. He was simply Turple the magnificent.

"One fine day," said Wee Winnie, "or rather, one day that began fine, a merry party made an excursion into the country. Sybil Hotspur and her *fiancé*, Guy Fledgely, (and of course the baronet) were of the party. After picknicking on the grass, the party broke up into twos till tea-time. The baronet was good enough to pair off with an unattached young lady, and so Sybil and Guy were free to wander away into a copse. The sun was very hot, and the young man had not spared the fizz. First he took off his coat, to be cooler, then with an afterthought he converted it into a pillow and went to sleep. Meantime Sybil, under the protection of her parasol, steadily perused one of Addiper's early works, chaster in style than in substance, and sneering in exquisitely chiselled epigrams at the weaknesses of his sex. Sybil stole an involuntary glance at Guy—sleeping so peacefully like a babe in the wood, with the squirrels peeping at him trustfully. She felt that Addiper was a jaundiced cynic—that her Guy at least would be faithful unto death. At that instant she saw a folded sheet of paper on the ground near Guy's shoulder. It might have slipped from the inner pocket of the coat on which his head was resting, but if it had she could not put it back without disturbing his slumbers. Besides, it might not belong to him at all. She picked up the paper, opened it, and turned pale as death. This is what she read.

"Manager of *Daily Hurrygraph*. Please insert enclosed series, in order named, on alternate days, commencing to-day week. Postal order enclosed."

"'1. Dearest, dearest, dearest. Remember the grotto.—POPSY.

"'2. Dearest, dearest, dearest. This is worse than silence. Sobs are cheap to-day.—POPSY.

"'3. Dearest, dearest, dearest. Only Anastasia and the dog. Thought I should have died. Cruel heart, hope on. The white band of hope! Watchman, what of the night? Shall we say 11.15 from Paddington since the sea will not give up its dead? I have drained the dregs. The rest is silence. Answer to- morrow or I shall dree my weird.—POPSY.'

"There was no signature to the letter, but the writing was that which had hitherto borne to poor Sybil the daily assurances of her lover's devotion. She looked at the sleeping traitor so savagely that he moved uncomfortably, even in his sleep. Like a serpent that scrap of paper had entered into her Eden, and she put it in her bosom that it might sting her. Unnoticed, the shadows had been lengthening, the sky had grown gray, as if in harmony with her blighted hopes. Roughly she roused the sleeper, and hastily they wended their way back to the rendezvous, to find tea just over and the rush to the station just beginning. There was no time to talk till they were seated face to face in the railway carriage. The party had just caught the train, and bundling in anyhow had become separated. Sybil and Guy were alone again.

"Then Sybil plucked from her breast the serpent and held it up.

"'Guy,' she said. 'What is this?'

"He turned pale. 'W—w—here did you get that from?' he stammered.

"'What is this?' she repeated, and read in unsympathetic accents: 'Dearest, dearest, dearest. Remember the grotto.—POPSY.'

"'Who is "dearest"?' she continued.

"'You, of course,' he said with ghastly playfulness.

"Dearest, is you," he said with ghastly playfulness.

"'Indeed. Then allow me to say, sir, I *will* remember the grotto. I shall never forget it, Popsy. If you wish to communicate with me, a penny postage stamp is, I believe, adequate. Perhaps I am also Anastasia, to say nothing of the dog. Or shall we say the 11-15 from Paddington, Popsy?'

"'Sybil, darling,' he broke in piteously. 'Give me back that paper, you wouldn't understand.'

"Sybil silently replaced the serpent in her bosom and leant back haughtily.

"'I can explain all,' he cried wildly.

"'I am listening,' Sybil said.

"'The fact is—I—I——' The young man flushed and stammered. Sybil's pursed lips gave him no assistance.

"'It may seem incredible—you will not believe it.'

"Sybil made no sign.

"'I—I—am the victim of a disease.'

"Sybil stared scornfully.

"'I—I—don't look at me like that, or I can't tell you. I—I—I didn't like to tell you before, but I always knew you would have to know some day. Perhaps it is better it has come out before our marriage. Listen!'

"The young man leant over and breathed solemnly in her ear: *'I suffer from an hereditary tendency to advertise in the agony column.'*

"Sybil made no reply. The train drew up at a station. Without a word Sybil left the carriage and rejoined her friends in the next compartment."

"What an extraordinary excuse," exclaimed Lillie.

"So Sybil thought," replied Wee Winnie. "From that day to this—almost a week—she has never spoken to him. And yet Guy persists in his explanation, even to me; which is so superfluous that I am almost inclined to believe in its truth. At any rate I will now read you his letter:—

"'DEAR SYBIL:—

"'Perhaps for the last time I address you thus, for if after reading this you still refuse to believe me, I shall not trespass upon your patience again. But for the sake of our past love I beg you to read what follows in a trusting spirit, and if not in a trusting spirit, at least to read it. It is the story of how my father became a baronet, and when you know that, you will perhaps learn to pity and to bear with me.

"'When a young man my father was bitten by the passion for contributing to the agony column. Some young men spend their money in one way, some in another; this was my father's dissipation. He loved to insert mysterious words and sentences in the advertisement columns of the newspapers, so as to enjoy the sensation of giving food for speculation to a whole people. To sit quietly at home and with a stroke of the pen influence the thoughts of millions of his countrymen—this gave my father the keenest satisfaction. When you come to analyze it, what more does the greatest author do?

"'The agony column is the royal road to successful authorship, if the publication of fiction in leading newspapers be any test of success; for my father used sometimes to conduct whole romances by correspondence, after the fashion of the then reigning Wilkie Collins.

And the agony column is also the most innocuous method for satisfying that crave for supplying topics of conversation which sometimes leads people to crime. I make this analysis to show you that there was no antecedent improbability about what you seem to consider a wild excuse. The desire to contribute to this department of journalism is no isolated psychical freak; it is related to many other manifestations of mental activity, and is perfectly intelligible. But this desire, like every other, may be given its head till it runs away with the whole man. So it was with my father. He began—half in fun—with a small advertisement, one insertion. Unfortunately—or fortunately—he made a little hit with it. He heard two men discussing it in a café. The next week he tried again— unsuccessfully this time, so far as he knew. But the third advertisement was again a topic of conversation. Even in his own office (he was training for an architect), he heard the fellows saying, "Did you see that funny advertisement this morning—'Be careful not to break the baby.'"

"'You can imagine how intoxicating this sort of thing is and how the craving for the secret enjoyment it brings may grow on a man. Gradually my father became the victim of a passion fiercer than the gambler's, yet akin to it. For, he never knew whether his money would procure him the gratification he yearned for or not; it was all a fluke. The most promising mysteries would attract no attention, and even a carefully planned novelette, that ran for a week with as many as three characters intervening, would fall still-born upon the tapis of conversation. But every failure only spurred him to fresh effort. All his spare coin, all his savings, went into the tills of the newspaper cashiers. He cut down his expenses to the uttermost farthing, living abstemiously and dressing almost shabbily, and sacrificing everything to his ambitions. It was lucky he was not in a bank; for he had only a moderate income, and who knows to what he might have been driven? At last my father struck oil. Tired of the unfruitful field of romance, whose best days seemed to be over, my father returned to that rudimentary literature which pleases the widest number of readers, while it has the never-failing charm of the primitive for the jaded disciples of culture. He wrote only polysyllabic unintelligibilities.

"'Thus for a whole week in every morning agony column he published in large capitals the word:

"'Paddlepintospheroskedaddepoid.

This was an instantaneous success. But it was only a *succès d'estime*. People talked of it, but they could not remember it. It had no seeds of permanence in it. It could never be more than a nine days' wonder. It was an artificial, esoteric novelty, that might please the cliques but could never touch the masses. It lacked the simplicity of real greatness, that unmistakable elemental *cachet* which commends things to the great heart of the people. After a bit, this dawned upon my father; and, profiting by his experience, he determined to create something which should be immortal.

"'For days he racked his brains, unable to please himself. He had the critical fastidiousness of the true artist, and his ideal ever hovered before him, unseizable. Grotesque words floated about him in abundance, every current of air brought him new suggestions, he lived in a world of strange sounds. But the great combination came not.

"'Late one night, as he sat brooding by his dying fire, there came a sudden rapping at his chamber door. A flash of joy illumined his face, he started to his feet.

"'"I have it!" he cried.

"'"Have what?" said his friend Marple, bursting into the room without further parley.

"'"Influenza," surlily answered my father, for he was not to be caught napping, and Marple went away hurriedly. Marple was something in the city. The two young men were great friends, but there are some things which cannot be told even to friends. It was not influenza my father had got. To his fevered onomatopœic fancy, Marple's quick quadruple rap had translated itself into the word: Olotutu.

"'At this hour of the day, my dear Sybil, it is superfluous to say anything about this word, with which you have been familiar from your cradle. It has now been before the public over a quarter of a century, and it has long since won immortality. Little did you think when we sat in the railway carriage yesterday, that the "Olotutu" that glared at you from the partition was the far-away cause of the cloud now hanging over our lives. But it may be interesting to you to learn that in the early days many people put the accent on the second syllable, whereas all the world now knows, the accent is on the first, and the "o" of "ol" is short. When my father found he had set the Thames on fire, he was almost beside himself with joy. At the office the clerks, in the intervals of wondering about "Olotutu" wondered if he had come into a fortune. He determined to follow up his success: to back the winning word, to consecrate his life to "Olotutu," to put all his money on it. Thenceforwards for the next three months you very rarely opened a paper without seeing the word, "Olotutu." It stood always by itself, self-complete and independent, rigid and austere, in provoking sphynx-like solitude. Sybil, imagine to yourself my father's rapture! To be the one man in all England who had the clue to the enigma of "Olotutu!" At last the burden of his secret became intolerable. He felt he must breathe a hint of it or die. One night while Marple was smoking in his rooms and wondering about "Olotutu," my father proudly told him all.

""""Great heavens!" exclaimed Marple. "Tip us your flipper, old man! You are a millionaire."

""""A what?" gasped my father.

""""A millionaire!"

""""Are you a lunatic?"

""""Are you an idiot? Don't you see that there is a fortune in 'Olotutu'?"

""""A fortune! How?"

""""By bringing it out as a Joint Stock Company." """"But—

but—but you don't understand. 'Olotutu' is only——"

""""Only an income for life," interrupted Marple excitedly. "Look here, old boy, I'll get you up a syndicate to run it in twenty-four hours."

""""Do you mean to say——?"

""""No, I mean to do. I'm an ass not to quietly annex it all to myself, but I always said I was too honest for the City. Give me 'Olotutu' and we'll divide the profits. Glory! Hooray!"

"'He capered about the floor wildly.

""""But what profits? Where from?" asked my father, still unenlightened, for, outside architecture, he was a greenhorn.

"'Marple sang the "Ba, ba, ba, boodle-dee" of the day, and continued his wild career.

"'My father seized him by the throat and pushed him into a chair.

""""Speak, man," he cried agitatedly. "Stop your tomfoolery and talk sense."

""""I am talking cents—which is better," said Marple, with a boisterous burst of laughter. "A word that all the world is talking about is a gold-mine—a real gold-mine. I mean, not one on a prospectus. Don't you see that 'Olotutu' is a household word, and that everybody imagines it is the name of some new patent, something which the proprietor has been keeping dark? I did myself. When at last 'Olotutu' *is* put upon the market it will come into the world under the fierce light that beats upon a boom, and it will be snapped up like currant cake at a tea-fight. Why, Nemo's Fruit Pepper, which has been on every hoarding for twenty years, is not half so much talked about as 'Olotutu.' What you achieved is an immense preliminary advertisement—and you were calmly thinking of stopping there! Within sight of Pactolus!"

""""I had achieved *my* end!" replied my father with dignity. "Art for art's sake—I did not work for money."

""""Then you refuse half the profits?"

""""Oh, no, no! If the artist's work brings him money, he cannot help it. I think I catch your idea now. You wish to put some commodity upon the market attached to the name of 'Olotutu.' We have a pedestal but no statue, a cloak but nothing to cover."

""""We shall have plenty to cover soon," observed Marple winking. And he sat himself unceremoniously at my writing-desk and began scribbling away for dear life.

""""I suppose then," went on my father, "we shall have to get hold of some article and manufacture it."

""""Nonsense," jerked Marple. "Where are we to get the capital from?"

""""Oh, I see you will get the syndicate to do it?"

""""Good gracious, man!" yelped Marple. "Do you suppose the syndicate will have any capital? Let me write in peace."

""""But who *is* going to manufacture 'Olotutu' then?" persisted my father.

""""The British Public of course," thundered Marple. My father was silenced. The feverish scratching of Marple's pen continued, working my father up to an indescribable nervous tension.

""""But what will 'Olotutu' be?" he inquired at last. "A patent medicine, a tobacco, a soap, a mine, a comic paper, a beverage, a tooth- powder, a hair-restorer?"

""""Look here, old man!" roared Marple. "How do you expect me to bother about details? This thing has got to be worked at once. The best part of the Company season is already over. But 'Olotutu' is going to make it up. Mark my words the shares of 'Olotutu' will be at a premium on the day of issue. Another sheet of paper, quick."

""""What for?"

""""I want to write to a firm of Chartered Accountants and Valuers to give an estimate of the profits!"

""""An estimate of the profits?"

""""Don't talk like a parrot!"

""""But how can they estimate the profits?"

""""How? what do you suppose they're chartered for? You or I couldn't do it; of course not. But it's the business of accountants! That's what they're for. Pass me more writing-paper—reams of it!"

The public curiosity amounted to frenzy.

"'Marple spent the whole of that night writing letters to what he called his tame guinea-pigs; and the very next day large bills bearing the solitary word "Olotutu" were posted up all over London till the public curiosity mounted to frenzy. The bill-posters earnt many a half-crown by misinforming the inquisitive. Marple worked like a horse. First he drew up the Prospectus, leaving blanks for the Board of Directors of the Company. Then he filled up the blanks. It was not easy. One lord was only induced to serve on Marple's convincing representations of the good 'Olotutu' would do to the masses. When the Board was complete, Marple had still to get the Syndicate from which the Directors were to acquire "Olotutu," but he left this till the end, knowing there would be no difficulty there. I have never been able to gather from my father exactly what went on, nor does my father profess to know exactly himself, but he tells with regret how he used to worry Marple daily by inquiring if he had yet decided what "Olotutu" was to be, as if Marple had not his hands full enough without that. Marple turned round on him one day and shrieked: "That's your affair, not mine. You're selling 'Olotutu' to me, aren't you? I can't be buyer and seller, too."

"'This, by the way, does not seem to be as impossible as it sounds for, according to my father, when the company came out, Marple bought and sold "Olotutu" in the most mysterious manner, rigging the market, watering the shares, cornering the bears, and doing other extraordinary things, each and all at a profit. He was not satisfied with his share of the price paid for "Olotutu" by the syndicate, nor with his share of the enormously higher price paid to the syndicate by the public, but went in for Stock Exchange manœuvres six-deep, coming out an easy winner on settling day. One of my father's most treasured collections is the complete set of proofs of the prospectus. It went through thirteen editions before it reached the public; no author could revise his book more lovingly than Marple revised that prospectus. What tales printers could tell to be sure! The most noticeable variations in the text of my father's collection are the omission or addition of cyphers. Some of the editions have £120,000 for the share capital of the Company, where others have £1,200,000 and others £12,000. Sometimes the directors appear to have extenuated "nought," sometimes to have set down "nought" in malice. As for the number of debenture shares, the amounts to be paid up on allotment, the contracts with divers obscure individuals, the number of shares to be taken up by the directors and the number to be accepted by the vendors in part payment, these vary indefinitely; but in no edition, not even in those still void of the names of the directors, do the profits guaranteed by the directors fall below twenty-five per cent. Sometimes the complex and brain-baffling calculations that fill page three result in a bigger profit, sometimes in a smaller, but they are always cheering to contemplate.

"'There is not very much about "Olotutu" itself even in the last edition, but from the very first, there is a great deal about the power of the company to manufacture, import, export, and deal in all kinds of materials, commodities, and articles necessary for and useful in carrying on the same; to carry on any other operations or business which the company might from time to time deem expedient in connection with its main business for the time being; to purchase, take in exchange, or on lease, hire, or otherwise, in any part of the world, for any estate, or interests, any lands, factories, buildings, easements, patent rights, brands and trademarks, concessions, privileges, machinery, plant, stock-in-trade, utensils, necessary or convenient, for the purposes of the company, or to sell, exchange, let or rent royalty, share of profits, or otherwise use and grant licenses, easements and other rights of and over, and in any other manner deal with or dispose of the whole or any part of the undertaking, business and property of the Company, and in consideration to accept cash or shares, stock, debenture or securities of any company whose objects were or included objects similar to those of the Company.

"'The actual nature of "Olotutu" does not seem to have been settled till the ninth edition, but all the editions include the analyst's report, certifying that "Olotutu" contains no injurious ingredients and is far purer and safer than any other (here there was a blank in the first eight editions in the market). From this it is evident that Marple has made up his mind to something chemical, though it is equally apparent that he kept an open mind regards its precise character, for in the ninth edition the blank is filled up with "purgative," in the tenth with "meat extract," in the eleventh with "hair-dye," in the twelfth with "cod liver oil," and it is only in the thirteenth edition that the final decision seems to have been arrived at in favor of "soap." This of course, my dear Sybil, you already know. Indeed, if I mistake not, "Olotutu," the only absolutely scentless soap in the market, is your own pet soap. I hope it will not shock you too much if I tell you in the strictest confidence that except in price, stamp, and copious paper-wrapping, "Olotutu" is simply bars of yellow soap chopped small. It was here, perhaps, that Marple's genius showed to the highest advantage. The public was overdone with patent scented soaps; there seemed something unhealthy or at least molly-coddling about their use; the time was ripe for return to the rude and primitive. "Absolutely scentless" became the trademark of "Olotutu" and the public, being absolutely senseless (*pace*, my dear Sybil), somehow concluded that because the soap was devoid of scent it was impregnated with sanitation.

"'Is there need to prolong the story? My father, so unexpectedly enriched, abandoned architecture and married almost immediately. Soon he became the idol of a popular constituency, and, voting steadily with his party, was made a baronet. I was born a few months after the first dividend was announced. It was a dividend of thirty-three per cent, for "Olotutu" had become an indispensable adjunct to every toilet-table and the financial papers published leaders, boasting of having put their clients up to a good thing, and "Olotutu" was on everybody's tongue and got into everybody's eyes.

"'Can you wonder, then, that I was born with a congenital craving for springing mysteries upon the public? Can you still disbelieve that I suffer from an hereditary tendency to advertise in the agony column?

"'At periodic intervals an irresistible prompting to force uncouth words upon the universal consciousness seizes me; at other times I am driven to beguile the public with pseudo-sensational communications to imaginary personages. It was fortunate my father early discovered my penchant and told me the story of his life, for I think the very knowledge that I am the victim of heredity helps me to defy my own instincts. No man likes to feel he is the shuttlecock of blind forces. Still they are occasionally too strong for me, and my present attack has been unusually severe and protracted. I have been passing through my father's early phases and conducting romances by correspondence. Complimentary to the series of messages signed Popsy, I had prepared a series signed Wopsy to go in on alternate days, and if you had only continued your search in my coat-pocket you would have discovered these proofs of my innocence. May I trust it is now re-established, and that "Olotutu" has washed away the apparent stain on my character? With anxious heart I await your reply.

"'Ever yours devotedly,

"'GUY

"Sybil's reply was: 'I have read your letter. Do not write to me again.' She was so set against him," concluded Miss Nimrod, "she would not even write this but wired it."

"Then she does not believe the story of how Guy Fledgely's father became a baronet," said Lord Silverdale.

"She does not. She says 'Olotutu' won't wash stains."

"Well, I suppose you will be bringing her up," said the President.

"I will—in the way she should go;" answered Wee Winnie. "To-day is Saturday; I will bring her on Monday. Meantime as it is getting very late, and as I have finished my lemonade, I will bid you good afternoon—have you

215

used 'Olotutu?'" And with this facetious inquiry Miss Nimrod twirled her stick and was off.

An hour later Lillie received a wire from Wee Winnie.

"*Olotutu. Wretches just reconciled. Letter follows.*"

And this was the letter that came by the first post on Monday.

"MY POOR PRESIDENT:

"We have lost Sybil. She takes in the *Hurrygraph* and reads the agony column religiously. So all the week she has been exposed to a terrible bombardment.

"As thus (Tuesday.) 'My lost darling. A thousand demons are knocking at my door. Say you forgive me or I will let them in.—BOBO.'

"Or thus. (Wednesday.) 'My lost darling. You are making a terrible mistake. I am innocent. I am writing this on my bended knees. The fathers have eaten a sour grape. Misericordia.—BOBO.'

"The bitter cry of the outcast lover increased daily in intensity, till on Saturday it became delirious.

"'My lost darling. Save, O Save! I have opened the door. They are there—in their thousands. The children's teeth are set on edge. The grave is dug. Betwixt two worlds I fall to the ground. Adieu forever.—BOBO.'

"Will you believe that the poor little fool thought all this was meant for her, and that in consequence she thawed day by day till on Saturday she melted entirely and gushed on Guy's shoulder? Guy admitted that he had inserted these advertisements, but he did not tell her (as he afterwards told me in confidence, and as I now tell you in confidence) that they had been sent in before the quarrel occurred and constituted his Agony Column romance for the week, the Popsy Wopsy romance not being intended for publication till next week. He had concocted these cries of despairing passion without the least idea they would so nearly cover his own case. But he says that as his hereditary craze got him into the scrape, it was only fair his hereditary craze should get him out of it.

"So that's the end of Sybil Hotspur. But let us not lament her too much. One so frail and fickle was not of the stuff of which Old Maids are made. Courage! Wee Winnie is on the warpath.

"Yours affectionately,

"NELLY."

CHAPTER XVI.

THE CLUB BECOMES POPULAR.

The influence of Wee Winnie on the war-path was soon apparent. On the following Wednesday morning the ante-room of the Club was as crowded with candidates as if Lillie had advertised for a clerk with three tongues at ten pounds a year. Silverdale had gone down to Fleet Street to inquire if anything had been heard of Miss Ellaline Rand's projected paper, and Lillie grappled with the applicants single-handed.

Turple the magnificent, was told to usher them into the confessional one by one, but the first two candidates insisted that they were one, and as he could not tell which one he gave way.

It is said that the shepherd knows every sheep of his flock individually, and that a superintendent can tell one policeman from another. Some music-hall managers even profess to distinguish between one pair of singing sisters and all the other pairs. But even the most trained eye would be puzzled to detect any difference between these two lovely young creatures. They were as like as two peas or two cues, or the two gentlemen who mount and descend together the mirror-lined staircase of a restaurant. Interrogated as to the motives of their would-be renunciation, one of them replied: "My sister and myself are twins. We were born so. When the news was announced to our father, he is reported to have exclaimed, 'What a misfortune!' His sympathy was not misplaced, for from our nursery days upward our perfect resemblance to each other has brought us perpetual annoyance. Do what we would, we never could never get mistaken for each other. The pleasing delusion that either of us would be saddled with the misdeeds of the other has got us into scrapes without number. At school we each played all sorts of pranks, making sure the other would be punished for them. Alas! the consequences have always recoiled on the head of the guilty party. We were not even whipped for neglecting each other's lessons. It was always for neglecting our own. But in spite of the stern refusal of experience to favor us with the usual imbroglio, we always went on hoping that the luck would turn. We read Shakespeare's *Comedy of Errors*, and that confirmed us in our evil courses. When we grew up, it would be hard to say which was the giddier, for each hoped that the other would have to bear the burden of her escapades. You will have gathered from our friskiness that our parents were strict Puritans, but at last they allowed an eligible young curate to visit the house with a view to matrimony. He was too good for us; our parents were as much as we wanted in that line. Unfortunately, in this crisis, unknown to each other, the old temptation seized us. Each felt it a unique chance of trying if the thing wouldn't work. When the other was out of the room, each made love to the unwelcome suitor so as to make him fall in love with her sister. Wretched victims of mendacious farce-writers! The result was that he fell in love with us both!"

She paused a moment overcome with emotion, then resumed. "He proposed to us both simultaneously, vowed he could not live without us. He exclaimed passionately that he could not be happy with either were t'other dear charmer away. He said he was ready to become a Mormon for love of us."

He was willing to become a Mormon.

"And what was your reply?" said Lillie anxiously.

The fresh young voices broke out into a duet: "We told him to ask papa."

"We were both so overwhelmed by this catastrophe," pursued the story-teller, "that we vowed for mutual self-protection against our besetting temptation to fribble at the other's expense, never to let each other out of sight. In the farces all the mistakes happen through the twins being on only one at a time. Thus have we balanced each other's tendencies to indiscretion before it was too late, and saved ourselves from ourselves. This necessity of being always together, imposed on us by our unhappy resemblance, naturally excludes either from marriage."

Lillie was not favorably impressed with these skittish sisters. "I sympathize intensely with the sufferings of either," she said slily, "in being constrained to the society of the other. But your motives of celibacy are not sufficiently pure, nor have you fulfilled our prime condition, for even granting that your reply to the eligible young Churchman was tantamount to a rejection, it still only amounts to a half rejection each, which is fifty per cent. below our standard."

She rang the bell. Turple the magnificent ushered the twins out and the next candidate in. She was an ethereal blonde in a simple white frock, and her story was as simple.

"Read this Rondeau," she said. "It will tell you all."

Lillie took the lines. They were headed

THE LOVELY MAY—AN OLD MAID'S PLAINT.

The lovely May at last is here,
    Long summer days are drawing near,
And nights with cloudless moonshine rich;
    In woodlands green, on waters clear,
Soft-couched in fern, or on the mere,
    Gliding like some white water-witch,
Or lunching in a leafy niche,
    I see my sweet-faced sister dear,
        The lovely May.

She is engaged—and her career
    Is one of skittles blent with beer,
While I, plain sewing left to stitch,
    Can ne'er expect those pleasures which,
At this bright season of the year,
        The lovely may.

Lillie looked up interrogatively. "But surely *you* have nothing to complain of in the way of loveliness?" she said.

"No, of course not. *I am* the lovely May. It was my sister who wrote that. She died in June and I found it among her manuscripts. Remorse set in at the thought of Maria stitching while I was otherwise engaged. I disengaged myself at once. What's fair for one is fair for all. Women should combine. While there's one woman who can't get a husband, no man should be allowed to get a wife."

"Hear, hear!" cried Lillie enthusiastically. "Only I am afraid there will always be blacklegs among us who will betray their sex for the sake of a husband."

"Alas, yes," agreed the lovely May. "I fear such was the nature of my sister Maria. She coveted even my first husband."

"What!" gasped the President. "Are you a widow?"

"Certainly! I left off black when I was engaged again, and when I was disengaged I dared not resume it for fear of seeming to mourn my *fiancé*."

"We cannot have widows in the Old Maids' Club," said Lillie regretfully.

"Then I shall start a new Widows' Club and Old Maids shall have no place in it." And the lovely May sailed out, all smiles and tears.

The newcomer was a most divinely tall and most divinely fair brunette with a brooding, morbid expression. Candidate gave the name of Miss Summerson.

Being invited to make a statement, she said: "I have abandoned the idea of marrying. I have no money. Ergo, I cannot afford to marry a poor man. And I am resolved never to marry a rich one. I want to be loved for myself, not for my want of money. You may stare, but I know what I am talking about. What other attraction have I? Good looks? Plenty of girls with money have that, who would be glad to marry the men I have rejected. In the town I came from I lived with my cousin, who was an heiress. She was far lovelier than I. Yet all the moneyed men were at my feet. They were afraid of being suspected of fortune-hunting and anxious to vindicate their elevation of character. Why should I marry to gratify a man's vanity, his cravings after cheap quixotism?"

"Your attitude on the great question of the age does you infinite credit, but as you have no banking account to put it to, you traverse the regulation requiring a property qualification," said the President.

"Is there no way over the difficulty?"

"I fear not: unless you marry a rich man, and that disqualifies you under

222

another rule." And Miss Summerson passed sadly into the outer darkness, to be replaced by a young lady who gave the name of Nell Lightfoot. She wore a charming hat and a smile like the spreading of sunshine over a crystal pool. "I met a young Scotchman," she said, "at a New Year's dance, and we were favorably impressed by each other. On the fourteenth of the following February I received from him a Valentine, containing a proposal of marriage and a revelation of the degradation of masculine nature. It would seem he had two strings to his bow—the other being a rich widow whom he had met in a Devonshire lane. Being a Scotchman he had for economy's sake composed a Valentine which with a few slight alterations would do for both of us. Unfortunately for himself he sent me the original draft by mistake and here is his

VERACIOUS VALENTINE.

Though the weather is snowy and dreary
        And a shiver careers down my spine,
Yet the heart in my bosom is cheery,
        For I feel I've exchanged mine for thine.
Do not call it delusion, my dearie,
        But become my own loved Valentine.

For that { stormy June day you } remember,
        { New Year's dance you must }
When we { sheltered together from rain,
        { waltzed to a languorous strain,
While the sky, like the Fifth of November, }
And our souls glowed despite 'twas December }
        Gleamed with lightening outrivalling P { ain. }
        With a burning but glorious p { ain.}
Ah me! In my fire's dying ember
        I can see that { dank Devonshire lane.
                { bright ball-room again.

And } I spoke { of the love that I } bore you,
Yet }   { not then, fearing to }
        And of how for a widow I   } yearned,
        Though for maidenly love my heart }
Not a schoolgirl { and fealty I swore you,
                { I'd gazed on before you,
        And you listened till sunshine re- } turned,
        Had my heart with such sweet madness }
Then { you } parted { from me who } adore you,
        { we }   { but still I }
        And my heart and umbrella you spurned.   }
        Though you may not my love have discerned, }
Not repelled by { hoarded-up } money,
                { having no }
        I adore you, my { Belle, } for yourself,
                { Nell, }
You are sweeter than music or honey;
        And Dan Cupid's a sensuous elf,
Who is drawn to the fair and the sunny,
        And is blind unto nothing but pelf.

Need we feel a less genuine passion Because
        we { shall } live in May-fair?
                { can't }

Love { blooms rich } in the hothouse of fashion,
         { oft fades }
    'Tis { an orchid that flourishes there;
        { a moss-rose that needs the fresh air;
Yet I would not my own darling lass shun
    Were she even as { poor } as she's { fair.
        { rich } { rare.

There are fools who adore a complexion
    That's like strawberries mingled with cream. }
    As with Nubian blacking a gleam }
A brunette } is my own predilection,
But a blonde }
    And the glances from { dark } eyes that beam
        { blue }
Then refuse not my deathless affection,
    Neither shatter my amorous dream.

You're the very first { woman } who's thrilled me
        { maiden }
    With the passion that tongue cannot tell.
Of none else have I thought since you filled me
    With { despair in that Devonshire dell. }
        { unrest when the waltz wove its spell. }
When your final refusal has killed me.
    On my heart will be found graven { Belle.
        { Nell.

"How strange!" said Lillie. "You combine the disqualifications of two of the previous candidates. You are apparently poor and you have received only half a proposal."

A flaming blonde, whose brow was crowned with an aurora of auburn hair, was the next to burst upon the epigrammatic scene. She spoke English with an excellent Parisian accent. "One has called me a young woman in a hurry," she said, "and the description does not want of truth. I am impatient; I have large ideas; I am ambitious. If I were a grocer I should contract for the Sahara. I fall in love, and when Alice Leroux falls in love it is like the volcano which goes to make eruption. Figure to yourself that my man is shy—but of a shyness of the most ridiculous—that it is necessary to make a thousand sweet eyes at him before he comprehends that he loves me. And when he comprehends it, he does not speak. *Mon Dieu*, he does not speak, though I speak, me, with fan, my eyes, my fingers, almost with my lips. He walks with me—but he does not speak. He takes me to the spectacle—but he does not speak. He promenades himself in boat with me—but he does not speak. I encircle him with my arms, and I speak with my lips at last—one, two, three, four, five, kisses. Overwhelmed, astonished, he returns me my kisses—hesitatingly, stupidly, but in fine, he returns them And then at last—with our faces together, my arm round his graceful waist—he speaks. The first words of love comes from his mouth—and what think you that he say? Say then."

I encircle him with my arms and speak with my lips.

"I love you?" murmured Lillie.

"A thousand thunders! No! He says: 'Miss Leroux—Alice; may I call you Alice?'"

"I see nothing to wonder at in that," replied Lillie quietly. "Remember that for a man to kiss you is a less serious step than for him to call you Alice. That were a stage on the road to marriage, and should only be reached through the gate of betrothal. Changes of name are the outward marks of a woman's development as much as changes of form accompany the growth of the caterpillar. You, for instance, began life as Alice. In due course you became Miss Alice; if you were the eldest daughter you became Miss Leroux at once; if you were not, you inherited the name only on your sister's death or marriage; when you are betrothed you will revert to the simple Alice, and when you are married you will become Mrs. Something Else; and every time you get married, if you are careful to select husbands of varying patronymics, you will be furnished with a change of name as well as of address. Providence, which has conferred so many sufferings upon woman, has given her this one advantage over man, who in the majority of instance is doomed to the monotony of ossified nomenclature, and has to wear the same name on his tombstone which he wore on his Eton collar."

"That is all a heap of galimatias," replied the Parisienne with the flaming hair "If I kiss a man, I, surely he may call me Alice without demanding it? Bah! Let him love your misses with *eau sucrée* in their veins. When he insulted me with his stupidity, I became furious. I threw him—how you say? —overboard on the instant."

"Good heavens!" gasped Lillie. "Then you are a murderess!"

"Figure you to yourself that I speak at the foot of the letter? Know you not the idioms of your own barbarian tongue? It seems to me you are as mad as he. Perhaps you are his sister."

"Certainly. Our rules require us to regard all men as brothers."

"*He!* What?"

"We have rejected the love of all men; consequently we have to regard them all as our brothers."

"That man there my brother!" shrieked Alice. "Never! Never of my life! I would rather marry first!" And she went off to do so.

The last of these competitors for the Old Maiden Stakes was a whirlwind in petticoats who welcomed the President very affably. "Good-morning, Miss Dulcimer," she said. "I've heard of you. I'm from Boston way. You know I travel about the world in search of culture. I'm spending the day in Europe, so I thought I'd look you up. Would you be so good as to epitomize your scheme in twenty words? I've got to see the Madonna del Cardellino in the Uffizi at Florence before ten to-morrow, and I want to hear an act of the *Meistersingers* at Bayreuth after tea."

"I'm rather tired," pleaded Lillie, overwhelmed by the dynamic energy radiating from every square inch of the Bostonian's superficies. "I have had a hard morning's work. Couldn't you call again to-morrow?"

"Impossible. I have just wired to Damietta to secure rooms commanding a view of Professor Tickledroppe's excavations on the banks of the Nile. I dote on archæological treasures and thought I should like to see the Old Maids. Are they on view?"

"No, they are not here," said Lillie evasively. "But do you want to join us?"

"Shall I have time? I remember I once wasted a week getting married. Some women waste their whole lives that way. Marriage is an incident of life's novel—they make it the whole plot. I don't say it isn't an interesting experience. Every woman ought to go through it once, but with the infinite possibilities of culture lying all round us it's mere Philistinism to give one husbandman more than a week of your society. Mine is a physician practising in Philadelphia. Judging by the checks he sends me he must be a successful man. Well, I am real glad to have had this little talk with you, it's been so interesting. I will become an Honorary Member of your charming Club with pleasure."

"You cannot if you are married. You can only be a visitor."

"What's my being married got to do with it?" inquired the American in astonishment. "This is the first time I have ever heard that the name of a club has anything to do with the membership. Are the members of the Savage Club savages, of the Garrick Garricks, of the Supper Club suppers?"

"We are not men," Lillie said haughtily. "I could pass over your relation to the hub of the universe, but when it comes to having a private hub I have no option."

"Well, this may be your English idea of hospitality to travellers of culture," replied the Bostonian warmly, "but if you come to our crack Crank Club in the fall you shall be as welcome as a brand new poet. Good-bye. Hope we shall meet again. I shall be in Hong Kong in June if you like to drop in. Good-bye."

"Good-bye," said Lillie, pressing one hand against the visitor's and the other to her aching forehead.

Silverdale found her dissolved in tears. "In future," he said, when she had explained her troubles, "I shall hang the rules and by-laws in the waiting room. The candidates will then be able to eliminate themselves. By the way, Ellaline Rand's *Cherub* is going to sit up aloft,—on a third floor in Fleet Street."

CHAPTER XVII.

A MUSICAL BAR.

When Turple the magnificent, looking uneasy, brought up Frank Maddox's card, Lillie uttered a cry of surprise and pleasure. Frank Maddox was a magic name to her as to all the elect of the world of sweetness and light. After a moment of nervous anxiety lest it should not be *the* Frank Maddox, her fears were dispelled by the entry of the great authority on art and music, whose face was familiar to her from frontispiece portraits. Few critics possessed such charms of style and feature as Frank Maddox, who had a delicious *retroussé* nose, a dainty rosebud mouth, blue eyes, and a wealth of golden hair.

Lillie's best hopes were confirmed. The famous critic wished to become an Old Maid. The President and the new and promising candidate had a delightful chat over a cup of tea and the prospects of the Club. The two girls speedily became friends.

"But if you join us, hadn't you better go back to your maiden name?" inquired Lillie.

"Perhaps so," said Frank Maddox thoughtfully. "My pen-name does sound odd under the peculiar circumstances. On the other hand to revert to Laura Spragg now might be indiscreet. People would couple my name with Frank Maddox's—you know the way of the world. The gossips get their facts so distorted, and I couldn't even deny the connection."

"But of course you *have* had your romance?" asked Lillie. "You know one romance per head is our charge for admission?"

"Oh, yes! I have had my romance. In three vols. Shall I tell it you?"

"If you please."

"Listen, then. Volume the First: Frank Maddox is in her study. Outside the sun is setting in furrows of gold-laced sagging storm-clouds, dun and——"

"Oh, please, I always skip that," laughed Lillie. "I know that two lovers cannot walk in a lane without the author seeing the sunset, which is the last thing in the world the lovers see. But when the sky begins to look black, I always begin to skip."

"Forgive me. I didn't mean to do it. Remember I'm an habitual art-critic. I thought I was describing a harmony of Whistler's or a movement from a sonata. It shall not occur again. To the heroine enter the hero—shabby, close-cropped, pale. Their eyes meet. He is thunderstruck to find the heroine a woman; blushes, stammers, and offers to go away. Struck by something of innate refinement in his manner, she presses him to avow the object of his visit. At last, in dignified language, infinitely touching in its reticence, he confesses he called on Mr. Frank Maddox, the writer he admires so much, to ask a little pecuniary help. He is starving. Original, isn't it, to have your hero hungry in the first chapter? He speaks vaguely of having ambitions which, unless he goes under in the struggle for existence may some day be realized. There are so many men in London like that. However, the heroine is moved by his destitute condition and sitting down to her desk, she writes out a note, folds it up and gives it to him. 'There!' she says, 'there's a prescription against starvation.' 'But how am I to take it?' he asked. 'It must be taken before breakfast, the first thing in the morning,' she replied, 'to the editor of the *Moon*. Give him the note; he will change it for you. Don't mention my name.'

"There's a prescription against starvation."

"He thanked me and withdrew."

"And what was in the note?" asked Lillie curiously.

"I can't quite remember. But something of this sort. 'The numerous admirers of Frank Maddox will be gratified to hear that she has in the press a volume of essays on the part played by color-blindness in the symphonic movements of the time. The great critic is still in town but leaves for Torquay next Tuesday.' For that the editor of the *Moon* gave him half-a-crown."

"Do you call that charity?" said Lillie, astonished.

"Certainly. Charity begins at home. Do many people give charity except to advertise themselves? Philanthropy by paragraph is a perquisite of fame. Why, I have a pensioner who comes in for all my *Acadæum* paragraphs. That *Moon* part saved our hero from starvation. Years afterwards I learnt he had frittered away two-pence in having his hair cut."

"It seems strange for a starving man to get his hair cut," said Lillie.

"Not when you know the cause," replied Frank Maddox. "It was his way of disguising himself. And this brings me to Volume Two. The years pass. Once again I am in my study. There is a breath of wind among the elms in the front garden, and the sky is strewn with vaporous sprays of apple-blossom
——I beg your pardon. Re-enter the hero, spruce, frock-coated, dignified. He recalls himself to my memory—but I remember him only too well. He tells me that my half-crown saved him at the turning-point of his career, that he has now achieved fame and gold, that he loves my writing more passionately than ever, and that he has come to ask me to crown his life. The whole thing is so romantic that I am about to whisper 'yes' when an instinct of common sense comes to my aid and my half-opened lips murmur instead: 'But the name you sent up— Horace Paul—it is not known to me. You say you have won fame. I, at least, have never heard of you.'

"'Of course not,' he replies. 'How should you? If I were Horace Paul you would not marry me; just as I should certainly not marry you if you were Frank Maddox. But what of Paul Horace?'"

"Paul Horace," cried Lillie. "The great composer!"

"That is just what I exclaimed. And my hero answers: 'The composer, great or little. None but a few intimates connect me with him. The change of name is too simple. I always had a longing—call it morbid if you will—for obscurity in the midst of renown. I have weekly harvests of hair to escape any suspicion of musical attainments. But you and I, dearest—think of what our life will be enriched by our common love of the noblest of the arts. Outside, the marigolds nod to the violets, the sapphire—excuse me, I mean to say——'

thus he rambled on, growing in enthusiasm with every ardent phrase, the while a deadly coldness was fastening round my heart. For I felt that it could not be."

"And why?" inquired Lillie in astonishment. "It seems one of the marriages made in heaven."

"I dared not tell him why; and I can only tell you on condition you promise to keep my secret."

"I promise."

"Listen," whispered the great critic. "I know nothing about music or art, and I was afraid he would find me out."

Lillie fell back in her chair, white and trembling. Another idol shivered! "But how——?" she gasped.

"There, then, don't take on so," said the great critic kindly. "I did not think you, too, were such an admirer of mine, else I might have spared you the shock. You ask how it is done. Well, I didn't set out to criticise. I can at least plead that in extenuation. My nature is not wilfully perverse. There was a time when I was as pure and above criticism as yourself." She paused and furtively wiped away a tear, then resumed more calmly, "I drifted into it. For years I toiled on, without ever a thought of musical and art criticism sullying my maiden meditations. My downfall was gradual. In early maidenhood I earnt my living as a type-writer. I had always had literary yearnings, but the hard facts of life allowed me only this rough approximation to my ideal. Accident brought excellent literature to my machine, and it required all my native honesty not to steal the plots of the novelists and the good things of the playwrights. The latter was the harder temptation to resist, for when the play was good enough to be worth stealing from, I knew it would never be produced and my crime never discovered. Still in spite of my honesty, I benefited indirectly by my type-writing, for contact with so much admirable work fostered the graceful literary style which, between you and me, is my only merit. In time I plucked up courage to ask one of my clients, a journalist, if he could put some newspaper work in my way. 'What can you do?' he asked in surprise. 'Anything,' I replied with maiden modesty. 'I see, that's your special line,' he said musingly. 'Unfortunately we are full up in that department. You see, everyone turns his hand to that—it's like schoolmastering, the first thing people think of. It's a pity you are a girl, because the way to journalistic distinction lies through the position of office- boy. Office-girl sounds strange. I doubt whether they would have you except on a Freethought organ. Our office-boy has to sweep out the office and review the novels, else you might commence humbly as a critic of literature. It isn't a bad post either, for he supplements his income by picking rejected matter out of the waste paper basket and surreptitiously lodging it in the printer's copy pigeonhole. His income in fees from journalistic aspirants must be considerable. Yes, had you been a boy you might have made a pretty good thing out of literature! Then there is no chance at all for me on your paper?' I inquired desperately. 'None,' he said sadly. 'Our editor is an awful old fogey. He is vehemently opposed to the work of outsiders, and if you were to send him his own leaders in envelopes he would say they were rot. For once he would be a just critic. You see, therefore, what your own chance is. Even I, who have been on the staff for years, couldn't do anything to help you. No, I am afraid there is no hope for you unless you approach our office-boy.' I thanked him warmly for his advice and encouragement, and within a fortnight an article of mine appeared in the paper. It was called 'The Manuscripts of Authors,' and revealed in a refined and ladylike way the secrets of the chirographic characteristics of the manuscripts I had to type-write. My friend said I was exceedingly practical——"

"Exceedingly practical," agreed Lillie with a suspicion of a sneer.

"Because most amateur journalists write about abstract principles, whereas I had sliced out for the public a bit of concrete fact, and the great heart of the people went out to hear the details of the way Brown wrote his books, Jones his jokes, and Robinson his recitations. The article made a hit, and annoyed the authors very much."

"So, I should think," said Lillie. "Didn't they withdraw their custom from you instanter?"

The office boy edits the paper.

"Why? They didn't know it was I. Only my journalistic friend knew; and he was too much of a gentleman to give away my secret. I wrote to the editor under the name of Frank Maddox, thanking him for having inserted my article, and the editor said to my friend, 'Egad, I fancy I've made a discovery there. Why, if I were to pay any attention to your idea of keeping strictly to the old grooves, the paper would stagnate, my boy, simply stagnate.' The editor was right, for my friend assured me the paper would have died long before, if the office-boy had not condescended to edit it. Anyhow, it was to that office-boy I owed my introduction to literature. The editor was very proud of having discovered me, and, being installed in his good graces, I passed rapidly into dramatic criticism, and was even allowed to understudy the office-boy as literary reviewer. He could not stomach historical novels, and handed over to me all works with pronouns in the second person. Gradually I rose to higher things, but it was not until I had been musical and art critic for over eighteen months that the editor learnt that the writer whose virile style he had often dilated upon to my friend was a woman."

"And what did he do when he learnt it?" asked Lillie.

"He swore——"

"Profane man!" cried Lillie.

"That he loved me—me whom he had never seen. Of course, I declined him with thanks; happily there was a valid excuse, because he had written his communication on both sides of the paper. But even this technical touch did not mollify him, and he replied that my failure to appreciate him showed I could no longer be trusted as a critic. Fortunately my work had been signed, my fame was established. I collected my articles into a book and joined another paper."

"But you haven't yet told me how it is done?"

"Oh, that is the least. You see, to be a critic it is not essential to know anything—you must simply be able to write. To be a great critic you must simply be able to write *well*. In my omniscience, or catholic ignorance, I naturally looked about for the subject on which I could most profitably employ my gift of style with the least chance of being found out. A moment's consideration will convince you that the most difficult branches of criticism are the easiest. Of musical and artistic matters not one person in a thousand understands aught but the rudiments: here, then, is the field in which the critical ignoramus may expatiate at large with the minimum danger of discovery. Nay, with no scintilla of danger; for the subject matter is so obscure and abstruse that the grossest of errors may put on a bold face and parade as a profundity, or, driven to bay, proclaim itself a paradox. Only say what you have not got to say authoritatively and well, and the world shall fall down and worship you. The place of art in religion has undergone a peculiar historical development. First men worshipped the object of art; then they worshipped the artist; and nowadays they worship the art critic."

"It is true," said Lillie reflectively. "This age has witnessed the apotheosis of the art critic."

"And of all critics. And yet what can be more evident than that the art of criticism was never in such a critical condition? Nobody asks to see the critic's credentials. He is taken at his own valuation. There ought to be an examination to protect the public. Even schoolmasters are now required to have certificates; while those who pretend to train the larger mind in the way it should think are left to work their mischief uncontrolled. No dramatic critic should be allowed to practise without an elementary knowledge of human life, law, Shakespeare, and French. The musical critic should be required to be able to perform on some one instrument other than his own trumpet, to distinguish tune from tonality, to construe the regular sonata, to comprehend the plot of *Il Trovatore*, and to understand the motives of Wagner. The art critic should be able to discriminate between a pastel and a water-color, an impressionist drawing and a rough sketch, to know the Dutch school from the Italian, and the female figure from the male, to translate morbidezza and chiaroscuro, and failing this, to be aware of the existence and uses of a vanishing point. A doctor's certificate should also be produced to testify that the examinee is in possession of all the normal faculties; deafness, blindness, and color-blindness being regarded as disqualifications, and no one should be allowed to practise unless he enjoyed a character for common honesty supplemented by a testimonial from a clergyman, for although art is non- moral the critic should be moral. This would be merely the passman stage; there could always be examinations in honors for the graduates. Once the art critics were educated, the progress of the public would be rapid. They would no longer be ready to admire the canvases of Michael Angelo, who, as I learnt the other day for the first time, painted frescoes, nor would they prefer him, as unhesitatingly as they do now, to Buonarotti, which is his surname, nor would they imagine Raffaelle's Cartoons appeared in *Puncinello*. All these mistakes I have myself made, though no one discovered them; while in the realm of music no one has more misrepresented the masters, more discouraged the overtures of young composers."

"But still I do not understand how it is done," urged Lillie.

"You shall have my formula in a nutshell. I had to be a musical critic and an art critic. I was ignorant of music and knew nothing of art. But I was a dab at language. When I was talking of music, I used the nomenclature of art. I spoke of light and shade, color and form, delicacy of outline, depth and atmosphere, perspective, foreground and background, nocturnes and harmonies in blue. I analyzed symphonies pictorially and explained what I saw defiling before me as the music swept on. Sunsets and belvedere towers, swarthy Paynims on Shetland ponies, cypress plumes and Fra Angelico's cherubs, lumps of green clay and delicate pillared loggias, fennel tufts and rococo and scarlet anemones, and over all the trail of the serpent. Thus I created an epoch in musical criticism. On the other hand, when I had to deal with art, I was careful to eschew every suggestion of the visual vocabulary and to confine myself to musical phrases. In talking of pictures, I dwelt upon their counter-point and their orchestration, their changes of key and the evolution of their ideas, their piano and forte-passages, and their bars of rest, their allegro and diminuendo aspects, their suspensions on the dominant. I spoke of them as symphonies and sonatas and masses, said one was too staccato and another too full of consecutive sevenths, and a third in need of transposition to the minor. Thus I created an epoch in art criticism. In both departments the vague and shifting terms I introduced enabled me to evade mistakes and avoid detection, while the creation of two epochs gave me the very first place in contemporary criticism. There is nothing in which I would not undertake to create an epoch. I do not say I have always been happy, and it has been a source of constant regret to me that I had not even learnt to play the piano when a girl and that unplayed music still remained to me little black dots."

"And so you did not dare marry the composer?"

"No, nor tell him why. Volume Three: I said I admired him so much that I wanted to go on devoting critical essays to him, and my praises would be discounted by the public if I were his wife. Was it not imprudent for him to alienate the leading critic by marrying her? Rather would I sacrifice myself and continue to criticise him. But I love him, and it is for his sake I would become an Old Maid."

"I would rather you didn't," said Lillie, her face still white. "I have found so much inspiration in your books that I could not bear to be daily reminded I ought not to have found it."

Poor president! The lessons of experience were hard! The Club taught her much she were happier without.

That day Lord Silverdale appropriately intoned (with banjo obligato) a patter-song which he pretended to have written at the Academy, whence he had just come with the conventional splitting headache.

AFTER THE ACADEMY—A JINGLE.
(NOT BY ALFRED JINGLE.)

Brain a-whirling, pavement twirling,
Cranium aching, almost baking,
Mind a muddle, puddle, fuddle.
Million pictures, million mixtures,
Small and great 'uns, Brown's and Leighton's,
Sky and wall 'uns, short and tall 'uns,
Pseudo classic for, alas! *Sic*

Transit gloria sub Victoriâ),
Landscape, figure, white or nigger,
Steely etchings, inky sketchings,
Genre, portrait (not one caught trait),
Eke historic (kings plethoric),
Realistic, prize-fight-fistic,
Entozoic, nude, heroic,
Coarse, poetic, homiletic,
Still-life (flowers, tropic bowers),
Pure domestic, making breast tick
With emotion; endless ocean,
Glaze or scrumble, craze and jumble,
Varnish mastic, sculpture plastic,
Canvas, paper (oh, for taper!)
Oil and water, (oh, for slaughter!)
Children, cattle, 'busses, battle,
Seamen, satyrs, lions, waiters,
Nymphs and peasants, peers and pheasants,
Dogs and flunkeys, gods and monkeys
Half-dressed ladies, views of Hades,
Phillis tripping, seas and shipping,
Hearth and meadow, brooks and bread-dough,
Doves and dreamers, stars and steamers,
Saucepans, blossoms, rags, opossums,
Tramway, cloudland, wild and ploughed land,
Gents and mountains, clocks and fountains,
Pan and pansy—these of fancy
Have possession in procession
Never-ending, ever blending,
All a-flitter and a-glitter,
Ever prancing, ever dancing,
Ever whirling, ever curling,
Ever swirling, ever twirling,
Ever bobbing, ever throbbing.
Ho, some brandy—is it handy?
Air seems tainting, I am fainting.
Hang all—no, *don't* hang all—painting!

CHAPTER XVIII.

THE BEAUTIFUL GHOUL.

Wee Winnie called at the Club, while the President was still under the cloud of depression, and Lillie had to force herself to look cheerful, lest Miss Nimrod should mistake the melancholy, engendered by so many revelations of the seamy side of life, for loss of faith in the Club or its prospects.

Avid of experience as was the introspective little girl, she felt almost fated for the present.

Miss Nimrod was astonished to hear of the number of rejections, and to learn that she had whipped up the Writers, and the Junior Widows, and her private friends to such little purpose. But in the end she agreed with Lillie that, as no doubt somewhere or other in the wide universe ideal Old Maids were blooming and breathing, it would be folly to clog themselves up in advance with inferior specimens.

The millionaire, who was pottering about in blue spectacles, strolled into the club while Wee Winnie was uttering magnificent rhapsodies about the pages the Club would occupy in the histories of England, but this time Lillie was determined the dignity of the by-laws should be maintained, and had her father shown out by Turple the magnificent. Miss Nimrod went, too, and so Lord Silverdale had the pleasure of finding Lillie alone.

"You ought to present me with a pair of white gloves," he said, gleefully.

"Why?" asked Lillie.

"I haven't had a single candidate to try for days."

"No," said Lillie with a suspicion of weariness in her voice. "They all broke down in the elementary stage."

Even as she spoke Turple the magnificent ushered in Miss Margaret Linbridge. Lord Silverdale, doubly vexed at having been a little too previous in the counting of his chickens, took up his hat to go, but Lillie murmured: "Please amuse yourself in the library for a quarter of an hour, as I may want you to do the trying at once."

"How do you expect me to amuse myself in the library?" he grumbled. "You don't keep one of my books."

Miss Margaret Linbridge's story was simple, almost commonplace.

"I had spent Christmas with a married sister in Plymouth," she said, "and was returning to London by the express on the first of January. My prospects for the New Year were bright—or seemed so to my then unsophisticated eyes. I was engaged to be married to Richard Westbourne—a good and good-looking young man, not devoid of pecuniary attractions. My brother, with whom I lived and on whom I was dependent, was a struggling young firework-manufacturer, and would, I knew, be glad to see me married, even if it cost him a portion of his stock to express his joy. The little seaside holiday had made me look my prettiest, and when my brother-in-law saw me into a first-class carriage and left me with a fraternally-legal kiss, I rather pitied him for having to go back to my sister. There was only one other person in the carriage beside myself—a stern old gentleman, who sat crumpled up in the opposite corner and read a paper steadily.

"The train flew along the white frosty landscape at express rates, but the old gentleman never looked up from his paper. The temperature was chill and I coughed. The old gentleman evinced no symptom of sympathy. I rolled up my veil the better to see the curmudgeon, and smiled to think what a fool he was, but he betrayed no sign of sharing my amusement.

"At last, as he was turning his page, I said in my most dulcet tones: 'Oh, pray excuse my appropriating the entire foot-warmer. I don't know why there is only one, but I will share it with you with pleasure.'

"'Thank you,' he said gruffly, 'I'm not cold.'

"'Oh, aren't you!' I murmured inwardly, adding aloud with a severe wintry tone, 'Gentlemen of your age usually are.'

"'Yes, but I'm not a gentleman of my age,' he growled, mistaking the imbecile statement for repartee.

"'I beg your pardon,' said I. 'I was judging by appearances. Is that the *Saturday Slasher* you have there?'

"He shook himself impatiently. 'No, it is not.'

"'I beg your pardon,' said I. 'I was again judging by appearances. May I ask what it is?'

"'*Threepenny Bits!*' he jerked back.

"'What's that?' I asked. 'I know *Broken Bits*.'

"'This is a superior edition of *Broken Bits* at the price indicated by the title. It contains the same matter, but is issued at a price adapted to the means of the moneyed and intellectual classes. No self-respecting person can be seen reading penny weeklies—it throws doubt not only on his income, but on his mental calibre. The idea of this first-class edition (so to speak) should make the fortune of the proprietor, and deservedly so. Of course, the thousand pound railway assurance scheme is likewise trebled, though this part of the paper does not attract me personally, for my next-of-kin is a hypocritical young rogue. But imagine the horror of being found dead with a penny weekly in one's pocket! You can't even explain it away.'

"He had hardly finished the sentence before a terrible shock, as of a ton of dynamite exploding under the foot-warmer, lifted me into the air; the carriage collapsed like matchwood, and I had the feeling of being thrown into the next world. For a moment I recovered a gleam of consciousness, just enough to show me I was lying dying amid the *débris*, and that my companion lay, already dead, in a fragment of the compartment, *Threepenny Bits* clenched in his lifeless hand.

"With a last fond touch I smoothed my hair, which had got rather ruffled in the catastrophe, and extracting with infinite agony a puff from my pocket I dabbed it spasmodically over my face. I dared not consult my hand-mirror, I was afraid it would reveal a distorted countenance and unnecessarily sadden my last moments. Whatever my appearance, I had done my best for it, and I wanted to die with the consciousness of duty fulfilled. Murmuring a prayer that those who found my body would not imitate me in judging by appearances, if they should prove discreditable after all, I closed my eyes upon the world in which I had been so young and happy. My whole life passed in review before me, all my dearly loved bonnets, my entire wardrobe from infancy upwards. Now I was an innocent child with a white sash and pink ribbons, straying amid the sunny meadows and plucking the daisies to adorn my hats; anon a merry maiden sporting amid the jocund schoolboys and receiving tribute in toffy; then again a sedate virgin in original gowns and tailor-made jackets. Suddenly a strange idea jostled through the throng of bitter-sweet memories. *Threepenny Bits!*

"The old gentleman's next-of-kin would come in for three thousand pounds! I should die and leave nothing to my relatives but regrets; my generous brother would be forever inconsolable now, and my funeral might be mean and unworthy. And yet if the old misogynist had only been courteous enough to lend me the paper, seeing I had nothing to read, it might have been found on my body. *De mortuis nil nisi bonum.* Why reveal his breach of etiquette to the world? Why should I not enable him to achieve posthumous politeness! Besides, his heir was a hypocritical rogue, and it were a crime against society to place so large a sum at his disposal. Overwhelmed as I was by the agonies of death, I steeled myself to this last duty. I wriggled painfully towards the corpse, and stretching out my neatly-gloved fingers, with a last mighty effort I pulled the paper cautiously from the dead hand which lay heavy upon it. Then I clasped it passionately to my heart and died."

I pulled the paper from the dead hand.

"Died?" echoed Lillie excitedly.

"Well—lost consciousness. You are particular to a shade. Myself I see no difference between a fainting fit and death except that one attack of the latter is fatal."

"As to that," answered Lillie. "I consider we die every night and dream we are alive. To fall asleep is to die painlessly. It is, perhaps, a pity we are resurrected to tea and toast and toilette. However, I am glad you did not really die. I feared I was in for a tale of re-incarnation or spooks or hypnotism or telepathy or astral bodies. One hears so many marvellous stories, now that we have left off believing in miracles. Really, man's credulity is the perpetual miracle."

"I have not left off believing in miracles," replied Miss Linbridge seriously. "How could I? Was I not saved by one? A very gallant miracle, too, for it took no trouble to save my crusty old fellow-traveller, while it left me without a scratch. I am afraid I should not have been grateful for salvation without good looks. To face life without a pretty face were worse than death. You agree with me?"

"Not entirely. There are higher things in life than beautiful faces," said Lillie gravely.

"Certainly. Beautiful bonnets," said the candidate with laughing levity. "And lower things—beautiful boots. But you would not seriously argue that there is anything else so indispensable to a woman as beauty, or that to live plain is worth the trouble of living?"

"Why not? Plain living and high thinking!" murmured Lillie.

"All nonsense! We needn't pretend—we aren't with men. You would talk differently if you were born ugly! Goodness gracious, don't we know that a girl may have a whole cemetery of virtues and no man will look at her if she is devoid of charms of face or purse. It's all nonsense what Ruskin says about a well-bred modest girl being necessarily beautiful. It is only a pleasing fiction that morality is invaluable to the complexion. Of course if Ruskin's girl chose to dress with care, she could express her goodness less plainly; but as a rule goodness and dowdiness are synonymous. I think the function of a woman is to look well, and our severest reprobation should be extended to those conscienceless creatures who allow themselves to be seen in the company of gentlemen in frumpish attire. It is a breach of etiquette towards the other sex. A woman must do credit to the man who stakes his reputation for good taste by being seen in her society. She must achieve beauty for his sake, and should no more leave her boudoir without it than if she were an actress leaving her dressing-room."

"That the man expects the woman to make his friends envy him is true," answered Lillie, "and I have myself expressed this in yonder epigram, *It is man who is vain of woman's dress*. But were we created merely to gratify man's vanity?"

"Is not that a place in nature to be vain of? We are certainly not proud of him. Think of the average husband over whom the woman has to shed the halo of her beauty. It is like poetry and prose bound together. It is because I intend to be permanently beautiful that I have come to cast in my lot with the Old Maids' Club. Your rules ordain it so—and rightly."

"The Club must be beautiful, certainly, but merely to escape being twitted with ugliness by the shallow; for the rest, it should disdain beauty. However, pray continue your story. It left off at a most interesting point. You lost consciousness!"

"Yes, but as my chivalrous miracle had saved me from damage, I was found unconsciously beautiful (which I have always heard is the most graceful way of wearing your beauty). I soon came to myself with the aid of a dark-eyed doctor, and I then learnt that the old gentleman had been too weak to sustain the shock and that his poor old pulse had ceased to beat. My rescuers had not disturbed *Threepenny Bits* from its position 'twixt my hand and heart in case I should die and need it; so when the line was cleared and I was sent on to London after a pleasant lunch with the dark-eyed doctor, I had the journal to read after all, despite the discourtesy of the deceased. When I arrived at Paddington I found Richard Westbourne walking the platform like Hamlet's ghost, white and trembling. He was scanning the carriages feverishly, as the train glided in with its habitual nonchalance.

"'My darling!' he cried when he caught sight of my dainty hat with its sweet trimmings. 'Thank Heaven!' He twisted the door violently open and kissed me before the crowd. Fortunately I had my lovely spotted veil all down, so he only pressed the tulle to my lips.

"'What is the matter?' I said ingenuously.

"'The accident!' he gasped. Weren't you in the accident?'

"'Of course I was. But I was not very much crumpled. If I had sat in the other corner I should have been killed!"

"'My heroine!' he cried. 'How brave of you!' He made as if he would rumple my hair but I drew back.

"'Were you waiting for me?' I asked.

"'Of course. Hours and hours. O the agony of it! See, here is the evening paper! It gives you as dead.'

"'Where?' I cried, nervously. His trembling forefinger pointed to the place. 'A beautiful young lady was also extricated in an unconscious condition from this carriage.'

"'Isn't it wonderful the news should be in London before me?' I murmured. 'But I suppose they will have names and fuller particulars in a later edition.'

"'Of course. But fancy my having to be in London, unable to get to you for love or money!'

"'Yes, it was very hard for me to be there all alone,' I murmured. 'But please run and see after my luggage, there are three portmanteaus and a little black one, and three bonnet boxes, and two parasols, and call a hansom, oh— and a brown paper parcel, and a long narrow cardboard box—and get me the latest editions of the evening papers—and please see that the driver isn't drunk, and don't take a knock-kneed horse or one that paws the ground, you know those hansom doors fly open and shoot you out like rubbish—I do so hate them—and oh! Richard, don't forget those novels from Mudie's,—they're done up with a strap. Three bonnet boxes, remember, and *all* the evening papers, mind.'

"When we were bowling homewards he kept expressing his joy by word and deed, so that I was unable to read my papers. At last, annoyed, I said: 'You wouldn't be so glad if you knew that my resurrection cost three thousand pounds.'

"'How do you mean?'

"'Why, if I had died, somebody would have had three thousand pounds. This number of *Threepenny Bits* would have been found on my body, and would have entitled my heir to that amount of assurance money. I need not tell you who my heir is, nor to whom I had left my little all.'

"I looked into his face and from the tenderness that overflowed it I saw he fancied himself the favored mortal. There is no end to the conceit of young men. A sensible fellow would have known at once that my brother was the only person reasonably entitled to my scanty belongings. However, there is no good done by disturbing a lover's complacency.

"'I do not want your money,' he answered, again passionately pressing my tulle veil to my lips. 'I infinitely prefer your life.'

"'What a bloodthirsty highwayman!'

"'I shall steal another kiss. I would rather have you than all the gold in the world.'

"'Still, gold is the next best thing,' I said, smiling at his affectionateness which my absence had evidently fostered. 'So being on the point of death, as I thought, I resolved to make death worth dying, and leave a heap of gold to the man I loved. This number of *Threepenny Bits* was not mine originally. When the crash occurred it was being read by the old gentleman in the opposite corner but his next of kin is a hypocritical young scapegrace (so he told me) and I thought it would be far nicer for *my* heir to come in for the money. So I took it from his body the very instant before I fainted dead away!'

"'My heroine!' he cried again. 'So you thought of your Richard even at the point of death. What a sweet assurance of your love!'

"'Yes, an assurance of three thousand pounds,' I answered, laughing merrily. 'And now, perhaps, you will let me read the details of the catastrophe. The reporters seem to know ever so much more about it than I do. It's getting dusk and I can hardly see—I wonder what was the name of old grizzly-growler—ah! here it is—"The pocket-book contained letters addressed to Josiah Twaddon, Esquire, and——"'

"'Twaddon, did you say?' gasped Richard, clutching the paper frantically.

"'Yes—don't! You've torn it. Twaddon, I can see it plainly.'

"'Does it give his address?' Richard panted.

"'Yes,' I said, surprised. I was just going on to read that, '4, Bucklesbury Buildings——"'

"'Great heavens!' he cried.

"'What is it? Why are you so pale and agitated? Was he anything to you. Ah, I guess it—by my prophetic soul, your uncle!'

"'Yes,' he answered bitterly. 'My uncle! My mother's brother! Wretched woman, what have you done?'

"My heart was beating painfully and I felt hot all over, but outwardly I froze.

"'You know what I have done,' I replied icily.

"'Yes, robbed me of three thousand pounds!' he cried.

"'How dare you say that?' I answered indignantly. 'Why, it was for you I meant them.'

"The statement was not, perhaps, strictly accurate, but my indignation was sufficiently righteous to cover a whole pack of lies.

"'Your intentions may have been strictly honorable,' he retorted, 'but your behavior was abominable. Great heavens! Do you know that you could be prosecuted?'

"'Nonsense!' I said stoutly, though my heart misgave me. 'What for?'

"'What for? You, a plunderer of the dead, a harpy, a ghoul, ask what for?'

"'But the thing was of no value!' I urged.

"'Of no intrinsic value, perhaps, but of immense value under the peculiar circumstances. Why, if anyone chose to initiate a prosecution, you would be sent to jail as a common thief.'

"'Pardon me,' I said haughtily. 'You forget you are speaking to a lady. As such, I can never be more than a kleptomaniac. You might make me suffer from hysteria yesterday, but the worst that could befall me now would be a most interesting advertisement. Prosecute me and you will create for me an army of friends all over the world. If it is thus that lovers behave, it is better to have friends. I shall be glad of the exchange.'

I can never be more than a kleptomaniac.

"'You know I could not prosecute you,' he answered more gently.

"'After your language to me you are capable of anything. Your uncle called you a rogue with his dying breath, and statements made with that are generally veracious. Prosecute me if you will—I have done you out of three thousand pounds and I am glad of it. Only one favor I will ask of you—for the sake of our old relations, give me fair warning!'

"'That you may flee the country?'

"'No, that I may get a new collection of photographs.'

"'You will submit to being taken by the police?' "'Yes—

after I have been taken by the photographer.' "'But look

at the position you will be in?'

"'I shall be in six different positions—one for each of the chief illustrated papers.'

"'Your flippancy is ill-timed, Margaret,' said Richard sternly.

"'Flippant, good heavens! Do you know me so little as to consider me capable of flippancy? Richard, this is the last straw. You have called me a thief, you have threatened to place me in the felon's dock, and I have answered you with soft words, but no man shall call me flippant and continue to be engaged to me!'

"'But, Maggie, darling!' His tone was changing. He saw he had gone too far. 'Consider! It is not only I that am the loser by your—indiscretion, your generous indiscretion——'

"'My indiscreet generosity,' I corrected.

"He accepted my 'indiscreet generosity' and went on. 'Cannot you see that, as my future wife, you will also suffer?'

"'But surely you will come in for something under your uncle's will all the same,' I reminded him.

"'Not a stiver. He never made a will, he never saved any money. He was the most selfish brute that ever breathed. All the money he couldn't spend on himself he gave away in charity so as to get the kudos during his lifetime, pretending that there was no merit in post-mortem philanthropy. And now all the good he might have done by his death you have cancelled.'

"I sat mute, my complexion altered for the worse by pangs of compunction.

"'But I can make amends,' I murmured at last.

"'How?' he asked eagerly.

"'I can tell the truth—at least partially. I can make an affidavit that *Threepenny Bits* belonged to my fellow-passenger, that he lent it me just before the accident, or that, seeing he was dead, I took it to hand over to his relatives.'

"For a moment his face brightened up, then it grew dark as suddenly as if it had been lit by electricity. 'They will not believe you,' he said. 'Even if you were a stranger, the paper would contest my claim. But considering your relation to me, considering that the money would fall to you as much as to me, no common-sense jury would credit your evidence.'

"'Well, then, we must break off our engagement.'

"'What would be the good of that? They would ferret out our past relations, would suspect their resumption immediately after the verdict.'

"'Well, then, we must break off our engagement,' I repeated decisively. 'I could never marry a prosecutor in posse—a man in whose heart was smouldering a petty sense of pecuniary injury.'

"'If you married me, I should cease to be a prosecutor in posse,' he said soothingly. 'As the law stands, a husband cannot give evidence against his wife in criminal cases.'

"'Oh, well, then you'd become a persecutor in esse,' I retorted. 'You'd always have something to throw in my teeth, and for my part I could never forgive you the wrong I have done you. We could not possibly live together.'

"My demeanor was so chilling, my tone so resolute that Richard was panic-stricken. He vowed, protested, stormed, entreated, but nothing could move me.

"'A kindly accident has shown me your soul,' I answered, 'and the sight is not encouraging. Fortunately I have seen it in time. You remember when you took me to see *The Doll's House*, you said that Norah was quite right in all she did. I daresay it was because the actress was so charming—but let that pass. And yet what are you but another Helmer? Just see how exact is the parallel between our story and Ibsen's. Norah in all innocence forged her husband's name in order to get the money to restore him to health. I, in all innocence, steal a threepenny paper, in order to leave you three thousand pounds by my death. When things turn out wrong, you turn round on me just as Helmer turned round on Norah—forgetting for whose sake the deed was done. If Norah was justified in leaving her husband, how much more justified must I be in leaving my betrothed!'"

"The cases are not quite on all fours," interrupted the President who had pricked up her ears at the mention of the "Woman's Poet." "You must not forget that you did not really sin for his sake but for your brother's."

"That is an irrelevant detail," replied the beautiful ghoul. "He thought I did —which comes to the same thing. Besides, my telling him I did only increases the resemblance between me and Norah. She was an awful fibber, if you remember. Richard, of course, disclaimed the likeness to Helmer, though in doing so he was more like him than ever. But I would give him no word of hope. 'We could never be happy together,' I said. 'Our union would never be real. There would always be the three thousand pounds between us.'

"'Well, that would be fifteen hundred each,' he answered with ghastly jocularity.

"'This ill-timed flippancy ends all,' I said solemnly. 'Henceforth, Mr. Westbourne, we must be strangers.'

"He sat like one turned to stone. Not till the cab arrived at my brother's house did he speak again.

The Old Maid arrives.

"Then he said in low tones: 'Maggie, can I never become anything to you but a stranger?'

"'The greatest miracle of all would have to happen then, Richard,' I quoted coldly. Then, rejecting his proffered assistance, I alighted from the vehicle,

253

passed majestically across the threshold and mounted the stairs with stately step, not a sign, not the slightest tremor of a muscle betraying what I felt. Only when I was safe in my own little room, with its lavender-scented sheets and its thousand childish associations did my pent-up emotions overpower me. I threw myself upon my little white bed in a paroxysm of laughter. I had come out of a disagreeable situation agreeably, leaving Dick in the wrong, and I felt sure I could whistle him back as easily as the hansom."

"And what became of Richard?" asked Lillie.

"I left him to settle with the cabman. I have never seen him since."

Lillie gave a little shudder. "You speak as if the cabman had settled with him. But are you sure you are willing to renounce all mankind because you find one man unsatisfactory?"

"All. I was very young when I got engaged. I did not want to be a burden on my brother. But now his firework factory is a brilliant success. He lives in a golden rain. Having only myself to please now, I don't see why I should have to please a husband. The more I think of marriage the less I think of it. I have not kept my eyes open for nothing. I am sure it wouldn't suit me. Husbands are anything but the creatures a young girl's romantic fancy pictures. They have a way of disarranging the most careful toilettes. They ruffle your hair and your temper. They disorder the furniture—and put their feet on the mantelpiece. They scratch the fenders, read books and stretch themselves on the most valuable sofas. If they help in the household they only make more work. The trail of tobacco is over all you prize. All day long the smoke gets into your eyes. Filthy pipes clog your cabinets, your window- curtains reek of stale cigars. You have bartered your liberty for a mess of cigar-ash. There is an odor of bar saloons about the house and boon companions come to welter in whiskey and water. Their talk is of science and art and politics and it makes them guffaw noisily and dig one another in the ribs. There is not a man in the world to whom I would trust my sensitive fragility—they are all coarse, clumsy creatures with a code of morals that they don't profess and a creed of chivalry that they never practise. Falsehood abides permanently in their mouth like artificial teeth and corruption lurks beneath the whited sepulchres of their shirt-fronts. They adore us in secret and deride us when they are together. They feign a contempt for us which we feel for them." These sentiments re-instated Miss Linbridge in the good opinion of the President, conscious heretofore of a jarring chord. She ordered in some refreshments to get an opportunity of whispering to Turple the magnificent that the Honorary Trier might return.

"Oh, by the way," said Miss Linbridge, "I hunted out that copy of *Threepenny Bits* before coming out. I've kept it in a drawer as a curiosity.

Here it is!"

Lillie took the paper and examined it anxiously.

"What's that? *You* reading *Threepenny Bits*?" said Silverdale coming in.

"It is only an old number," said Lillie, "whereby hangs a tale. Miss Linbridge was in a railway accident with it."

"Miss Linbridge, Lord Silverdale."

The Honorary Trier bowed.

"Oh what a pity it was an old number," he said. "Miss Linbridge might have had a claim for damages."

"How very ungallant," said Lillie. "Miss Linbridge could have had no claim unless she had been killed."

"Besides," added Miss Linbridge laughing at Lillie's bull, "it wasn't an old number then. The accident happened on New Year's Day."

"Even then it would have been too old," answered Silverdale, "for it is dated December 2d and the assurance policy is only valid during the week of issue."

"What is that?" gasped Miss Linbridge. Her face was passing through a variety of shades.

"Yes," said Lillie. "Here is the condition in print. You don't seem to have noticed it was a back number. But of course I don't wonder at that—there's no topical interest whatever, one week's very much like another. And see! Here is even 'Specimen Copy' marked on the outside sheet. Richard's uncle must have had it given to him in the street."

"The miracle!" exclaimed Miss Linbridge in exultant tones, and repossessing herself of the paper she darted from the Club.

CHAPTER XIX.

"LA FEMME INCOMPRISE.

Lord Silverdale had gone and there was now no need for Lillie to preserve the factitious cheerfulness with which she had listened to his usual poem, while her thoughts were full of other and even more depressing things. Margaret Linbridge's miracle had almost undermined the President's faith in the steadfastness of her sex; she turned mentally to the yet unaccepted Wee Winnie for consolation, condemning her own half-hearted attitude towards that sturdy soul, and almost persuading herself that salvation lay in spats. At any rate long skirts seemed the last thing in the world to find true women in.

But providence had not exhausted its miracles, and Lillie was not to spend a miserable afternoon. The miracle was speeding along towards her on the top of an omnibus—a miracle of beauty and smartness. On reaching the vicinity of the Old Maid's Club, the miracle, which was of course of the female gender, tapped the driver amicably upon the hat with her parasol and said "Stop please." The *petite* creature was the spirit of self-help itself and scorned the aid of the gentleman in front of her, preferring to knock off his hat and crush the driver's so long as the independence of womanhood was maintained. But she maintained it charmingly and without malice and gave the conductor a sweet smile in addition to his fare as she tripped away to the Old Maids' Club.

Amicably said, "Stop please."

Lillie was fascinated the instant Turple the magnificent announced "Miss Wilkins" in suave tones. The mere advent of a candidate raised her spirits and she found herself chatting freely with her visitor even before she had put her through the catechism. But the catechism came at last.

"Why do I want to join you?" asked the miracle. "Because I am disgusted with my lover—because I am a *femme incomprise*. Oh, don't stare at me as if I were a medley of megrims and fashionable ailments, I'm the very opposite of that. Mine is a buoyant, breezy, healthy nature, straightforward and simple. That's why I complain of being misunderstood. My lover is a poet—and the misunderstanding I have to endure at his hands is something appalling. Every man is a bit of a poet where woman is concerned, and so every woman is more or less misunderstood, but when you are unfortunate enough to excite the affection of a real whole poet—well, that way madness lies. Your words are twisted into meanings you never intended, your motives are misconstrued, and your simplest actions are distorted. Silverplume, for it is the well-known author of 'Poems of Compassion' that I have had the misfortune to captivate, never calls without laying a sonnet next day; in which remarks, that must be most misleading to those who do not know me, occur with painful frequency. His allowance is two kisses per day—one of salutation, one of farewell. We have only been actually engaged two months, yet I have counted up two hundred and thirty-nine distinct and separate kisses in the voluminous 'Sonnet Series' which he has devoted to our engagement, and, what is worse, he describes himself as depositing them.

"'Where at thy flower-mouth exiguous
The purple passion mantles to the brim.'

It sounds as if I was berouged like a dowager. Purple passion, indeed! I let him kiss me because he appears to like it and because there seems something wrong about it—but as for really caring a pin one way or another, well, you Miss Dulcimer, know how much there is in that! This 'Sonnet Series' promises to be endless, the course of our acquaintanceship is depicted in its most minute phases with the most elaborate inaccuracy—if I smile, if I say: 'How do you do?' if I put my hand to my forehead, if I look into the fire, down go fourteen lines giving a whole world of significance to my meanest actions, and making Himalayas out of the most microscopic molehills. I am credited with thoughts I never dreamed of and sentiments I never felt, till I ask myself whether any other woman was ever so cruelly misunderstood as I? I grow afraid to do or say anything, lest I bring upon my head a new sonnet. But even so I cannot help *looking* something or the other; and when I come to read the sonnet I find it is always the other. Once I refused to see him for a whole week, but that only resulted in seven 'Sonnets of Absence,' imaginatively depicting what I was saying and doing each day, and containing a detailed analysis of his own sensations, as well as reminiscences of past happy hours together. Most of them I had no recollection of, and the only one I could at all share was that of a morning we spent on the Ramsgate cliffs where Silverplume put his handkerchief over his face and fell asleep. In the last line of the sonnet it came out:

"'There mid the poppies of the planisphere,
I swooned for very joy and wearihead.'

But I knew it by the poppies. Then, dear Miss Dulcimer, you should just see the things he calls me—'Love's gonfalon and lodestar' and what-not. Very often I can't even find them in the dictionary and it makes me uneasy. Heaven knows what he may be saying about me! When he talks of

"'The rack of unevasive lunar things'

I do not so much complain, because it's their concern if they are libelled. It is different with incomprehensible remarks flung unmistakably at my own head such as

"'O chariest of Caryatides.'

It sounds like a reproach and I should like to know what I have done to deserve it. And then his general remarks are so monotonously unintelligible. One of his longest poetical epistles, which is burnt into my memory because I had to pay twopence for extra postage, began with this lament:

"'O sweet are roses in the summer time
And Indian naiads' weary walruses
And yet two-morrow never comes to-day.'

I cannot see any way out of it all except by breaking off our engagement. When we were first engaged, I don't deny I rather liked being written about in lovely-sounding lines but it is a sweet one is soon surfeited with, and Silverplume has raved about me to that extent that he has made me look ridiculous in the eyes of all my friends. If he had been moderate, they would have been envious; now they laugh when they read of my wonderful charms, of my lithe snake's mouth, and my face which shames the sun and my Epipsychidiontic eyes (whatever that may be) and my

"'Wee waist that holds the cosmos in its span,'

and say he is poking fun at me. But Silverplume is quite serious—I am sure of that, and it is the worst feature of the case. He carries on just the same in conversation, with the most improper allusions to heathen goddesses, and seems really to believe that I am absorbed in the sunset when I am thinking what to wear to-morrow. Just to give you an idea of how he misinterprets my silence let me read to you one of his sonnets called:

"'MOONSHINE.

"'Walking a space betwixt the double Naught,
The What Is Bound to Be and What Has Been,
How sweet with Thee beneath the moonlit treen,
O woman-soul immaculately wrought,
To sit and catch a harmony uncaught
Within a world that mocks with margarine,

In chastened silence, mystic, epicene,
Exchanging incommunicable thought.

"'Diana, Death may doom and Time may toss,
And sundry other kindred things occur,
But Hell itself can never turn to loss,
Though Mephistopheles his stumps should stir,
That day, when introduced at Charing Cross,
I smiled and doffed my silken cylinder.'

"Another distressing feature about Silverplume—indeed, I think about all men—is their continuous capacity for love-making. You know, my dear Miss Dulcimer, with us it is a matter of times and seasons—we are creatures of strange and subtle susceptibilities, sometimes we are in the mood for love and ready to respond to all shades of sentimentality, but at other moments (and these the majority) men's amorous advances jar horribly. Men do not know this. Ever ready to make love themselves they think all moments are the same to us as to them. And of all men, poets are the most prepared to make love at a moment's notice. So that Silverplume himself is almost more trying than his verses."

"But after all you need not read them," observed Lillie. "They please him and they do not hurt you. And you have always the consolation of remembering it is not you he loves but the paragon he has evolved from his inner consciousness. Even taking into account his perennial affectionateness, your reason for refusing him seems scarcely strong enough."

"Ah, wait a moment—You have not heard the worst! I might perhaps have tolerated his metrical misinterpretations—indeed on my sending him a vigorous protest against the inaccuracies of his last collection (they came out so much more glaringly when brought all together from the various scattered publications to which Silverplume originally contributed them) he sent me back a semi-apologetic explanation thus conceived:

"'TO CELIA.'

"(You know of course my name is Diana, but that is his way.)

"''Tis not alone thy sweet eyes' gleam
     Nor sunny glances,
For which I weave so oft a dream
     Of dainty fancies.

"''Tis not alone thy witching play
     Of grace fantastic
That makes me chant so oft a lay

261

Encomiastic.

"'Both editors and thee I see,
     Thy face, their purses.
I offer heart and soul to thee,
     To them my verses.'

"I was partially mollified by this, for if his poems were not merely complimentary, and he really got paid for them, one might put up with inspiring them. We were reconciled and he took me to a reception at the house of a wealthy friend of his, a fellow-member of the Sonneteers' Society. It was here that I saw a sight that froze my young blood and warned me upon the edge of what a precipice I was standing. When we got into the drawing-room, the first thing we saw was an awful apparition in a corner—a hideous, unkempt, unwashed man in a dressing-gown and slippers, with his eyes rolling wildly and his lips moving rhythmically. It was the host.

"'Don't speak to him,' whispered the hostess. 'He doesn't see us. He has been like that all day. He came down to look to the decorations this morning, when the idea took him and he has been glued to the spot ever since. He has forgotten all about the reception—he doesn't know we're here and I thought it best not to disturb him till he is safely delivered of the sonnet.'

"'You are quite right,' everybody said in sympathetic awestruck tones and left a magic circle round the poet in labor. But I felt a shudder run through my whole being. 'Goodness gracious, Silverplume,' I said, 'is this the way you poets go on?'"

"'No, no, Diana,' he assured me. 'It is all tommyrot (I quote Silverplume's words). The beggar is just bringing out a new volume, and although his wife has always distributed the most lavish hospitality to the critics, he has never been able to get himself taken seriously as a poet. There will be lots of critics here to-night and he is playing his last card. If he is not a genius now, he never will be.'

The poet plays his last card.

"'Oh, of course,' I replied sceptically, 'two of a trade.' I made him take me away and that was the end of our engagement. Even as it was, Silverplume's neglect of his appearance had been a constant thorn in my side, and if this was so before marriage, what could I hope for after? It was all very well for him to say his friend was only shamming, but even so, how did I know he would not be reduced to that sort of thing himself when his popularity faded and younger rivals came along."

Lillie, who seemed to have some *arrière-pensée*, entered into an animated defence of the poet, but Miss Wilkins stood her ground and refused to

263

withdraw her candidature.

"I don't want you to withdraw your candidature," said Lillie, frankly. "I shall be charmed to entertain it. I am only arguing upon the general question."

And, indeed, Lillie was enraptured with Miss Wilkins. It was the attraction of opposites. A matter-of-fact woman who could reject a poet's love appealed to her with irresistible piquancy. Miss Wilkins stayed on to tea (by which time she had become Diana) and they gossiped on all sorts of subjects, and Lillie gave her the outlines of the queerest stories of past candidates and in the Old Maids' Club that afternoon all went merry as a marriage bell.

"Well, good-bye, Lillie," said Diana at last.

"Good-bye, Diana," returned Lillie. "Now *I* understand you I hope you won't consider yourself a *femme incomprmise* any longer."

"It is only the men I complained of, dear."

"But we must ever remain *incomprises* by man," said Lillie. "*Femme incomprise*—why, it is the badge of all our sex."

"Yes," answered Diana. "A woman letting down her back hair is tragic to a man; to us she only recalls bedroom gossip. Good-bye."

And nodding brightly the brisk little creature sallied into the street and captured a passing 'bus.

CHAPTER XX.

THE INAUGURAL SOIREE.

"Oh, Lord Silverdale," cried Lillie exultantly when he made his usual visit the next afternoon. "At last I have an unexceptional candidate. We shall get under weigh at last. I am so pleased because papa keeps bothering about that inaugural *soirée*. You know he is staying in town expressly for it. But what is the matter?—You don't seem to be glad at my news."

"I am afraid you will be grieved at mine," he replied gravely. "Look at this in to-day's *Moon*."

Sobered by his manner, she took the paper. Then her face grew white. She read, in large capitals:

"The Old Maids' Club.
"Interview with the President.
"Sensational Stories of Skittish Spinsters.
"Wee Winnie and Lillie Dulcimer."

"I called at the Old Maids' Club yesterday," writes a *Moon* woman, "to get some wrinkles, which ought to be abundant in such a Club, though they are not. Miss Dulcimer, the well-known authoress, is one of the loveliest and jolliest girls of the day. Of course I went as a candidate, with a trumped-up story about my unhappy past, which Miss Dulcimer will, I am sure, forgive me, in view of the fact that it was the only way of making her talk freely for the benefit of my readers."

Lillie's eye glanced rapidly down the collection of distortions. Then she dropped the *Moon*.

"This is outrageous," she said. "I can never forgive her."

"Why, is this the candidate you were telling me about?" asked Silverdale in deeper concern.

"I am afraid it is!" said Lillie, almost weeping. "I took to her so, we talked ever so long. Even Wee Winnie did not possess the material for all these inaccuracies."

"What is this woman's name?"

"Wilkins—I already called her Diana."

"Diana?" cried Silverdale. "Wilkins? Great heavens, can it be?"

"What is the matter?"

"It must be. Wilkins has married his Diana. It was Mrs. Diana Wilkins who called upon you—not Miss at all."

"What *are* you talking about? Who are these people?"

"Don't you remember Wilkins, the *Moon*-man that I was up in a balloon with? He was in a frightful quandary then about his approaching marriage. He did not know what to do. It tortured him to hear anyone ask a question because he was always interviewing people and he got to hate the very sound of an interrogation.—I told you about it at the time, don't you remember?— and he knew that marriage would bring into his life a person who would be sure to ask him questions after business hours. I was very sorry for the man and tried to think of a way out, but in vain, and I even promised him to bring the Old Maids' Club under the notice of his Diana. Now it seems he has hit on the brilliant solution of making her into a Lady Interviewer, so that her nerves, too, shall be hypersensitive to interrogatives, and husband and wife shall sit at home in a balsamic restfulness permeated by none but categorical propositions. Ah me! well, I envy them!"

"You envy them?" said Lillie.

"Why not? They are well matched."

"But you are as happy as Wilkins, surely."

"Query. It takes two to find happiness."

"What nonsense!" said Lillie.

She had been already so upset by the treachery and loss of the misunderstood Diana, that she felt ready to break down and shed hot tears over these heretical sentiments of Silverdale's. He had been so good, so patient. Why should he show the cloven hoof just to-day?

"Miss Dolly Vane," announced Turple the magnificent.

A strange apparition presented itself—an ancient lady quaintly attired. Her dress fell in voluminous folds—the curious full skirt was bordered with velvet, and there were huge lace frills on the elbow-sleeves. Her hair was smoothed over her ears and she wore a Leghorn hat. There were the remains of beauty on her withered face but her eyes were wild and wandering. She curtseyed to the couple with old-fashioned grace, and took the chair which Lord Silverdale handed her.

Lillie looked at her inquiringly.

"Have I the pleasure of speaking to Miss Dulcimer?" said the old lady. Her tones were cracked and quavering.

"I am Miss Dulcimer," replied Lillie. "What can I do for you?"

"Ah, yes, I have been reading about you in the *Moon* to-day. Wee Winnie and Lillie Dulcimer! Wee Winnie! It reminds me of myself. They call me Little Dolly, you know." She simpered in a ghastly manner.

Lillie's face was growing pale. She could not speak.

"Yes, yes of course," said Silverdale smiling. "They call you Little Dolly."

"Little Dolly!" she repeated to herself, mumbling and chuckling. "Little Dolly."

"So you have been reading about Miss Dulcimer!" said Silverdale pleasantly.

"Yes, yes," said the old lady, looking up with a start. "Little Lillie Dulcimer. Foundress of the Old Maids' Club. That's the thing for me, I thought to myself. That'll punish Philip. That'll punish him for being away so long. When he comes home and finds Little Dolly is an old maid, won't he be sorry, poor Philip? But I can't help it. I said I would punish him and I will."

All the blood had left Lillie's cheek—she trembled and caught hold of Lord Silverdale's arm.

"I shan't have you now, Philip," the creaking tones of the old lady continued after a pause. "The rules will not allow it, will they, Miss Dulcimer? It is not enough that I am young and beautiful, I must reject somebody—and I have nobody else to reject but you, Philip. You are the only man I have ever loved. Oh my Philip! My poor Philip!"

She began to wring her hands. Lillie pressed closer to Lord Silverdale and her grasp on his arm tightened.

"Very well, we will put your name on the books at once," said the Honorary Trier, in bluff, hearty tones.

Little Dolly looked up smiling. "Then I'm an old maid!" she cried ecstatically. "Already! Little Dolly an old maid! Already! Ha! ha! ha! ha! ha!"

She went off into a burst of uncanny laughter. Lord Silverdale felt Lillie shuddering violently. He disengaged himself from her grasp and placed her on the sofa. Then offering his arm to Miss Dolly Vane, who accepted it with a charming smile, and a curtsey to Miss Dulcimer, he led her from the apartment. When he returned Lillie was weeping half-hysterically on the sofa.

"My darling!" he whispered. "Calm yourself." He laid his hand tenderly on her hair. Presently the sobs ceased.

"Oh, Lord Silverdale!" she said in a shaken voice. "How good you are! Poor old lady! Poor old lady!"

"Do not distress yourself. I have taken care she shall get home safely."

"Little Dolly! how tragic it was!" whispered Lillie.

"Yes, it was tragic. Probably it is not now so sad to her as it is to us, but it is tragic enough, heaven knows. Lillie,"—he trembled as he addressed her thus for the first time—"I am not sorry this has happened. The time has come to put an end to all this make-believe. This Old Maids' Club of yours is a hollow mockery. You are playing round the fringes of tragedy—it is like warming your hands at a house on fire, wherein wretched beings are shrieking for help. You are young and rich and beautiful—Heaven pity the women who have none of these charms. Life is a cruel tragedy for many—never crueller than when its remorseless laws condemn gentle loving women to a crabbed and solitary old age. To some all the smiles of fortune, the homage of all mankind—to others all the frowns of fate and universal neglect, aggravated by contumely. You have felt this, I know, and it is as a protest that you conceived your club. Still can it ever be a serious success? I love you, Lillie, and you have known it all along. If I have entered into the joke, believe me, I have sometimes taken it as seriously as you. Come! Say you love me, too, and let us end the tragi-comedy."

Lillie was obstinately silent for a moment, then she dried her eyes, and with a wan little smile said, in tones which she vainly strove to render those of the usual formula: "What poem have you brought me to-day?"

"To-day I have brought no poem, but I have lived one," said Lord Silverdale, taking her soft unresisting hand. "But, like Lady Clara Vere de Vere, you put strange memories in my head, and I will tell you some verses I made in the country in my callow youth, when the world was new.

"PASTORAL.

"A rich-toned landscape, touched with darkling gold
        Of misty, throbbing corn-fields, and with haze
Of softly-tinted hills and dreaming wold,
        Lies warm with raiment of soft summer rays,
And in the magic air there lives a free
And subtle feeling of the distant sea.

"The perfect day slips softly to its end,
        The sunset paints the tender evening sky,
The shadows shroud the hills with gray, and lend
        A softened touch of ancient mystery,

And ere the silent change of heaven's light
I feel the coming glory of the night.

"O for the sweet and sacred earnest gaze
    Of eyes divine with strange and yearning tears
To feel with me the beauty of our days,
    The glorious sadness of our mortal years
The noble misery of the spirit's strife,
The joy and splendour of the body's life."

Lillie's hand pressed her lover's with involuntary tenderness, but she had turned her face away. Presently she murmured:

"But think what you are asking me to do? How can I, the President of the Old Maid's Club, be the first recreant?"

"But you are also the last to leave the ship," he replied, smiling. "Besides, you are not legally elected. You never came before the Honorary Trier. You were never a member at all, so have nothing to undo. If you had stood your trial fairly, I should have plucked you, my Lillie, plucked you and worn you nearest my heart. It is I who have a position to resign—the Honorary Triership—and I resign it instanter. A nice trying time I have had, to be sure!"

"Now, now! I set my face against punning!" said Lillie, showing it now, for the smiles had come to hide the tears.

"Pardon, Rainbow," he answered.

"Why do you call me Rainbow?"

"Because you look it," he said. "Because your face is made of sunshine and tears. Go and look in the glass. Also because—well, wait and I will fashion my other reason into rhyme and send it you on our wedding morn."

"Poetry made while you wait," said Lillie, laughing. The laugh froze suddenly on her lips, and a look of horror overswept her face.

"What is it, dearest?" cried her lover, in alarm.

"Wee Winnie! How can we face Wee Winnie?"

"There is no need to break the truth to her—we can simply get rid of her by telling her she has never been elected, and never will be."

"Why," said Lillie, with a comic *moue*, "that would be harder to tell her than the truth. But we must first of all tell father. I am afraid he will be dreadfully disappointed at missing that inaugural *soirée* after all. You know he has been staying in town expressly for it. We have some bad quarters of an hour before us."

They sought the millionaire in his sanctum but found him not. They inquired of Turple the magnificent, and learned that he was in the garden. As they turned away, the lovers both simultaneously remarked something peculiar about the face of Turple the magnificent. Moved by a common impulse, they turned back and gazed at it. For some seconds they could not at all grasp the change that had come over it—but at last, and almost at the same instant, they realized what was the matter.

Turple the magnificent was smiling.

Filled with strange apprehensions, Silverdale and Lillie hurried into the garden, where their vague alarm was exchanged for definite consternation. The millionaire was pacing the gravel-paths in the society of a strange and beautiful lady. On closer inspection, the lady turned out to be only too familiar.

"Why it's Wee Winnie masquerading as a woman!" exclaimed Lord Silverdale.

And so it proved—Nelly Nimrod in all the flush of her womanly beauty, her mannish attire discarded.

"Why, what is this, father?" murmured Lillie.

"My child," said the millionaire solemnly. "As *you* have resolved to be an Old Maid, I—I—well I thought it only *my* duty to marry. Even the poorest millionaire cannot shirk the responsibilities of wealth."

"But father!" said Lillie in dismay. "I have changed my mind. I am going to marry Lord Silverdale."

"Bless ye, my children!" said the millionaire. "You are a woman, Lillie, and it is a woman's privilege to change her mind. But I am a man and have no such privilege. I must marry all the same."

"But Miss Nimrod has changed her mind, too," said Lillie, quite losing her temper. "And *she* is not a woman."

"Gently, gently," said the millionaire. "Respect your stepmother to be, if you have no respect for my future wife."

"Lillie," said Miss Nimrod appealingly, "do not misjudge me. I have *not* changed my mind."

"But you said you could never marry, on the ground that while you would only marry an unconventional man, an unconventional man wouldn't want to marry you."

"Well? Your father is the man I sought. He *didn't* want to marry me," she explained frankly.

"Oh," said Lillie, taken utterly aback, and regarding her father commiseratingly.

"It is true," he said, laughing uneasily. "I fell in love with Wee Winnie, but now Nelly says she wants to settle down."

"You ought to be grateful to me, Lillie," added Nelly, "for it was solely in the interest of the Old Maid's Club that I consented to marry your father. He was always a danger to the Club; at any moment he might have put forth autocratic authority and wound it up. So I thought that by marrying him I should be able to influence him in its favor."

"No doubt you *will* make him see the desirability of women remaining old maids," retorted Lillie unappeased.

"Come, come, Lillie, be sensible!" said the millionaire. "Nelly shall give Lillie a good dinner at the Junior Widows, one of those charming dinners you and I have had there, and Lillie please send out the cards for the inaugural *soirée*. I am not going to be done out of that and nothing can now be gained by delay."

"But, sir, how can we inaugurate a Club which has never had any members?" asked Silverdale.

"But what does that matter? Aren't there plenty of candidates without them? Besides, nobody'll know. Each of the candidates will think the others are the members. Tell you what, boy, they shall all dance at Lillie's wedding, and we'll make that the inaugural *soirée*."

"But that would be to publish my failure to the world," remonstrated Lillie.

"Nonsense, dear. It'll be published without that. Trust the *Moon*. Isn't it better to take the bull by the horns?"

"Well, yes, perhaps you're right," said Lillie hesitating. "But I hope the world will understand that it is only desperation at the collapse of the Old Maids' Club that has driven me to commit matrimony."

She went back to the Club to write out the cards.

"What do you think of my stepmother?" she inquired pathetically of the ex-Honorary Trier.

"What do I think?" said Lord Silverdale seriously. "I think she is the punishment of Providence for your interference with its designs."

The explanatory poem duly came to hand on Lillie's wedding morn. It was written on vellum in the bridegroom's best hand and ran—

RAINBOW.

Ah, why I call you "Rainbow," sweet?
The shadows 'fore your eyes retreat,
The ground grows light beneath your feet.

You smile in your superior way,
A Rainbow has no feet, you say?
Nay, be not so precise to-day.

Created but to soothe and bless,
You followed logic to excess,
Repressing thoughts of tenderness.

My life was chilled and wan and hoary,
You came, the Bow of ancient story,
To kiss the grayness into glory.

And now, as Rainbow fair to see,
A promise sweet you are to me
Of sorrow never more to be.

Besides the friends of the happy pair, nearly all the candidates were present
at the inaugural *soirée* of the Old Maids' Club. Not quite all—because Lillie
who was rapidly growing conventional did not care to have Clorinda Bell even
accompanied by her mother, or by her brother, the Man in the Ironed Mask.
Nor did she invite the twins, nor the osculatory Alice. But she conquered her
prejudices in other instances, and Frank Maddox, the art critic, came under the
convoy of the composer, Paul Horace, and Miss Mary Friscoe was brought by
Bertie Smythe. The Writers' Club also sent Ellaline Rand, and an account of the
proceedings appeared in the first number of the *Cherub*. The "Princess" was
brought by Miss Primpole, and Captain Athelstan and Lord Arthur came
together in unimpaired friendship. Eustasia Pallas and her husband, Percy
Swinshell Spatt, both their faces full of the peace that passeth understanding,
got a night off for the occasion and came in a hansom paid for out of the week's
beer-money. Turple the magnificent, who had seen them at home in the
servants' hall, was outraged in his deepest instincts and multiplied occasions
for offering them refreshments merely for the pleasure of snorting in their
proximity. The great Fladpick (Frank Gray), accompanied by his newly-won
bride, Cecilia, made the evening memorable by the presence of the English
Shakespeare, Guy Fledgely brought Miss Sybil Hotspur, and his father, the
baronet, was under the care of Miss Jack. The lady from Boston wired
congratulations on the success of the Club from Yokohama whither she had
gone to pick up lacquer-work. Poor Miss Summerson, the lovely May, and the
victim of the Valentine were a triad that was much admired. Miss Fanny
Radowski, whose Oriental loveliness excited much attention, came,

with Martin. Winifred Woodpecker was accompanied by her mother, the resemblance between the two being generally remarked, and Miss Margaret Linbridge seemed to afford Richard Westbourne copious opportunities for jealousy. Even Wilkins was there with his Diana, in an unprofessional capacity, Lillie having relented towards her interviewer on learning that she had been really engaged to Silverplume once and that she had not entirely drawn on the stores of journalistic fancy. Silverplume himself was there, unconscious to what he owed the invitation, and paying marked attention to the unattached beauties. Miss Nimrod promenaded the rooms on the arm of the millionaire. She had improved vastly since she had become effeminate, and Lillie felt she could put up with her, now she would not have to live with her. Even Silverdale's aunt, Lady Goody-Goody Twoshoes could find no fault with Nelly now.

It was a brilliant scene. The apartments of the Old Maids' Club had been artistically decked with the most gorgeous flowers that the millionaire could afford, and the epigrams had been carefully removed so as to leave the rooms free for dancing. As Lillie's father gazed around, he felt that not many millionaires could secure such a galaxy of beauty as circled in the giddy dance in his gilded saloon. It was, indeed, an unexampled gathering of pretty girls— this inaugural *soirée* of the Old Maids' Club, and the millionaire's shirt-front heaved with pride and pleasure and the Letter-Day Cupid that still hung on the wall seemed to take heart of grace again.

"You got my verses this morning, Rainbow mine?" said Silverdale, when the carriage drove off, and the honeymoon began.

It was almost the first moment they had had together the whole day.

"Yes," said Lillie softly. "And I wanted to tell you there are two lines which are truer than you meant."

"I am indeed, a poet, then! Which are they?"

Lillie blushed sweetly. Presently she murmured,

"'You followed logic to excess,
Repressing thoughts of tenderness.'

"How did you know that?" she asked, her brown eyes looking ingenuously into his.

"Love's divination, I suppose."

"My father didn't tell you?"

"Tell me what?"

"About my discovery in the algebra of love?"

"Algebra of love?"

"No, of course he didn't. I don't suppose he ever really understood it," said Lillie with a pathetic smile. "I think I ought to tell you now what it was that made me so—so—you understand."

She put her little warm hand lightly into his and nestled against his shoulder, as if to make amends.

After a delicious silence, for Lord Silverdale betrayed no signs of impatience, Lillie confessed all.

"So you see I have loved you all along!" she concluded. "Only I did not dare hope that the chance would come to pass, against which the odds were 5999."

"But great heavens!" cried Lord Silverdale, "do you mean to say this is why you were so cold to me all those long weary months?"

"It is the only reason," faltered Lillie. "But would you have had me defy the probabilities?"

"No, no, of course not. I wouldn't dream of such a thing. But you have miscalculated them!"

"Miscalculated them?"

Lillie began to tremble violently.

"Yes, there is a fallacy in your ratiocination."

"A fallacy!" she whispered hoarsely.

"Yes, you have calculated on the theory that the probabilities are independent, whereas they are interdependent. In the algebra of love this is the typical class of probabilities. The two events—your falling in love with me, my falling in love with you—are related; they are not absolutely isolated phenomena as you have superficially assumed. It is our common qualities which make us gravitate together, and what makes me love you is the same thing that makes you love me. Thus the odds against our loving each other are immensely less than you have ciphered out."

Lillie had fallen back, huddled up, in her corner of the carriage, her face covered with her hands.

"Forgive me," said Lord Silverdale penitently. "I had no right to correct your mathematics on your wedding-day. Say two and two are six and I will make it so."

"Two and two are not six and you know it," said Lillie firmly, raising her

275

wet face. "It is I who have to ask forgiveness for being so cruel to you. But if I have sinned, I have sinned in ignorance. You will believe that, dearest?"

"I believe anything that comes from my Rainbow's lips," said Lord Silverdale. "Why, they are quite white! Let me kiss them rosy again."

Like a naughty child that has been chastened by affliction she held up her face obediently to meet his. The lips were already blushing.

"But confess," she said, while an arch indefinable light came into the brown eyes, "confess we have had a most original courtship."